THE FERGUS

Tori Grant Welhouse

THE FERGUS

Tori Grant Welhouse

Santa Clarita, CA

Tori Grant Welhouse
2967 School Lane
Green Bay, WI 54313
www.torigrantwelhouse.com

ISBN: 979-8-218-38503-3

Illustration & Cover Design by Mick Koller

Originally Published by Skyrocket Press

Ordering Information:

Quantity sales. Special discounts are available on quantity purchases by corporations, associations, and others. For details, contact the author at torigrantwelhouse@gmail.com.

Be happy while you're living, for you're a long time dead.
— Scottish Proverb

TABLE OF CONTENTS

DEADEND

GHOST SIGNS

LAST CITATION

COURIER PROJECT

DEADEND

Prologue

"LOONIE, HOLD MY ARM," said Rork's gran.

He caught up to her and held out his arm, wondering at her asking for help. She was a small, compact woman, less than five feet tall, agile and energetic into her eighties. Rork towered over her, and she had to reach up to take his arm. It was rare for her to ask for help. He noticed she was flushed, her lips pursed with breathlessness.

She'd insisted he drive her to forage for nettles in the woodlands surrounding their Highland village. They walked slowly through the spring-soaked grass, one of her hands in the crook of his elbow, the other resting in the pocket of her pinny as her sturdy shoes crunched windfallen leaves. *Heg-beg*, she called nettles, and lopped the tops to use in concocting a tonic they drank each spring — Rork, his father, and his gran.

Rork scrabbled for his smartphone in the back pocket of his jeans. He wanted to write a few notes to help him code later.

His gran squeezed his arm. "Rork, the Fergus," she said, "that machine language will wait. Right now, I need you to keep an eye out for —"

She was interrupted by a thought or a spasm and stopped walking for a moment, standing still and closing her eyes.

"Gran, are you —?"

"Don't," said his gran, holding up a hand. "I can't abide any fussing. It's why I —"

She didn't finish her sentence.

Chastened, Rork kept silent. Her urgency unnerved him, and he concentrated on looking for nettles, a tall plant with serrated leaves and stinging hairs. The plants were not easy to harvest, which was why he carried a pair of gardening gloves and kitchen shears in his backpack.

His gran dragged on his arm. Rork slowed his step. The muted sun pierced the cathedral of oak, pine, and ash trees, casting into beatific light a small clearing to their right. His gran breathed out with effort. She gave Rork a reassuring smile and linked her arm tighter with his.

Rork and his gran stood under the canopy of trees for long seconds, minutes, inhaling the tang of ancient pine. His gran relaxed her grip on his arm, her eyes flitting about the clearing like Small Blue butterflies, rare and striking with their bright blue wings, white margin, and dark fringe. Rork loved his gran's curiosity, her interest in the things around her. Even the nettles were worthy of her wonder. But worry prickled the back of his neck. She seemed slighter. Less. Should he say something to his father? His stomach knotted anxiously. His father was the opposite of curious. His cold indifference made Rork want to run away from home. If it wasn't for his gran, he might have.

His gran's eyes, like balefire, found his. "I especially feel your grandfather in the woods, in doing the tasks we used to do," she said with a shake of her pin-curled head. Rork had only a dim memory of his grandfather, how he used to tease Rork about his tousled head of hair like flame flower.

"Life and death go side-by-side, you know, loonie," said his gran. She chuckled softly. "How that man *could* natter."

Woodland light burst into smaller particles, twinkling.

Rork didn't understand. It wasn't like his gran to dwell on the deceased. Usually she only remembered them during the high holidays, and he felt her wavering at his side, like a boundary was blurring between past and present. What was she trying to tell him? What was she preparing him for?

Rork tried to lead his gran to a fallen tree to rest. She braced herself with one hand on the tree but remained insistent, pointing to a clump of nettles just off the path. While she waited, she lifted her face to the sun-dappled light of the clearing, her other hand resting on the front of her pinny, fingers poised near her throat.

Rork crouched down to pluck the veined leaves. Although semi-cultivated, nettles grew best in patches near busy areas of a trail or outbuilding. The garden gloves stretched tightly on his hands but protected him from the many stinging hairs. He followed the vine-like stems, crawling along the loose earth to reach for more leaves. In warm weather, the plant's catkins would grow tall with budding brown or yellow flowers. He hoped his gran would be happy with the harvest. He thought it'd make enough tonic to see them through the winter. Maybe she was in need of tonic? Was that the purpose of the outing? He hoped so. He was concerned about her. She didn't seem herself, and Rork hoped the tonic would restore her. He was looking forward to an afternoon in the kitchen with her.

The kitchen was his gran's domain, a place where she was quietly and emphatically in charge, and Rork had many happy memories of helping her bake bread or oatcakes, cauldrons of soup or mince and tatties. Endless cups of tea. Steam from the stove and fragrant food, much laughter. Rork and his father had only basic kitchen skills. When his father was home, he would wander into the farmhouse kitchen for a cup of tea and a taste of whatever they were making. Rork would catch his father's eye over the head of his gran, and there'd be a moment. An out of the ordinary, isolated moment. A moment when they felt like a family. Rork was happiest in his gran's kitchen. She was the connection between his father and him. The only language they spoke.

In the woodlands, Rork sat back on his heels to gently arrange the plants in his backpack, careful not to crush the soft leaves. They reminded Rork a little of mint but without the distinct smell. Still, they were wonderfully fresh and green, like shade on a hot day. He got to his feet unsteadily, his hiking boots shifting in the soil.

"Gran," he said, opening the pack wide for her to see the verdant pickings. Looking up, he saw her perfectly illuminated by the sun's rays, light dispersing around her in a hazy halo that seemed somehow to also buzz. Or maybe Rork imagined it, but words stuck in his throat at the unexpected sight of his gran — glowing.

"Och," she said, barely above a whisper, as if in surprise. "Are you coming for me, then?"

Rork grew alarmed. *Who* was she talking to?

Suddenly, his gran folded to the ground and lay peacefully on her side, head pillowed on the bend of one elbow.

"No!" yelled Rork, startling the birds from the trees. He cinched the backpack and flung it onto his back. In three frantic strides, he was lifting his gran in his arms, holding her gently under her knees and head. Her cheek rested on his chest. He lifted her, lurching back the way they'd come, willing the car to come into sight. She was heavy with collapse, and fear made Rork's heart race. The sound of his own panting was loud in his ears.

"No, no, no," he kept saying. With superhuman effort, he got her into the backseat, laying her tenderly on the cushion, using the backpack as a bolster against the door. As he made final adjustments, his gran gripped his hand fiercely. Surprised, Rork sucked in a breath and stared into her opened eyes.

"Find a way —" said his gran. Rork leaned nearer. He could hardly hear her.

"What?" he asked.

"Find. A. Way. To. Connect," she said, haltingly. Her eyes stuttered and closed, and the strange buzzing from before returned.

Rork climbed into the driver's seat in shock, not sure what to do or where to go. His clumsy thumbs could hardly operate his phone. "Da," he said, his voice breaking as his father answered. "It's gran!"

"Bring her home," said his father, abrupt as always, somehow understanding what Rork was too incoherent to put into words.

"But Da —"

"*Bring. Her. Home*," repeated his father, and then added in a gentler tone, "I'll call the doctor."

1: Keening

A CHATTER OF VOICES finally roused Rork from an abyss of sleep. Where were the voices coming from? His eyes flicked around his bedroom. Had he left the TV on? No, the screen was blank. Computer? Was his Beta group trying to connect with him? No, he saw zero bubbles of dialogue. Were there guests in the house? Immediately he dismissed that thought. The house creaked with emptiness. He knew he was alone.

His eyes blinked and blinked, sticky with sleep. No, the voices were originating from *inside* his head, a fact that might have caused him more alarm had he not been numb with loneliness and grief. Rork forced himself to remain motionless on his feather pillow while he listened to the insistent wail between his ears.

The babble wasn't unpleasant exactly. His head didn't hurt. He felt no screaming or piercing pain, but the clamor did make him feel slightly bristly, as if something important was just out of reach, like the year of the Boer War, which Rork had missed on a pop quiz the previous Monday at Bellie High School, the only secondary school in his small village on the North Sea coast of Scotland. It was a date he should have remembered since it was the year his gran had been born.

Thinking of his gran caused Rork's heart to squeeze. He had a vision of her in the light of the kitchen window, her face a crescent of smiles each and every morning. Like layers of buttery, his favorite Highland pastry. For Rork, food and memory always seemed to intertwine.

He levered his legs out of bed, the reality returning that his gran had passed away two long, desolate weeks ago. His days were now empty of light, empty of smiles. His eyes were covered by a film of sorrow. Even food was tasteless without her.

He rattled around, alone, in the large, draughty former boarding house he and his gran used to share with the brooding threat of his father's regular arrivals and departures. His father was a mason and traveled with a crew, often staying away for days, weeks at a time. He was his gran's only child, arriving later in her life. She had admitted to indulging him, letting him "go wild."

There was nothing *wild* about Rork, who considered himself cerebral, appreciating the math and algorithms needed for programming language. His father was the opposite. *He* was physical, taking up all the space, all the air in a room.

Rork bustled around his bedroom and tried to ignore the prattle of voices. It had only been his gran and him during his father's long absences, and now he had no one. He definitely couldn't confide the strange voices to his father because his father already thought Rork was a hopeless headcase.

Yet the keening persisted.

Rork heard it while he ate breakfast, sitting in the gloom of the back kitchen with a bottle of new milk, which he poured over his oatmeal in a smooth, white stream. His gran had always saved him the cream.

He heard it as he got dressed, splashing his face in the sink as he hopped from foot to foot on the cold tile floor in the bathroom he shared with his father. His gran used to say he had a chin that could cut glass. Chiseled and prominent like his father's, it made him look more resolved than he usually felt. Yet it was one familiar feature in the mirror during this changeling phase of his life — no longer a boy but not quite a man.

Rork sat on the closed toilet seat and clutched his head. He began to wonder if something was seriously wrong with him. Maybe he had an ear infection? Or a brain tumor? He ran his hands through his thick, ginger hair, which sprang out from his head in erratic coils. His skin was hot to the touch, flushed by spots of color. Rork groaned. The last thing he needed today of all days was to get sick. His father was expected. Later today his father would wheel his gray ghost of a car into a parking spot in front of their terraced corner house, and his broad shoulders would shadow their front door. It was hard enough enduring his military-like interrogations without feeling peely-wally.

Rork was having a tough time adjusting to life without his gran. Mornings were the worst, coming down to the kitchen to find it chilly and bleak. No gran. No whistling teakettle. No fiddle music. Rork would duck beneath the doorframe, clutching his upper arms and steeling himself against the silent void. His green and briny eyes would fix on the kitchen window, life going past without his gran. He missed her wrinkled cheeks. He missed her twinkling eyes. Her pin-curls. Her head so downy he could see the pinkness of her scalp when he'd bend down to kiss her good morning. But most of all he missed her laugh. That clear, gleeful peal that gave joy to his awkward, wretched teenaged life. Without her, each day was a purgatory. He'd give anything for a chance to reunite with her, if only for a cyber-moment.

Rork put the kettle on the stove to boil. Still, the papers needed fetching. The dog needed walking. Perhaps some fresh air would help him clear his head. His father wasn't expected until almost dinnertime. Also, he felt — although he'd never admit it out loud — that the voices were compelling him somewhere. The voices were strident, foreign, and calling over each other like a street bazaar in a strange city. Rich with intrigue and excitement but also confusing, incomprehensible, putting him on alert.

Rork reached for his jacket and shoes in the back hall. His gran's housecoat hung on a hook by the door next to the dog's leash. She'd called it a pinny. He hesitated on seeing it. His gran had been the conduit between his father and him, especially after Rork's mother passed. His gran had been the only one who could manage his father, playfully teasing him into seeing how rigid and impossible he was being. She conceded that the service and life had changed his father. His gran always shook her head at this, making a *tsk*ing noise with her teeth. She never went into detail, but Rork had always wondered. His father, she'd said, had been such a carefree loon, mad about soccer, disappearing after dinner to the fields behind the school, coming home long after dusk. Gran would cajole Rork's father into the bath with the promise of thick, hot chocolate, which would send him into a spent sleep, dreaming about soccer.

Rork had a hard time imagining his father as a carefree schoolboy. His mind was fixed on the memory of bringing his gran home after foraging for nettles. How they'd helplessly watched her slip away. How stubborn his father had been about keeping her at home. It was easier for Rork to be angry with his father than deal with her loss. While they'd hovered helplessly, his gran had spoken softly to herself, but the words hadn't made any sense, as if she spoke to an unseen someone, reliving moments of her life. As a young Scottish lass or quinie. A wifey. A mother. The doctor offered no help. She was of an age, he'd said, but she'd looked so small in her confection of a bed. Rork had lain as close as he dared on one side of her, almost stupefied with worry, while his father paced between the candy pink walls.

"How she delighted in this room," he'd said. "I promised her she could die here. It was what she wanted. I promised." Rork wondered who he was trying to convince.

In the small hours of the night, his father finally succumbed to exhaustion. He carefully laid down next to his mother on her other side, looping an arm lightly across her body, which managed to encompass Rork's shoulder. Rork was aware of the presence of his father's hand, the warmth of it. The physical contact was a jolt after years of distance. Ever since his mother disappeared from Rork's life, his father had retreated into the maze of his body, denying himself any kind of sensory connection, threatening Rork with his world of deprivation. His gran presented their only lifeline.

Breathing sonorously, Rork and his father lay near his gran like bookends throughout a long, lingering night as the moon and the sun switched places in the sky. Rork watched his gran's eyes move rapidly behind their lids, her face twitching in a range of gestures. Joy. Determination. Sorrow. Longing. Rork knew she'd lived a full life, and she'd always been there for him. Rork dozed, dreaming of the sun and buzzing. By morning she was cold, taking light, laughter, and language with her.

Since that night, his father gave little away. Stern. Unbending. In truth, Rork wondered sometimes if his father even *liked* him. Or wanted him around. His father's piercing blue eyes would sweep over Rork, veiled with something. Regret? Disdain? Rork shuddered as the stoniness leeched into his bones. He feared dismissal from his father, so he protected himself by shutting down around him, his conversation reduced to monosyllables, grunts. It was a terrible pattern. Rork grew more and more recalcitrant, while his father grew more and more autocratic. Only his gran could have helped them break the cycle and teach them how to communicate with each other.

Frustrated, Rork grabbed the leash and slapped it in the palm of his hand.

Rork's father was perennially stoic, never showing emotion of any kind, which made Rork even more self-conscious, embarrassed even, at just how much he missed his gran. Her absence was a daily punch to the solar plexus. He could hardly breathe. He felt like the shell of a person. Worse, thoughts of regret nagged at him. Why hadn't he noticed how sick she was? Why hadn't he made himself more useful to her? She'd tried to prepare him at the end, and he'd been oblivious. In his own world, as his father said. He'd wondered, too, what her last, mysterious words had meant. "Find. A. Way. To. Connect." Find a way to connect with others? Connect with his heritage? What *had* she meant? And *who* was she talking to at the end? He wished he could ask his father, but the risk of scorn was too high, and he didn't know how he'd find the words. He wished he could go back, do-over, re-program his last moments with his gran, so she could tell him.

Pathetic.

"Angus," he whistled. The dog, a West Highland Terrier with curious, dark button eyes and permanently alert ears, skidded around a corner. Rork looped the leash around the dog's neck, and he and Angus stepped out into the street.

The village was hushed and quiet. The milk truck was still making its rounds, stopping and starting with that queer hum between the neighborhoods' terraced houses. Rork squinted into bright sunlight, his head scudding with the racket made by the voices, and turned away from the village, heading for the outer boundary where the road dead-ended. The colors in the sky hadn't resolved themselves yet and were trapped in splotches of pink, purple, and mauve above a rim of trees, but the air was bracing and a little breezy and carried with it, as always, a salty hint of the sea.

Rork stepped over the barricade and walked the Castle Farm path, his spirits lifted momentarily by the sudden change in landscape. One minute he walked along the stone dyke, bordering the sleepy village. The next he was in open fields and farm pasture. The only problem was he had to walk past the cemetery and Morag the Crazy One's gatehouse at the turn in the lane.

He kept his din-wracked head down, hoping to avoid contact with her, but of course, she was in the front garden, talking to herself while she tended to her marsh orchids and ragwort, her hair ethereal and white against the morning's low clouds. She usually wore her hair in a knot at the nape of her neck, but today it flowed past her shoulders in a floating curtain of hair.

"Aye, aye, Rork, the Fergus," she said, eyeing him with rheumy eyes.

"Aye, aye, Morag." Ferguson was his surname, and "the Fergus" was a pet name his gran had given him. It meant something in Gaelic, but he'd forgot. Morag and his gran had been great friends, though Rork could never figure out why. His gran would visit Morag at her cottage as the sun set on May Eve or Lammas, streaking the sky with confectionary light. She'd come home strange, touched almost, musing about her husband or mother when Rork would bring her nightly hot water bottle, as if Morag had somehow peeled back time.

Angus resisted the tug on his leash, interested as he was in rooting around and lifting his leg on every weed and tuft of grass, so Rork was forced to stand there, awkward and flustered as Morag stood in the jungle of her garden, her arms akimbo and looking to the woods in the distance. As she turned toward him, Rork could hear her singsong voice muttering a song, a chant, or some other incantation. There was something vaguely familiar about the lilting melody. Angus coiled the leash around Rork's feet, and Rork had to stoop to untangle himself.

Morag bobbed her head in his direction, a scowl between her eyes as she watched his face for some kind of reaction, but Rork didn't know what exactly to make of her nattering. And frankly, the less he knew about the inner workings of Morag's mind the better. Most adults he knew were superstitious, so he thought the ditty or chant might just be a sign of that. His gran would box his ears for leaving his shoes on the table. Bad luck, she'd say. His father, too, when he was home, was forever tossing salt over his shoulder.

But then Rork stopped thinking. The wailing in his head grew louder, filling his skull. What was happening? he wondered, shaking his head. Then a strange shaft of light opened behind his eyes, like a rip in a fabric, and he heard a distinct voice calling him.

He looked at Morag who was looking at him in a funny way. "Did you say something?" he asked.

She looked at him like he was a ghost or something. "No, loonie," she said. "It wasn't me."

Morag made a small movement towards him, but Rork backpedaled, sticking his hand in his pocket. He gripped and ungripped the flash drive that he had a habit of always carrying with him and impatiently tugged on Angus. Begrudgingly, Angus lifted his head, and they trotted away from the cottage and Morag.

Morag the Crazy One called after him. "Aye, aye, Rork. You hurry. She's calling you." Muttering to herself, she turned up the garden path. Rork was glad to see the back of her.

As the sun rose in the sky, the temperature soared to nearly ninety degrees, the windless air thick and humid. It was unusual weather for coastal Bellie at any time of year but especially late summer. The lane became hot and dusty, now skirting the pasture on the left and deep woods on the right. Saplings planted beside the lane only provided brief spots of shade.

Angus panted heavily. Rork struggled to get breath into his lungs as well. He felt pressure inside his head and out. The hot sun hit the back of his ginger head like an anvil. On the other side of the pasture, Rork caught a glimpse of one of the castle's towers, a tall, crenulated turret rising above the surrounding forest with a gleaming blue slate roof and pale, sun-bleached stone covered in ivy.

His classmates told stories about seeing a pale figure in the window of the turret on moonlit nights, insisting the castle was haunted by the tragic niece of the Duke, locked away in the tower because of a scandal no one really knew details about. Rork thought the tale too fanciful and didn't join in the embellishing, focusing instead on his sketchpad and computer.

At school, he was taking his "A's" in advanced technology and web development, and his instructor thought he might have real talent for web coding and design. As a matter of fact, he had a small cult following in the blogosphere where he went by the ironic epitaph "The Fergus." He would experiment with Beta sites, and his following would test and critique.

His gran hadn't understood Rork's fascination with what she called his machine language, but she had bought him his first computer. He won his next computer in a coding contest and built it custom to his needs.

His father complained that Rork always had "his head stuck in a screen." Rork spent hours in his room thinking, coding, recoding. Trying to get the sequencing he wanted. His father was more of an action-oriented man. Another way they were disconnected from each other. It was really too bad Rork couldn't develop a program for communicating with his gran in the afterlife so that she could continue to guide him.

Rork kicked a stone in the path. It thudded ahead of him. The keening was getting more insistent. He felt as if his head was going to explode. It throbbed with the ebb and swell of voices, unrelenting in their urgent need of him. The sun made it worse, as if all the solar rays were focused on him. He looked around. He was too far along the path to return home easily. If only he could get out of the sun. Get relief. He reached a wildly overgrown section of path where branches dangled, heavy with leaf clusters and seedpods, and where the forest exuded lushness like dense breath in his face. Rork bowed his head beneath the sharp branches and pushed his way off the path and deeper into the woods. Branches brushed against his chest, legs, and back, when suddenly the temperature changed. He got goosebumps from the swift transition — from sweltering heat to a cryptic coolness that seemed almost otherworldly. Briefly, he felt relief.

Then the sounds in his head grew shriller and more alarming. He couldn't see Angus, but he could hear him, growling at the end of the leash. Angus, acting more crazy than he'd ever acted in his life, dragged Rork farther away from the trail and deeper into the woods.

"Angus, stop. Stop!"

Rork's large feet tripped on a tangle of low plants and crosshatching tree roots. Off balance, he reached out and grabbed a sloping ash tree to steady himself. The tree's bark was chilled and damp to the touch. Despite the intensity of the sun beyond the trees, he could just glimpse Angus through the undergrowth, snuffling about in the dirt.

Rork blinked in the shadows, trying to get a sense of where he was. He'd only stepped off the path, but he felt half-lost in the thickness of the woodland. Glossy-leaved rhododendron overhung a rough trail, leading deeper into the trees. Rork walked a few paces forward, pushing aside the rhododendron's evergreen-like leaves, and came into an open area. A bog grove! The ground was spongy and loamish, carpeted in hummocks of sphagnum moss. The space was vaulted with trees, forming a thick cover that shielded the low-lying foliage of bog myrtle, heath rush, and the pale green twayblade, or fen orchid, tacky with its own kind of beauty.

A circular bench had been built around a large oak in the middle of the grove. The bench was gray, its wood split by age and neglect. Tree stumps ringed the grove in a loose circular pattern interspersed with white heather. The flowers were tiny points of light in the dark and shadowed space.

The keening sharpened inside Rork's skull. He stumbled forward and sat on the old bench, pressing his fingertips into his temple. One voice in the confusion of voices was growing higher-pitched and garbled.

On the far side of the grove, away from where he was sitting, was a large fire circle. Flat rocks had been moved out of neat geometry and were covered in moss. Rork saw indentations in the ground: a circle within a circle within a circle.

The bog grove gave him a feeling of awe. He wished he could show his gran. Even though she hadn't had much use for kirk, he thought she would appreciate the mysterious space. Despite its decay, the grove felt alive, filled with the loves, losses, and conflicts of people who had gathered here over time. The ground, carpeted with bog moss, was pungent with this other-feeling.

"Aye, aye, loonie," his gran would say. "Everything in this life has a story." She'd rub the middle of his forehead with the pad of her thumb. "All you have to do is pay attention."

How often had he stared at the bright blue eyes behind her gold-rimmed glasses, trying to read the network of fine, spidery veins in her cheeks, exquisite as a motherboard?

Rork peered deeper into the grove's gloom and saw a gap of light between two of the largest oak trees, flagstones barely visible, almost buried in mulchy earth. A path led beneath a tangled arbor. He got up, his long legs taking him across the grove in a few strides. Angus yipped and yipped, as if in warning, pulling at the cuffs of Rork's jeans in a dogged attempt to prevent him from following the light. Even Angus understood what was out of the ordinary.

2: Banshee

RORK DUCKED BENEATH a thorny arch and entered a forest room that emitted a warm glow. In the center of a patch of weedy grass he noticed a stone pier about waist-high on which stood a curious metal sphere that looked like a deconstructed globe. Bands of copper ringed the globe, creating multiple lines of circumference. There were also metal-stamped images of stars, planets, suns, and moons. The copper rings crisscrossed in a celestial framework of longitude and latitude. The rings of the sphere twisted and turned, rotating in and around each other, making a rhythmic grinding sound.

Standing next to the sphere was a luminous figure with the silhouette of a slight young woman no taller than five feet. She wore a long, flowing gown cloaked in a wrap of sheer drapery fabric tinted violet, the exact color of the sky in the last, lingering moments before the sun finally set. The figure was singing, twining her voice with the sphere's music, her notes crystalline, staccato, and piercing. Her singing made the pressure in Rork's head even more intense, like his skull was going to split. He felt as if the sound was going to spit his brain out of his cranium like a seed. He shielded his eyes as if that might shield him from the pain.

The figure turned at his arrival into the alcove. "At last," she said. "We were wondering what was taking you so long. We've been calling you all morning!"

She smiled at him, her eyes sheer blue, her face pale as bone. Her eyes reminded Rork of the clearie marbles he'd used to shoot as a boy. His eyes were drawn to the gap between her two front teeth.

Rork felt time skip. His jaw gaped. He felt his cheeks drain of color. Disbelief froze his body, locking his long legs at the knees. Soundlessly, he opened and closed his mouth. His entire body seized like an operating system that refused to work. Only his nose twitched. He smelled a sweet smell like butter-sugar.

The figure looked like a teenager, maybe the same age as him, seventeen-ish, but so fair she was almost transparent. Her skin was the blue-white of a bleached skeleton. She flung a corner of the wrap over her shoulder, covering the indent at the top of her throat, and raised an eyebrow as if waiting for Rork to say something. They stared at each other in the unreal tranquility of the forest room, the sphere's gritty whining in the background.

Finally, Rork swallowed as some sensation returned to his legs. "Who are you?" he croaked.

She cocked her head to one side, narrowing her eyes. "I am a banshee, messenger of the living and the dead." Her voice made him uncomfortable inside. She nodded her silvery head. "My name is Bryonna, but my friends and family call me Boo." Again, he got a glimpse of gap teeth.

Rork's brain went blank. He must not be hearing properly. Had the keening dislodged a small bone in his eardrum?

"Did. You. Hear. Me?" asked the figure.

Rork saw her mouth move, her eyes regarding him. The part in her hair shimmered in the low light, but the gist of what she was saying escaped him. He shook his head, wondering if he should just leave, push his way back through the trees to the safety of the path. The feeling of being lost intensified. Vaguely, he remembered letting Angus off the leash in the bog grove. Why had he done that?

"Did. You. Hear. Me?" the banshee asked again.

The words began to penetrate the fog in Rork's brain.

"Did. You. Hear. Me?" She stepped towards him.

"Aye, aye. Boo. A banshee," said Rork, holding a hand up, forcing himself to reply. He felt unreal. He stepped backwards a few steps.

"Yes," she said, "messenger of the dead."

"Banshee. Messenger. Living and dead," Rork replied, his voice not like his voice at all.

"Your gran sent me."

"My gran?" Rork heard his voice ascend into a higher register. He felt dizzy and light-headed. He wanted to sit down.

"Aye," said the banshee named Boo. "She thought we could help each other."

"Huh?"

Boo hesitated, eyeing him. "You're the Fergus, right?"

Rork nodded.

"And your gran passed a fortnight ago?"

Rork nodded again.

"Whew," she said. "For a minute there I thought I'd transmitted to the wrong grandson."

He stared at her. "That would be bad?" he asked, wondering.

"Very bad." The banshee grimaced, her heart-shaped face almost comical. "You see, I'm not actually a banshee yet. I'm only a banshee-in-training."

Rork raised his eyebrows.

Boo put one hand on her hip, watching him. "Your gran didn't tell me you were slow," she said.

"I'm *not* slow," said Rork. He squared his shoulders and glared at the banshee, puffing up his chest. Immediately, he wanted to prove to her his worth, but words stuck in his throat. She was a harbinger of death, and he knew enough about banshees to know he didn't want to get on her bad side.

"Well, I don't get why you're not understanding this. Didn't you wish to be reunited with her?"

Rork stared at her, letting the words sink in. "Iamnotslow," he repeated, feeling overcome despite his bravado. He sank to the ground, perching at an odd angle on the stone slab underneath the pier, legs splayed out in front of him.

"My gran?"

He ran his hands through his hair, a nervous habit, and the curls stuck out from his head in a disordered halo. The keening had settled into a low hum, superseded by Boo luminating.

"You're a banshee," he said, ticking off what he thought he had heard on one long, tapered finger. He looked to the banshee, his mind struggling for some sense of coherency.

The banshee nodded in quick bobs, her movement frenetic, charged by the strident energy of the voices. She crouched down next to him on the slab, peering closely but keeping her distance, the sugary-sweet smell of her filling Rork's nostrils.

"You've been in touch with my gran."

Boo nodded again.

"You shuttle between the living and the dead."

She smiled into Rork's face. The sweetness almost made his mouth water with a hunger that felt more like yearning.

"I must be dreaming or hallucinating or something," said Rork. He knocked on his forehead with the rounded end of one fist, flesh hammering the flat plane of his cranium. He found the pounding strangely calming.

He dropped his arm and looked sideways at the banshee. "Who did you say was calling me?" he asked.

Boo clasped her hands together in her lap. "The dead," she said. "Your gran. Others who have crossed."

Rork snorted, wanting to believe, at least in a way, feeling a glimmer of something. Maybe hope.

"It's true," Boo insisted.

"But it sounds like noise."

"You don't understand the language."

"It's a language?"

"Yes." The banshee slanted her clearie eyes at him.

Rork fidgeted, bouncing one extended knee. He levered himself upright and began to pace the grove. He glanced at the sky, the fading sun. He worried that his father would be looking for him. Keeping his father waiting was never a good idea. Their relationship was rocky enough. How could he explain what was happening to him? He could never seem to find the words his father wanted to hear. As he paced, the fingers of one hand tapped on his right thigh as if it were a keyboard, typing "o-k" over and over, while his brain attempted to process his thoughts and feelings. Find. A. Way. To. Connect.

He considered the banshee, Boo, watching him, pulling on a strand of her long silvery hair. He thought he must be going crazy. He'd heard loneliness could do that to a person. But there was another part of him that soared at the idea. What if the banshee really did exist? And she could make it possible for him to see his gran again? Wasn't that what he'd been wanting? Was the banshee the way?

Rork turned to Boo. "My gran was trying to reach me?"

"Yes," she replied.

"How is she?"

"At peace. Mostly. The other side is not all that different from this side, except there are no boundaries of time or chronology." The banshee let her wrap slip from her shoulders, bare skin shimmering. She added, "She wants to see you, too. She worries about you."

Rork grunted. "She's the one who died." He continued pacing, his boots scuffing the ground. Boo pleated the chiffon-like fabric of her gown between two fingers. "I don't get how I'm supposed to help you."

He swung his long arms, speaking to the trees and bushes rather than the…person? woman? Girl?…sitting calmly in the alcove's center. "You're a banshee, and I 'live in my own world,'" he said, regurgitating one of his father's favorite gripes.

"I'm only a banshee-in-training," said Boo, her eyes like two small crystal balls. Rork glimpsed the space between her front teeth, and the sight of it was a buoy to his growing optimism. Could he believe her?

"Besides," continued the banshee, "I need volunteers. Especially an intermediary. That is, someone with imagination who can hear the voices."

"What for?"

Boo sighed. The sound of her exhaling echoed between his ears louder than the cacophony of other voices.

"In order for me to become a fully-fledged banshee and earn my hood, I have to complete a couple of assignments that have to do with life and death. And Rork, you're the only one who can help!"

3: Message

"HUH?" ASKED RORK. He could hardly believe what he was hearing. A banshee, a fantastical being, needed his help with a life or death situation. What could she possibly mean?

The banshee narrowed her eyes at him. "One task is to come up with a project special enough that it affects the living and the dead."

Rork stared back, heavy brows beetling over his green eyes. "Who decides if it's special enough?" he asked.

"I report to a higher power," replied Boo, solemn-faced.

"God?" asked Rork, struck with a sudden sense of awe.

"No, silly." Her laughter trilled in the small space. "The Chief Banshee Officer."

As if in response, a great ruckus clamored in Rork's head. He grimaced and pointed to his temple. "Did you also say you could help me make sense of this commotion?"

"Yes, I can help you translate. But be warned. There's no system for who gets to speak in the afterlife. It can be a problem as sometimes they are anxious to be heard." The banshee pushed herself up from the stone slab and rearranged her gown. She wore dainty, pointy-toed slippers. "I've heard it can drive some intermediaries crazy," she continued. "Thank goodness, my messages are assigned."

Rork squeezed his head. "Help?" he said, his steps slowing.

"Okay, okay," said the banshee. "Tell me what you hear. Try to pick out one voice."

Rork stopped pacing, his face contorted in concentration. He let his brain scan through the confusion of shouting, searching for a voice he could distinguish from the noise. Finally, he identified a low baritone intoning the same thing over and over.

You were my life.
You were my life.

Rork rubbed his forehead and tried to decipher. "Effie if ewe erie ow," he said.

Boo looked at him blankly and then burst out laughing, covering her mouth with her hand. "Effie if ewe?" She shook her head.

"What?" asked Rork.

"The afterlife is the other world, Rork," said the banshee. "Some cultures call it the mirror world. Does that give you a clue about how to make sense of the language?" She rearranged the slippery wrap around her shoulders, her eyes intent on his.

He stared at her, trying to understand what she was telling him. A mirror world? Suddenly, he understood.

"Oh," said Rork. "Words are reversed?"

"Yes," said the banshee, her eyes shining.

Rork concentrated on the words again, tapping out their characters on his thigh. Backwards talking wasn't easy.

life

He imagined holding up a mirror next to what he was hearing. It took some acrobatic thinking, but his brain finally flipped the word.

life

"Life," he said, spreading his long arms wide in victory.

The banshee beamed at him. "I guess you're not so dumb after all," she said.

Rork scowled at her. "But what does it mean?"

"Well, I presume your dead person is trying to say something to somebody about his or her life. Do you think you can translate the rest?"

Rork scrunched up his face again, replaying the words in his head: forwards and then backwards. He wished he had a computer, or even a pad of paper. He was sure he could write some code that would help him translate the afterlife's mirror language. His fingers continued to tap away on his upper thigh. "You-were-my-," he said. "Life!"

"Very good," said Boo.

"He's not *my* dead person," said Rork. "I wonder who he's trying to reach."

"We'll probably never know," replied Boo. "There just aren't enough of us to carry all the messages." She fiddled with the celestial sphere, poking her hand into one of the metal rings.

Rork stared at her. "There's not enough banshees?"

"No," sighed Boo. "That's why it's so crucial I get my hood."

"You getting a hood makes a difference?"

"Yes!" said the banshee, spinning the armillary, which began to whine some more.

Rork winced at the unearthly noise.

"A hood is the highest achievement for a banshee. It has powers, helping us bridge the worlds, allowing us to come and go seamlessly. It's also a symbol of accomplishment, validating us, proving to our community that we've made a contribution to the life-death continuum." Boo's voice intensified.

"Why do you need to be validated as a banshee?" asked Rork.

She gave a lopsided smile, looking past him. "You see what I am, right?" she said. "It's my destiny. My mother is a banshee. My grandmother. Her grandmother."

"Wait a minute," said Rork, trying to manage his thoughts. "What kind of life and death projects?" Then, he asked, "Life and death are a continuum?" What was she saying? Rork struggled to understand. There was life, and there was death. There wasn't anything in-between, was there?

"Humans understand so little," said the banshee. She put out her hands to still the swinging bands of the armillary.

Rork couldn't disagree. He was feeling very much out of his depth.

"Death is a *progression*. Banshees' final projects are meant to add understanding to this progression. Some nuance. Some technique. Some development that might contribute to our knowledge base."

Rork didn't say anything, trying to comprehend, wrestling with the idea of banshees and knowledge base. If he could play some small part, wouldn't that be something? Wouldn't that validate something for him, too? He liked the idea of contributing to a knowledge base. The banshee was only a wisp of a thing, but she seemed so determined. He wished he was destined for a larger purpose. Or had a grand understanding of what he was meant to do. Most of the time he just felt confused, and since his gran's death, that had gotten worse.

Not to mention the fact that his father yelled at him constantly about being more practical, and now he had dead people also nattering at him in his head. What would having a purpose feel like?

The copper rings of the celestial sphere hummed faster, and the banshee seemed to get anxious, as if hurried.

"Now I have to come up with this act of inter-life moment, and I don't have any ideas. And that's after the bigger problem of —" The set of her mouth was mulish. She looked frantically left and right as if expecting somebody or something to crash into the secluded forest-room's space.

"I'm running out of time," she said. "Banshees are fleeting. Dispatch monitors our transmittal time. I'll be written up if I stay too long." The banshee cocked her head at Rork. "Will you come with me?" she asked.

"What?" Rork choked, swallowing hard, feeling like there was something lodged deep in his throat.

"I told you, I need you," pleaded Boo. "You could have more time with your gran. Help me find a way to complete my projects. Please?"

Rork stared at her suspiciously. He got the sense that 'please' did not come easily to her. "How did you know I wanted more time with my gran?" he asked.

The banshee pointed to herself. "Banshee. Remember? Humans almost always want more time with the people we shuttle."

The possibility of seeing his gran again bloomed large in Rork's mind. So many things were sliding out of his control. Like books off a shelf no longer anchored to the wall. His gran could help him put things to rights. She could. He knew she could.

"Oh," said the banshee, "I almost forgot. Your gran gave me something for you." She handed Rork a small jeweler's box like that made for a ring. An object rattled inside.

Rork opened the lid and found a sixpence resting on a small silk square. A token of good luck, the sixpence was his father's. It had been sewn behind his wings as aircrew in the Royal Air Force. His father credited the coin with bringing him home in one piece. His gran had promised it would be Rork's one day. His father wanted him to have it — for luck and legacy, she'd say — bringing it out whenever Rork was feeling particularly misunderstood or dismissed by his father.

Rork looked closer at the coin, at the floral pattern of rose, leek, shamrock and thistle and the words "FID DEF." *Defender of the faith*. Could Rork be the trooper his father was? Was meeting the banshee a test? Would he return home? Would he return home changed? One thing he knew for sure, he would need all the luck he could get.

Rork let the coin fall into the deep pocket of his jeans, opposite leg to the flash drive. Then he tucked the silk square back into the box and put the box in a side zipper of his backpack. The square smelled of the dried herbs from his gran's bedroom dresser drawer. Lavender. Geranium. Something woody, mysterious.

In their nightly bedtime ritual, he'd bring her a hot water bottle for her feet. She'd squeeze his hand in the high-vaulted chill of the back bedroom, pink as spring's first tulips, and whisper, "Love you forever, loon." Rork felt tears sting his lower eyelids. He turned a little away from the banshee, plucked a leaf from a tree overhead, and slowly ripped it to shreds.

The banshee didn't seem to notice. She continued, as if assuming his compliance. "Of course, I'll have to find you a minder, someone who can help you in-between. I'm only allowed to come and go, and intermediaries aren't very practical by nature. They also get distracted easily."

"What?" Rork asked, distracted. It was the second time she'd used the word 'intermediary.' Was that what he was? He rubbed the coin in his jean's pocket, reassured by the disk shape.

Boo shook her head at him. "S-l-o-w," she spelled, shaking out her wrap and rewinding it around her neck and shoulders.

"I am not slow," said Rork. He felt like he had to account for himself, like with his father. Then he was interrupted by a strange buzzing noise like a cellphone set to vibrate.

The banshee retrieved a heavy, silver comb from a pocket in her robe.

"Dispatch is calling."

She combed her silky hair with the comb, holding her head high. Her hair crackled with static electricity, an otherworldly energy. As Rork watched, he saw the banshee begin to fade, growing visibly less distinct against the leafy background of green foliage.

"Meet me here tomorrow," she said. He could hardly see her now. "The same time."

Her voice carried like the soughing of the wind. "Oh," she said, patting her robe again. "I have something else." She took out a slip of paper from what must be another pocket, "From your gran."

Rork's heart squeezed the breath out of him. He fixated on the slip of paper as he held out his hand, but the banshee was disappearing too fast. The slip blew out of her hand and skittered along the grove's deep grass. Rork grabbed it from the ground with a long sweep of his arm.

Looking over his shoulder, squinting, Rork could just make out the banshee's silhouette, watery-looking, as if he were peering through a glass jar, her eerie, see-through eyes the last to disappear.

"Tomorrow," she mouthed.

4: Misunderstanding

RORK STOOD IN THE GLOOMY forest room, staring at the spot where the banshee had disappeared, clutching the piece of paper. A hint of sweetness lingered. The sun was lower in the sky. Rork wondered how late it was. He hoped his father wasn't waiting for him. Suddenly, he got a sick feeling in his stomach. Did he want to face his father after what he'd just experienced? He shoved the paper down deep in the front pocket of his jeans, saving it for later when he had more time.

Panicked at the lateness, he batted at leaves. Somehow, he'd gotten turned around and couldn't tell where the opening in the trees was. Another of his failings: a terrible sense of direction. The banshee wasn't wrong. He did get distracted, lost at every turn. Angus dove out of the shadows and pounced at his feet.

"There you are," said Rork, relieved. "*Now* you show up." He bent down to stroke the scruffy white dog behind the ears. "Chicken," he said, under his breath. The dog's black button eyes gazed back adoringly.

The sun slipped like a lozenge below the horizon, and the unseasonable heat evaporated as the evening turned cool. Lights blinked on in the village. Rork walked back along the farm path, dragging his feet, the rabble of voices in his head subdued. He could hear the sound of a tractor working a field not too far away. There was no sign of Morag, just a spade left in the loose dirt of her patch of garden.

Rork could see the gate that marked the boundary of the village when he sniffed the acrid stink of a cigarette.

"Damn," he thought to himself. He was in a hurry, and the last thing he needed was to run into Hamish. Poor, tragic Hamish.

"Here comes Rorkie and his little dog," rasped Hamish from the shadows, crouched on the top railing. A studded wallet in his back pocket was linked to a front belt loop by a chain, which chinked softly.

"Aye, Aye, Hamish," said Rork. He gritted his teeth, willing himself not to engage. It was a miracle Hamish had even survived. If Rork could call it that. Hamish's hands — with their cross-stitching of scars — were a wrecked testimony to what he'd been through. There'd been so much shattered glass. Rork watched Hamish's hands float ghostly in the shuttering dusk. Lighting another cigarette. Opening and closing the steel lighter. Resting on the railing.

"What a doo-ti-ful son." Hamish slid from the railing and threw his cigarette into the gravel. He was skinny, almost emaciated, and wore baggy, grimy jeans.

If only the caustic tone of his voice didn't set Rork off. He bent down to untangle the leash from Angus's paws. It was twisted again. Hard to believe he and Hamish had once been friends. But that was before-the-accident Hamish, when he had hopes and dreams and two parents.

"What like?" asked Rork, the traditional greeting in their village. The skin around Hamish's bleak eyes was pouched and gray.

"The usual," replied Hamish. "Having a nip, waiting to die." He hacked a laugh, patting the top pocket of his frayed anorak.

Rork smelled the peat-y smell of whisky. "Oy, I thought your pen and ink for the senior opening was brilliant." Rork averted his gaze. Hamish hated it when Rork tried too hard, tried to resurrect some semblance of their former relationship. Like friendship could survive life's never-ending tragedies. "Dark," Rork added.

"Aye," said Hamish. "I'm all about the dark." His greasy, colorless hair hung in lank hunks. The only holdover from his old life was his mentorship with one of Bellie's art instructors. Rork understood Hamish even kipped on the teacher's sofa when his uncle was on a bender.

Rork felt Hamish's uncanny gaze on him and began to type on his upper thigh h-o-m-e.

"What's new with you?" Hamish asked.

"N-n-nothing," said Rork quickly, his voice hoarse.

"I heard about your gran," said Hamish, his tone clear, momentarily sincere, picking crumbs of tobacco from his tongue. "She was a rare dame."

"Aye, she was," said Rork, starting to choke up.

"And now she's gone."

"Aye."

"Just like my mum and da." Hamish took a long draw of whisky from a flask. Hissed.

Rork didn't dare answer. He wished Hamish would slink away, leave him alone. He hated how powerless he felt around him, worse because they'd once known each other so well.

Rork couldn't help but feel the dead-end waste of his drinking and talent. And there was no talking to him. He'd just give you that look, that hard look that said, "What do you know about anything?" It was a look Rork had difficulty withstanding. What *did* he know about anything? He thought of the banshee and her hopeful, glowing light. How could anything associated with death have a hopeful, glowing light?

"Where you coming from?" asked Hamish, his dark eyes probing, puckering the scar that stretched across his forehead, a relic from their friendlier days and one afternoon's misguided attempt to learn cricket. "It's late."

"Nowhere," said Rork. "Just me and Angus lost in the woods again." Angus snuffled on cue. Rork tried to laugh, but it sounded lame even to him. More frantic typing on his thigh. "Well…." he said. "I gotta get going." He started walking, inadvertently strangling Angus with his about-turn.

"Oh, aye," said Hamish, a hint of irony in his voice. "My uncle said something about your father coming home. I bet you can't wait. Say hi to him for me, will you?"

Angus growled. Rork nudged him along, feeling trail dust settle into every line of his face. He knew Hamish knew better. He'd witnessed first-hand enough tense moments between Rork and his father. Actually, Hamish had stood up for him once. Not something he'd likely repeat. His father had a way of making a person feel small if they showed they cared about anything he didn't agree with.

When he reached home, Rork kicked his heavy boots against the cement stoop, uncaking the mud collected in the treads. His father would scold him if he tracked dirt into the house, and he really didn't want to start things off that way.

Angus lifted his leg on a crack between the house and pavement where a small pile of pebbles had come loose from the stucco. "Have you no shame?" asked Rork distractedly.

Rork let Angus off the leash, and the dog clattered away down the long hallway to find his water bowl, his white tail swishing. Like a flag of surrender, thought Rork. He hung up his jacket and listened. He could hear the clock ticking on the mantel in the front room, the toilet gurgling in the bathroom, and at the far end of the hall the echo of a kitchen chair scraping against the stiff squares of linoleum.

Rork squared his shoulders, hoping for a cup of tea. Thankfully, the voices in his head had dulled. They were still there in the background, but not intruding too much on his thoughts or actions. He wished his gran were one of the voices he could hear. He could use her encouragement right about now. But he guessed there might be a trick to that.

"What like," he said, ducking under the kitchen door. The house was over two hundred years old, built solidly of field stone. When the kitchen had been added on, his father and other workers had discovered a stone lintel the size of a wheelbarrow above the old back door. There was no removing it without a lot of time, trouble and expense, so the doorway to the kitchen had stayed slightly lower than the rest of the doorways in the house.

His father sat at the kitchen table, his back to the patio door, his broad shoulders blocking out the minimal light their small back garden got, tacked on almost like an afterthought behind the house. In the garden, Rork could see Angus running around in circles on the paving stones.

The kitchen was a large room, extending the length of the house. Because his father favored more masculine décor and his gran bright colors, the kitchen was a disparate mix of paneling, red floral tile and flouncy curtains. Long lengths of red countertop created a horseshoe on either side of the sink, and his gran's old sideboard took up one wall opposite the dining table.

His father was stirring a teaspoon in his tea. "Aye, aye, Rork," he said, nodding to a corner of the kitchen. "Kettle's boiled. There's butteries, too."

Butteries were a local delicacy, a Highland version of the French croissant. On alert, Rork tried to read his father's face, his voice. His accent was thick and clipped, his "r's" rolling more pronounced when he was home, so his voice sounded like purring, an idling engine, or a deep-throated snarl, depending on his mood.

His father seemed calm enough, sanguine even. In Rork's life his father seemed to hold all the cards. Nervously, Rork sat at the kitchen table with a cup of tea filled to the brim with three teaspoonfuls of sugar. His chair bumped a leg of the table, and tea sloshed the table.

"Sorry," he said. He didn't dare look up. His father tossed him a napkin.

Silence ensued. His father was a man of few words. He did not natter, as his gran would say. It was a trait, Rork had noticed, shared by many of his father's ex-military friends. Perfectionism? Fastidiousness? An antiquated belief in black and white? His father rarely spoke of his time in the service. Rork knew he had served in the British Parachute Regiment stationed in Jordan and Cyprus for peacekeeping. Rork had found his beret in storage. To date, his father had only shared how delicious the grapes were.

"Where were you?" asked his father. He looked at Rork beneath heavy salt-and-pepper brows. Rork fidgeted. His father's eyes bore a hole right through him, his eyes so blazingly blue they looked white-hot. Fire-and-ice eyes, Rork thought. At the moment more ice than fire.

Rork's brain baulked at the thought of telling his father about the grove or the banshee. It was an otherworld experience, which he wanted to think about more when he was safely alone. His father would only think it was more of his fanciful nonsense.

"Walking Angus," he said.

"Did you get lost?" asked his father.

Rork drank his tea and did not respond. The question felt like a trap. Rork had too much on his mind today to fall for it.

His father pushed back from the table and crossed one leg over the other. Rork felt he was being assessed. His father's steel wool hair was slicked back with balsam oil in a pompadour-style that lifted off his high forehead. His face was windblown and craggy.

His father sighed heavily. "What are you doing with your life, Rork?"

"What do you mean, sir?" answered Rork.

"Ever since your gran died you've been mooning about the place or hiding away in your room, tapping away on that bloody computer."

"I miss her, sir."

His father was silent, sliding the rounded bowl of his teacup back and forth on the dining room table. It made a grating noise that got on Rork's nerves.

"It's about time you stop this grieving. What about a change?" said his father. "Get away, out of your own head." His father stood and clamped one hand on the soft flesh between Rork's neck and shoulder. He looked down at him.

"I've arranged for you to work with one of my mates in the Border Country. It'll be good for you. He needs a mason tender. It's a valuable trade, Rork. Honest, hard work. My mate will give you room and board, a decent wage."

"Sir, I don't want to go away." Rork struggled to keep the desolation out of his voice. His father wanted to send him away?

"Rork," said his father, moving towards the tea pot for a refill. "I believe I know what's best for you."

Rork clenched his jaw, grinding his teeth, as emotions coursed through him. He could feel the tumult in his body: loss, grief, sadness, frustration, regret. Now, added to all that, was a feeling of deep rejection that his father wanted to send him away. He could hardly bear it. And how could he explain himself to his father in a way he'd understand? He didn't know how. He didn't know if he had the language. This vexation seemed to burst the dam of emotions. Again, anger was easier.

"You do *not* know what's best for me!" said Rork, pushing away from the table. His chair tipped, hitting the kitchen floor with a loud smack. Rork stooped to pick it up, furiously biting his lower lip. He felt tears well up behind his eyes. "You don't even know me, so how could you know what's best for me? I don't want to stop feeling sad for my gran. I want to remember her."

Rork stomped out of the room in his stocking feet. He refused to let his father see him cry. When he got to his room, he sprawled face down on his bed, numbly listening to music on his computer, left on 24/7. He knew he had behaved childishly, but he didn't care. Well, he did care, but he pretended he didn't. His gran would not be proud of him and would have given him a chore that somehow aligned with his transgression. Perhaps weeding the garden? The act of pulling the tenacious clover and chickweed reminding him that some words were better left unsaid? What was it about his father that brought out the juvenile in him?

Rork rolled over and groaned. Mason tender? What was his father thinking? He was the farthest thing imaginable from a mason tender. Didn't they carry bricks on their backs with muck? He could only imagine what kind of a mess he'd make with that job.

In despair, he remembered the note the banshee had given him from his gran and dug it out of his pocket. Music riffed at the end of a song as he opened the piece of paper. He didn't know what to expect.

"It starts with the banshee and a wee shift," the note read in gran's spidery handwriting.

That was it. Rork smiled ruefully. It was so like her, cryptic and intriguing and sure to capture his interest. The note put him in mind of her last words. Find. A. Way. To. Connect. What starts with the banshee? What wee shift?

His gran's end had come so suddenly. Rork hadn't been prepared. Could he have been? Ever? She'd acted as if nothing were the matter, keeping her illness to herself. Rork knew she was willful, but why hadn't they noticed her slower step, her hand held out for steadying? He felt like he'd disappointed her. She must have known her time was near. Was that why she'd insisted on the nettle-hunting? Her way of creating a memory with him? Had she found a final moment with his father, too? Rork had never asked his father. Rork remembered carrying her to the car, the slightness of her, her strange murmurings. The long, interminable night of losing her.

The song on his computer flipped to a Celtic rock song. His web show interposed the song with images of drumsticks arranged in a stop-animation style: crossed drumsticks, uncrossed drumsticks, spotlight drumsticks, drumsticks in shadow, falling drumsticks, drumsticks spelling out "pain."

Rork air-drummed along to the song. His father wanted to send him away. Away. Not here. Gone. His gran was not here. Her note said it started with the banshee and a wee shift. What did she mean? Perhaps he should find out? If what the banshee said was true, and life and death were on a continuum, where was his gran? Her death felt final to him.

Was the banshee on the level? Was she real? Or had his imagination gotten the better of him in his grief? He also wondered about his own aptitude. Was he up for the challenge she'd hinted at? Or was he the disaster his father thought him to be? Should he even believe in the banshee?

The cadence of the song was heavy, mind-thumping, echoing in the small, back bedroom Rork inhabited. He continued to hear reverberation long after the song ended, percussive like rain.

You'll never know

Bang bang

unless you try.

Bang bang

The phrasing repeated in his head a number of times before he bolted to sitting, realizing that it was the voice of some dead person, rising above the din of the music. It was a woman with a mocking but urgent voice. Rork imagined a grandmotherly type with wavy white hair and freckled hands, knitting or reading in a rocking chair.

Rork raced to his computer, desperate for distraction. He had learned to type on an old-fashioned manual typewriter and continued to hit the keys harder than necessary. He knew he could figure out a string of code that would help him unmirror the language of the deceased, but he thought best with his fingers as he typed and untyped characters. Somehow, he could apprehend all the letters the dead spoke, as if recognizing a familiar pattern. He just couldn't assimilate the letters into spoken word without turning them this way and that in his head like puzzle pieces.

He worked furiously, putting his father, the banshee, the voices, and his needy self out of mind. "Aye," he said to himself. The code was tricky because he had to reverse engineer the language, without having mirror keys on his keyboard. But he figured out that if he ran the code in reverse order, he could lead the words in through the back door, so to speak, with them ultimately coming out the front door in the right order.

Rork sat back in his chair and gave a grunt of triumph.

You'll never know

unless you try.

He wondered who it was intended for. Daughter? Son? Granddaughter? It sounded like something his gran would say.

Rork tried his code sequence the other way, perversely typing in:

But if you don't try

you'll never know.

He heard a laugh that sounded loud and clear between his ears:

Chicken.

Rork didn't even have to run it through his code sequence. He knew the voice from the other side was right. Then his thoughts took an uncharacteristic turn. Why not just leave? Go with the banshee? Take his chances. Follow his gran's note and get out of the shadow his father cast with his un-Rork-like expectations. He wanted him to leave anyway, right? Could the impossible be possible? Mason tender indeed.

Maybe he could even make a difference, help the banshee, contribute to the knowledge base. Maybe.

5: Auditions

THE NEXT DAY, RORK RUSTLED his way back to the grove. When he first woke, he wasn't so sure about what he'd experienced in the grove or at his computer. The whole experience felt like a dream. His father was convinced his imagination was out of control most of the time. Rork wasn't absolutely sure his father was wrong. Then he remembered his gran bustling about the kitchen, talking to him with that lilt in her voice. She'd always had a feeling of possibility or magic about her.

Almost without thinking about what he was doing, Rork got up off the bed, got dressed, and headed downstairs. He was careful to avoid making any noise that would wake his father, and although Angus was more than ready to go with him as he slipped quietly toward the door, Rork left his loyal friend behind.

The morning in the Highlands was cool and clear, and Rork wore a quilted flannel shirt over a favorite T-shirt underneath his backpack. The leaves of the trees dripped moisture in the shadowed grove. His laptop was strapped to the outside of his pack with wide, buckled straps. Above him were sentinel trees, and as the sun rose in the sky, they created windows of light on the grove's floor. Rork missed Angus already, but he could hardly bring him, not knowing what to expect. The dog would be company for his father, or the neighbor.

Rork tore another leaf to shreds as he walked into the forest. He had left his father a message on his desktop screensaver, which was motion-activated and would play as soon as he entered his bedroom. Basically, it said he would take his father's advice and get away for a while. He planned to stay with friends in Wick and had left to take an early bus. He would call in a few days.

He did not think his father would worry about him. Much. After all, he was prepared to send him away. His father had his routine, his work, his crossword puzzles, and never-ending cups of tea. Mason was a fitting occupation for his father. The walls he built. Since his mom had died, his father had become a fortress. Rork hardly remembered his mother. His memories of her — mere sensations really — were fleeting. The sound of her voice in his ear as he drifted off to sleep. Her smell of rosewood as they lay next to each other. He remembered she always had a book nearby and read to him every night. Her voice rising and falling with the story, her American vowels like the square wheels of a wagon. He remembered his father would tease her about her "a's" or "r's." Rork had been learning his letters, too. She only laughed, slapping his father playfully. "I caaaan't help where I'm frrrrom," she'd reply, exaggerating the sounds.

Of course, his father did not speak of her, and Rork had been afraid to ask. His father had locked up his mother's things in a closet and turned the key. He'd taken his time, disappearing after their evening meal to fold her clothes, stack her books, and arrange her few pieces of jewelry and perfume bottles on rows of shelves. Rork wanted to go to him, but when he asked the question, his gran would shake her head. "Leave him be, loon." Then she'd open her arms wide and say, "Give us a hug."

Rork would walk into her arms, and gran would enfold him in a firm embrace. The loss was bottomless, his questions locked away with her things. He hardly cried. He felt dry as dust.

His gran smelled differently than his mother, but he grew to appreciate her smell, too, a mix of fresh plums and laundry. His father blamed himself for the accident. Rork's mother hadn't been much of a driver, and of course she'd learned to drive in the other lane. The bypass didn't exist then, and the motorway traffic through their village was high-speed and relentless. She had veered into the wrong lane. The metal of the car had crushed ugly and irrevocable. She'd died at the scene, a compendium of crossword puzzles on the bench seat.

In the grove, Rork looked around for the banshee. He saw no sign of her, just the deep green leaves of rhododendron and tiny-flowered white heather, perennial stars in the undergrowth. The doubts he'd had right after waking up intensified. Was he losing his sanity? He'd hate for his father to be right about him, but what if he was? Perhaps he *was* useless?

Since his mother died, Rork had existed in a strange tunnel of motherlessness. Other students avoided him as if motherlessness was something they could catch. He'd felt disconnected from others a lot of the time, despite a brief friendship with Hamish, until he'd disappeared into his own black tunnel. Rork could talk about what he remembered about his mother with his gran but not his father. He spent hours and hours alone, in the world of computers. His imagination was large and full of possibility. But what about the rest of him? Had he been stunted by life events and introspection? He no longer possessed any kind of objectivity about his skills or capabilities. And what about the voices? Would they compromise him? Or embolden him? Rork was contemplating stepping outside the only reality he knew, into something *other*. He must be mad. Or desperate. Or both. Yet despite his misgivings he knew the time had come to test himself, and he felt urged on by his gran's last words: Find. A. Way.

Rork entered the grove and heard the sphere music and the banshee's staccato voice. The pressure in his head mounted. In her piercing voice, the banshee seemed to be giving orders. But who could have joined her in the alcove? He ducked through the arch into the forest room and found himself face to face with an assortment of, well, *specimens* would be the only way to describe what he saw.

Rork paused, trying to take in what he was seeing. At first, he thought he was looking at aliens. Or perhaps kids dressed to look like aliens. But then he realized they were indeed humans, though the strangest-looking humans he'd ever seen. They looked extraterrestrial. One was paint splattered. One was flattened. One was shaped like a lightbulb with a head twice as large as his body. Their strange characteristics weren't just superficial. Paint penetrated the skin in multi-colored blotches. The flattening was physical. The kid could have slipped through the narrowest of openings like an envelope. The lightbulb had such a surprised look on her face, as if arrested at the moment of idea. Rork couldn't help but stare. He felt he'd walked into a side show at the circus. Where did these kids come from? What did their irregularities mean? Why were they here? The situation was beyond weird yet somehow within the realm of normal. But what he saw in the alcove undoubtedly stretched the realm of normal.

"Rork!" cried the banshee. "You came!" She hopped on her dainty toes, clapping her hands. "Your gran said you would, but I was fretting." She smiled her gap-teeth at him. "I'm glad you're here," she said.

Rork smiled back. Boo's gladness at seeing him was a balm to his hurt feelings at his father's rejection. Perhaps he was right to come. Like the day before, her sweet scent permeated the forest room.

"What's all this?" Rork asked.

"Tryouts," said Boo. "We have to find you a minder."

Rork's eyebrows lifted. "What for?"

Why did he need a minder? He thought they'd be working on an inter-life project. How did that warrant a need for protection?

The banshee stuck out her hip and placed her hand at her waist, looking a little like the handle of a teacup. "Rork, the Fergus," she said sternly as if she understood his apprehension. "You need a minder to enter Shufftie. They understand the path and will make sure you don't do anything *too* irreversible."

"Oh," he said, still mystified. What was the banshee talking about? He could hardly follow, but he became fixated on the idea of a new coding language. What kind of code? What did it do? Who wrote it? Here was the key to who he was. Rork was convinced.

"It's not advisable for an intermediary to journey alone," said Boo, preoccupied by the shuffle of bodies around her. "At least we find the results are more valuable when an intermediary is accompanied by a minder."

Wait a minute. Did she say 'Shufftie'? That 'intermediary' thing again? Journey where exactly? Would he leave the grove?

His village? The Highlands? He'd come despite his reservations, but the whole experience was becoming crazier and crazier, just the way his father would describe it, a product of his imagination.

The banshee had moved off before he could ask more questions. But then Rork remembered that she had said life *and death* projects, and he found that he rather welcomed the idea of a minder, someone to look out for him.

"Here are your candidates," said the banshee. She waved her arms at the strange assemblage, lining them up on one side of the alcove against the hedge of trees. She turned back to Rork. "You need to pick one."

Rork looked up and down the line, trying to make sense of the strangeness. Pick one? How would he do that? What was he looking for?

"Come on," said Boo, clapping her hands sharply. "We haven't got all day."

Rork leaned in closer to the banshee and whispered behind his hand. "Why do they all look so…so different?" He noticed this morning that the banshee smelled more like treacle or caramelized sugar, thick with urgency.

Boo looked up at Rork, shaking her head, already exasperated with him, it seemed. "All these young people," she said, "have been touched by a near-death experience in some way. The experience has left its mark." The banshee wriggled onto a bench at the far end of the alcove. "Sometimes the markings are literal," she said, pointing to one of the girls who mingled with the others, hieroglyphics tattooed in a ring around her wrist. "Sometimes not. Death can be very versatile, and, despite our work of centuries, we just don't know everything."

The banshee bounced in her seat impatiently. "Ask them each a few questions," she said, nodding forcefully at Rork. Rork was getting a little impatient himself. What was he getting himself into? For what felt like the millionth time, he asked himself if this was really real.

"What kind of questions?" asked Rork. "What exactly am I looking for?"

The banshee rearranged her cloak. "What do they remember about their experience that might be useful? Will you be compatible with their personality? You'll be together for a while."

Together for a while? Alarm bells exploded in Rork's head.

"How long?" he asked. He could hear the near-panic in his voice.

"As long as it takes," replied Boo inscrutably.

Rork paced in front of the candidates. He looked at them. What was he really seeing? They were so odd, hardly human. They eyed him warily. He hesitated, looking over at Boo. She bobbed her chin, pressing him to pick one already.

He stopped in front of a kid dressed all in black. He reminded Rork a little of Hamish, who also dressed all in black. The kid's head was bald, and his clothing was edged in char. Rork guessed he'd been involved in a fire. The kid looked angry, not afraid of anything. Useful? What was useful in Shufftie? Rork had no idea.

"What do you remember about your experience?" Rork asked him.

Charboy looked at him sullenly. He had a hoop in his right singed eyebrow. "I remember fire and smoke. I remember losing all my bleeding hair." Charboy had a London accent and an attitude. He blew puffs of smoke when he spoke. Rork coughed and moved on.

Next, he paused in front of a girl with hair curlier than his. Blondish strands corkscrewed around her face in a frizzy halo. "You?" he asked.

"I was struck by lightning," said the frizzy girl. "I remember a blinding light and a jolt through my bones." Her movements were a little spastic, as if her body had been short-circuited, and she spoke in a breathy, baby voice. Rork felt for her plight. It must have been traumatic, all that power coursing through her body. But the baby voice made him dismiss her.

He cast his eyes up and down the row of candidates. He could hear the banshee fidgeting. He felt at a complete loss. They all seemed too damaged to be of much assistance. The voices of the dead in his head weren't any help either. They started up a raucous as loud as when he first heard them, gossiping cattily about the youth today.

Rork did an about-turn at the end of the row, trying to buy more time. He had to think.

He tripped on a tuft of dandelion at his feet. It hadn't been there before, and then it was there, springing up spontaneously. He found himself nose to nose with a slim, long-legged Flower Girl type. She was as tall as him, if not a little taller. She blinked green eyelashes at him.

"Hi," she said. "I'm the storyteller's daughter." She held out her hand to shake his. Her nails were a dazzling sky-blue. "You can call me Deirdre."

"Who's the storyteller?" asked Rork.

"My mother," replied Deirdre, smiling. "I didn't know her."

"Oh," said Rork. He stood up straighter, claiming all of his five feet, ten inches. It seemed important that they be equal. Still, the Flower Girl looked him dead in the eyes. Hers were a sunny green-gold. She somehow seemed familiar, as if their paths had crossed before. School, maybe? Yet the lashes threw him off. He had never seen lashes like hers before.

"Do you remember anything?" he asked, stumbling over his words. "About your experience, I mean."

"I remember a yolky light," said Deirdre. "Trees, woods, a rough trail."

Deirdre closed her eyes. She was wearing a strange assortment of layers. Leggings, a skirt of some kind with corners like a handkerchief, a top he imagined a ballerina would wear, and a rainbow knit scarf made of a silky kind of yarn.

"The wind whistling," she added.

She opened her eyes. Rork stared into starburst irises. Her long, kinky hair was held back with a wide, yellow headband.

"I was only a child," continued Deirdre, her voice far away, innocent. "I was completely at home in the garden. I thought the plant fertilizer was sprinkling sugar." She shrugged one bony shoulder ruefully. "Now the plants tell me things."

Curious despite himself, Rork was just about to ask Deirdre a follow-up question when he heard a loud "Aha!" behind him. He spun around. A broad, muscular, gym-rat-looking banshee with the same blue-white skin as Boo had appeared out of nowhere. He wore sweat clothes in dusky violet. He sparked fury.

"I knew you'd be here," he accused Boo. "You pick the best grove, recruit the most capable minders. Your mentor," his voice dripped sarcasm, "helped you find an intermediary already. It's not fair."

"How dare you, Beck!" said Boo, her voice as furious as the gym rat's fury. Her hair crackled with aggravation. "You know I follow the rules. I earned my place the same as you. You're just jealous because I'm more resourceful than you. I can't help it if everybody compares you to your dead-charming big brother." Boo stalked across the copse toward the big banshee, her slippered feet winking beneath her gown.

"You leave my brother out of this," jeered the gym-rat. The sleeves of his sweatshirt had been cut off, revealing arms with incredible definition. Rork flexed his biceps, paltry by comparison. He felt self-conscious about how ordinary he was compared to the characters around him, which was a ridiculous thought. He might be ordinary, but he certainly found himself in an extraordinary situation.

The top of Boo's head came up only to Beck's breastbone. She tipped her chin up at him. Their anger escalated to another decibel level. They shrilled at each other in high-pitched shrieking. The other-worldly anger grew in waves of sound outside Rork's head, but inside his head the voices moaned with distress. Rork, Deirdre, and the other minder candidates pressed their hands against their ears. None of them could comprehend or tolerate the unearthly noises of the two banshees' voices.

Beck's face turned red, then purple. Neck muscles strained, coiling the silver rope chain clasped around his neck. Rork hadn't even noticed the chain until it glinted against the sudden redness of his neck. Boo's mouth and chin compressed into a sharp line of disdain. Their screeching became so high-pitched that Rork could no longer hear them, but he could feel a heightened pressure in the air, making his whole skull ache.

In frustration, Beck grabbed two sides of his sweatshirt and tore it apart with his bare hands, revealing a blue-white hairless chest. "This is not over," Beck said, glowering at Boo.

She glowered back.

Rork, fighting through a pounding headache, wished he were back in his room, anywhere other than where he was. The situation felt so outside what he was capable of. The banshee was fantastical enough, but now she had enemies? He watched the Flower Girl, how she reacted.

"I want him," said Beck, pointing to Charboy. The two seemed to share the same angry attitude.

Boo eyed him, assessing his request. She looked to Rork, who shrugged with one shoulder. He had no idea how he should react or why it mattered. "Fine," she said. "Take him and leave."

And then she added with irony, "Please."

Beck let the tatters of his sweatshirt fall to the ground and motioned to Charboy. The two left the copse in a cloud of smoke and bad temper. Bits of ash floated down out of the sky behind them. Rork could see Beck's blue-white skin flash between the leaves of the forest. What was left of his sweatshirt evaporated in the grass. The pressure in Rork's head lessened, but he still felt a dull ache. He surprised himself by not sprinting from the grove and heading toward home and safety.

"Who was that?" asked Rork, turning to Boo as soon as Beck and Charboy were out of sight.

Boo's chest heaved. She was clearly agitated. "I am so tired of bullies," she said, her voice drained of the shrillness that had been so overwhelming just a moment before.

"That Charboy," offered Rork, "is a lit fuse. I want to stay as far away from him as possible."

"Aye," said the Flower Girl, stepping out of line toward Rork and Boo. "A very destructive pair." She plucked at the scarf around her neck. "I'd like to help you."

Rork looked down again at her blue fingertips, trying to place her accent. The islands, for sure, he thought. Outer Hebrides? He watched, mesmerized, as a creeping vine entwined around her right ankle, sending green tendrils up her body and erupting in pert, yellow flowers at her knee, hip, and shoulder blade. A tiny bud opened behind her ear. Deirdre, nonplussed, opened and closed her bright green eyelashes at him.

"Since the accident," she explained, "plants find me. We help each other. Do you like plants?" Her voice sounded hopeful.

"My gran was a gardener," said Rork.

The banshee looked from Rork to Deirdre and back again. "Is this your minder, then?" she asked.

Rork felt the enormity of Boo's question. It was a turning point. By deciding, he would be committing to whatever strange sequence of events might happen: the unreality of battling banshees and minders of near death, whatever Shufftie was and would entail. Why had he come anyway? What had possessed him?

"Aye," decided Rork on the spot. Deirdre seemed less traumatized than some of the others, and her affinity with plants might come in handy. Then a deeper thought occurred to him. They could be motherless together, as he didn't really remember much about his mother either. The thought reminded him fleetingly of Hamish and his dark tunnel.

"Good," said the banshee. "We have lots to do." The banshee dismissed the other candidates who left in all directions, disappearing into the woodlands in a rustle of leaves, blurs of light or by simply vanishing.

Rork eyed Deirdre surreptitiously, hoping he'd made the right choice. She was tall and colorful and calm. At the very least they could keep pace with each other. He couldn't help but recall his father's words: "Rork, you can't move forward unless you make decisions." The recollection of his father seemed to reproach him, his father's eyes mocking the unreality into which he'd catapulted himself by missing his gran so fiercely.

Well, whether right or misguided, he *had* made a decision on this weirdly and otherworldly journey, his first decision as an intermediary, whatever that really meant.

The voices of the dead in his head gave him a polite round of applause.

6: Shufftie

INHALING DEEPLY, the banshee perched on a cushioned wicker chair and said, "I love a cup of tea."

"You're not actually drinking it," observed Rork.

Boo, Rork, and Deirdre sat huddled around a glass-topped, circular table in a Highland teashop benignly watched over by an elderly shopkeeper who had greeted the banshee warmly, beaming behind her spectacles.

"No," said the banshee, sadly. "I can only absorb it from the air."

The teashop had deep-welled windows overlooking the street that were full of flowers, lilies and dahlias and wilder willowherb in painted wood window boxes. Delicate blooms leaned imperceptibly towards Deirdre, extravagant in contrast to the simple, porch-style tearoom.

There was the clatter of spoons and china as Rork and Deirdre readied their teacups with sugar and cream. Rork removed the tea cozy and poured the dark Scottish Blend, stirring in three sugars for himself.

"You like yours sweet," said Boo, making conversation. She smiled, revealing her gap teeth, reminding Rork of the sun coming out from behind clouds.

The actual celestial sun was miraculously shining through tall, mullioned windows, cutting the green countryside into squares. Rork, oblivious to the landscape, lavishly buttered a scone and ate it in three bites.

"Cheers," said Deirdre, holding her teacup with two hands at chin level.

The banshee hummed beneath her breath, swinging her slippered feet beneath the table. Rork's wicker stool creaked under his weight. After a third scone, he relaxed and blew on his tea.

He eyed Boo beneath heavy brows. "Who's Beck?" he asked.

"Och. Just another banshee-in-training." She rearranged the folds of her wrap. "We don't get along."

Rork stared into her clearie eyes. "You don't say."

The banshee hiccupped, half-laughing.

"If you must know," she said, "Beck and I belong to two rival banshee families. We've been at odds for years."

Deirdre waggled a surprisingly large purple sneaker and looked from Rork to Boo.

"And?" said Rork.

"And he doesn't like me."

"Any particular reason?"

The banshee sighed, reluctant to share more. "His brother thought he should be CEO. The board determined otherwise. His brother blamed my mother, and as long as I can remember there has been this animosity between our families. Beck hates me on principle." She shrugged derisively. "I object to being hated for no good reason."

Rork sat back on his stool. His right hand twitched on his upper thigh, itching to type. W-h-a-t?

"There's a Board?" he asked. The unreality of sitting in a teashop drinking tea with a banshee and a near-death-experience girl talking about the politics of a fantastical world, a world his father would not acknowledge, made him feel light-headed.

"Yes," said Boo. She dug her blue-white chin into her palm. "There are thousands of banshees stationed all over the world. At some point in our vast history, we incorporated. Every century we elect a Board of Seers and a Chief Banshee Officer. There's even a mission statement."

"What's the mission statement?" asked Deirdre, looking up from her tea. Rork could see the sweeping lengths of her green eyelashes and the sprinkle of freckles across her nose and cheeks. She seemed really interested in what Boo was saying.

Deirdre intercepted his gaze. "Aren't you curious?" she said, her starburst eyes blazing.

Rork nodded, mute. He *was* curious.

The banshee recited airily, "Evolving the experience of death by transforming the way messages are given and received."

Rork felt new pressure in his head and moaned, holding his forehead.

Boo looked at him with concern. "The Board is big on training and," she paused, "new human technology."

"I know some herbs that might help with that headache," offered Deirdre.

"Thank you. I'll live," said Rork. He gave her what felt like a lopsided smile.

She gave him back a smile that was unusual, a smile that knew things that he didn't. Maybe promised, maybe not. Her smile was a little maddening, thought Rork, like she wanted to signal something but didn't quite know how.

"Are you ever going to tell us about Shuff-tie? Or this 'other stuff' you mentioned?" he asked Boo, suddenly anxious for details so he could better anticipate what was going to happen.

The banshee sat up, primly clasping her hands in her lap. "All banshees-in-training complete their banshee training with two final requirements."

Rork drained his tea and focused on Boo. "Like senior projects?"

"You could say," she replied. "First I have to guide humans through a trial death shuttle. We call it 'Shufftie.' I can choose an intermediary." She looked at Rork. "Essentially a grief-stricken human, attuned to the departed."

Rork gave her a comical expression. Mostly because he'd lost awareness of what his face was doing. Did he even have lips or a nose? The crowd in his head erupted with new urgency. Somehow Boo naming him 'intermediary' excited them, perhaps giving them new hope of being heard. Rork felt a deep schism in himself. Seriously, what had he signed up for? It sounded like the banshee was asking him to be her beta test for life-death messengering. He knew how volatile beta tests could be. They'd be at the mercy of misdirected action events while, if he hadn't joined the banshee, he'd be safely in his room right now, plugged into his computer, music and online community. Normally he sought solitude and craved time alone to think and work. His gran had encouraged connection with the larger world. Without her, Rork felt grief like a trapdoor he'd fallen through, risking all association with others. He felt the jeopardy in him as a vulnerability. Perhaps his father saw it, too, and deplored the weakness. That his grief now qualified him as an intermediary, a go-between, was ironic.

Rork swallowed down his misgivings, his mouth and throat dry as a desert, and nodded.

"As I've already said," continued Boo, "we have the best success with intermediaries when they are accompanied by a minder who helps with the getting in, the getting out, and the guiding in-between." The banshee smiled at Deirdre. "Humans who've experienced near-death come back with some transient ability." She clapped her small hands excitedly. "I can't wait to get started!"

Rork contemplated his tea. "Do we die?" asked Rork. He thought he was prepared for jeopardy, but he didn't want to die, although what *would* he sacrifice in order to see his gran again? He struggled to find a place in his pressurized head that gave him any kind of calm, and balanced what he was experiencing with normal reality.

The banshee straightened the front folds of her gown, looking away from Rork. "N-n-n-o-o-o," she finally said. "Shufftie is a short-lived oscillation. It allows non-banshees to slip between worlds." Her colorless eyes guilefully bored into Rork's. "The banshee's version of a simulation. A wee shift. Shufftie. Get it?"

Rork swallowed a gulp of tea. Wee shift? From his gran's note? The moment stretched momentous. "Is it dangerous?" he managed to choke out.

Boo fidgeted some more with her gown. Rork's fingers lapped the teacup. What was going on? What was she *not* saying?

"The engineers cause a ripple event, which will make things unstable for a while," said Boo. "I have heard of humans who don't come back. But things *usually* settle down, and we've never had a loss in this quadrant." She sat up straighter, as if that was assurance enough.

Rork ate another scone and licked his fingers. He wasn't exactly sure the banshee had answered his questions. Was she not capable of a straight answer?

"Do I even want to know what the other requirement is?" he asked.

"I want to know," said Deirdre.

"It's a Courier Project," said Boo.

"A what?" asked Deirdre, clinking her nails on the china cup.

Boo pressed her blue lips together before responding. "An interlife act of special moment. It's one of the Board's ideas for adapting to a new banshee future. Because there are fewer of us, the Board wants us to learn how to expand our influence. Operate in more than one dimension. Multitask."

"I am not sure I follow," said Rork. He felt way out of his depth.

"We could do the common thing and bring someone a message from a dead loved one, in a dream or hidden message. It would be passable, but not remarkable. The Board grades on a scale. The Chief Banshee Officer makes the final determination. The Board is looking for more than passable from me. Especially my mother."

"Your mother?" asked Deirdre. Deirdre, Rork noticed, had an encouraging way about her that was subtle and fascinating. She'd lean in slightly, fix you with those strange eyes of hers, and engage you with questions. And next? And next? The banshee must have felt her gentle urging, too.

"Yes, my mother. The Chief Banshee Officer. She's also my advisor."

Rork whistled. "That's got to be challenging."

"You don't know the half of it," said Boo.

For a moment, Rork forgot about food. "You love her but wish sometimes she wasn't your mother? That she wasn't so set on you becoming a certain kind of banshee? That you fear failure on an almost daily basis and wish for her support? That you wish you could turn back time to a more uncomplicated time?" Rork stared wistfully out the window, gradually bringing his eyes back to Boo.

"Yes," she sighed, meeting Rork's gaze, her face momentarily open and defenseless.

Deirdre seesawed between them, her eyes like the primrose blooms of willowherb bobbing in the window box.

Silently, Rork nursed the hurt of his father wanting to send him away, not understanding him. He felt for the outlines of the flash drive in his left pocket and the sixpence in his right. He wondered if he was becoming superstitious.

The banshee stacked their empty plates, sitting taller. "Remember a while ago there was all this publicity about seeing a bright light before death? Articles and news stories everywhere?"

Rork and Deirdre nodded.

"And a woman wrote a book about her experience of dying and coming back to life?"

Rork nodded again. The clamor in his head grew louder. He ignored it.

"I believe I read that book," said Deirdre.

"And a term was bandied about to describe the experience?"

Deirdre exhaled, the air in her vicinity becoming thick and hothouse-like.

"Near-death experiences?"

More nodding.

"Well, that was my mother's doing. There's even a Near Death Experience Foundation now." The banshee crossed her arms grumpily.

"That was a big thing?" asked Rork.

"A very big thing," said Boo. "And now I have to be remarkable."

Rork emptied the dregs of the teapot into his cup. Deirdre picked up table crumbs on the end of one of her blue-tipped fingers. Rork struggled to understand how he fit into the banshee's need to do something remarkable. He did not feel qualified. He felt, in fact, forgettable. He was a loner ghosting in the background. But wasn't that what he was trying to change? Overcome?

Rork's cup clattered in the saucer. "But first we have to get through Shufftie, right?" he said, pretending a confidence he didn't feel. "The wee shift?"

"Right," said the banshee.

"Let's worry about that first," said Rork, less concerned with the Courier Project, whatever that would turn out to be. He was more worried about Shufftie and acquitting himself in a way that didn't shame him or his gran.

"How do you 'get through Shufftie'?" asked Deirdre, licking her finger.

"When you die," said Boo, lowering her voice, her eyes intense, "you pass through levels of ghost experience based on your personality traits, your thoughts about dying, and whether or not you've had any previous ghost experience. We have to travel through the ghost levels and get out in the time allowed by the oscillation."

Rork noticed how closely Deirdre was paying attention. He wondered if she had a secret motive for volunteering. Did she hope to find something or someone in Shufftie?

"Trying to be remarkable is a lot of pressure," sighed Boo.

Rork was reminded of his own predicament. "My father has unrealistic expectations of me, too," he offered. "He thinks I should be someone I'm not. He can make me feel so, so, so… inadequate." He shifted on the wicker stool, feet planted, both hands poised above his thighs. Then he had a revelation about himself. "That's why I'm here," he said. "That's why I'm throwing in my lot. Why my gran suggested me."

"Because you're inadequate?" asked the banshee, the space between her teeth peeking out.

"No," said Rork, perfectly serious. "To show him I can look after myself away from my screens, even when the situation is not ordinary. To show him I can accomplish something. He doesn't get to decide my life. I can make my own decisions."

Rork had to admit to himself, however, that his father would not only have stocked up for the trip to Shufftie by now, but mapped out their itinerary, although Rork wasn't sure what an itinerary would look like in this case. His father did have a way of getting things done. Rork was more in the winging-it camp, which was probably something he should work on.

"When do we leave?" asked Rork.

"Today," said Boo.

Rork and Dierdre's heads swiveled.

"And you thought this was just a quaint teashop," said the banshee, impishly. "It's actually a Switch, a place where an oscillation can occur, providing access to Shufftie." She smiled mildly at Deirdre. "As long as you know where to look and have the sense."

Boo slid her hands beneath the back of her knees and swung her gowned legs in a faster cadence. "Banshees have an affinity for teashops," she said, looking around. "Coffee shops, too."

"Today?" asked Rork, surprised.

"Yes," said the banshee. "The energy feels right. The engineers are standing by."

"Don't we need supplies?" asked Deirdre, swirling the tea leaves in the bottom of her cup. Her amber eyes and yellow headband reminded Rork of a sunflower — tall, golden, rising up on a sturdy green stalk.

"You're in luck," said the banshee. "There's a supply shop around the corner. You should find what you need there."

"Yeah, lucky," said Rork hesitantly. The sun's shadow lengthened on the scuffed floor of the teashop. Rork heard Boo's comb vibrate.

"I have to go," she said, her voice abrupt, withdrawing the comb from its hidden pocket and spreading the tines. "Dispatch is calling. They keep track of us, you know." She began to comb her hair, which snapped and crackled as she faded. And then the banshee began to disappear, without notice or warning.

However, her voice lingered, eerily pitched, penetrating the small space of the teashop. "Rork," the banshee said, "Pay attention to what the shop clerk says."

Boo grew transparent as a glass etching. "Deirdre, look for a Sign. It will mark where the Switch can occur, giving access to Shufftie."

With that, the banshee disappeared. The gray-haired shopkeeper wiped down the empty tables, completely unperturbed by the comings and goings of the living and the not-so-living.

Deirdre and Rork looked at each other dumbfounded. Deirdre finally stirred, showing Rork the tea leaves at the bottom of her cup. "Look," she said.

Rork glanced in the teacup. Sodden flakes of tea swirled inside the white cup.

"'Long journey'," said Deirdre, her eyes bright and shining.

"I sure hope my gran knows what she's getting me into," muttered Rork, smelling the banshee's imperceptible sweetness left behind, a little cloying in the small confines of the teashop.

7: Supplies

NECESSARY AND DESIRABLE Supplies was one shop in a row of terraced shops. Picturesque. Stucco. Vinca vine hung in wire baskets from the upper story. 'Supplies' was large in wooden letters beneath the eaves. It was so inconspicuous they had passed it by without notice.

"Convenient," said Rork, opening the front door. A tiny bell chimed deep inside.

Rork blinked in the shop's gloom. He stood to one side of the doorframe so Deirdre could enter ahead of him. They both ducked beneath a wide wood lintel above the door opening.

Rork half-expected Middle Earth mining stuff: pickaxes and lighted hardhats. The shop was packed with all kinds of merchandise for camping and the outdoors. The aisles were narrow between displays of clothing, rucksacks, cooking supplies, and other equipment. A counter extended along the entire length of the back wall, with more shelves and cubbyholes rising to the ceiling, all bulging with merchandise. The counter, shelves, and uneven wood floorboards gleamed, worn and glossy from years of use.

"This is serious camping gear," said Rork, his eyebrows winching up into his hairline.

"Trails intertwine in the memory of my near-death experience," said Deirdre softly, fingering a rucksack.

A craggy, older man appeared behind the counter. He was white-skinned like a banshee, but Rork could detect the ghost of a tan. The clerk leaned forward, hands clasped prayer-like, and smiled at the two of them.

"Yes," said the clerk. "Also, many trails can be strenuous. Why, we've been trying to get the word out about the importance of cardiovascular exercise."

Rork heard a roar in his head. The dead crowd were vociferously reacting to the clerk and his words, making *a lot* of noise. Were they trying to get Rork's attention? Rork looked closer at the clerk.

The clerk rearranged a pile of thick wool socks as if he had all the time in the world. His eyes gleamed like dark agates beneath wild eyebrows. He had a long beard, streaked gray, which curled almost whimsically in front of his chin. He looked like he might have hiked a mile or two. Or two hundred.

Rork liked the shop's smell, an aromatic combination of wool, leather, tin, and pepper. He couldn't identify the other notes. Soap? Cedar? The colors in the shop were earth-tones, muted, like a stand of oak in wet autumn.

Rork fingered the clasps, buckles, and material of a display of rucksacks. He guessed they should start with the basics.

"Try this on?" he suggested to Deirdre, slipping the straps of a pack over her shoulders. He adjusted the waistband to the front, concentrating on pulling it tight. Deirdre looked down. Rork was very aware that his hands had touched her.

"What do you think?" he asked.

"Feels comfortable," she said.

"How about we give it a truer test?" suggested the clerk, his voice low, full of melody. He came out from behind the counter, gathering items in his arms, and began to slide them inside the opening at the top. A rolled-up shirt, a few pairs of socks, cooking utensils. Deirdre watched as the rucksack got full and fuller.

"Of course, there's an art to packing," the clerk said, his eyes crinkling. "You put anything soft or padded on the outside, square corners and hard surfaces on the inside." He tugged on the rucksack to better settle the items.

Deirdre teetered on her long legs, losing her balance. The clerk steadied her with two strong hands. "We're just trying to get a better idea, you understand," he said. "How does it feel?"

"How should it feel?" asked Rork, watching the clerk.

"Well, it's not like you can pretend it's not there," the clerk chuckled. "But the weight should be centered across the widest part of your back. Not pulling on your shoulders or hips."

Deirdre cinched the pack a little tighter across her hips and, tilting forward, maneuvered the weight more evenly across her back. "It feels good," she finally said.

"Good, good," said the clerk. "Now you." He turned to Rork with a larger, more proportioned rucksack. Rork dismissed a couple of styles but eventually chose one with a rain-flap that would protect his laptop.

The clerk walked back around the counter and reached for a clipboard from a collection hanging on nails up one side of the shelving unit. "There," he said, making a checkmark on the clipboard. "Now, let's help you find what else you might need." The clerk's dark eyes were conspicuous in the shop's gloom. He handed Rork the clipboard. "This will keep you organized," he said.

SUPPLIES FOR A LONGER JOURNEY it read along the top, detailing a checklist of gear and equipment they would need. Rork scanned the list; this was going to be more involved than he'd thought. Deirdre read the list over Rork's shoulder, a blue fingernail pointing down the list.

Supplies for a Longer Journey
PERSONAL KIT (TO CARRY)
__1x rucksack (as large as possible, yet comfortable)
__1x strong, large plastic bag (to line your rucksack)
__1x sleeping mat
__1x sleeping bag (in a waterproof stuffsack)
__1x personal first aid kit
__1x whistle
__1x notebook & pen/pencil
__1x flashlight or torch & spare battery
__1x emergency food rations (NOT to be eaten unless necessary, obviously)
__1x water bottle
__7x water purification tablets
__1x knife, fork, spoon
__1x pocketknife (small)
__1x plate/bowl
__1x mug
__1x box of matches (sealed in a dry container or bag)
__1x wash kit (small)
__1x towel (small)
PERSONAL KIT (TO WEAR)
__1x pair walking boots (broken in)
__1x thermal top or tee shirt
__1x sweater (woolen or fleece)
__1x walking trousers (warm, NOT jeans)

___1x jacket (it must be waterproof and windproof)

___7x pairs underwear

___7x pairs walking socks

___3x tee shirts

___1x spare sweater (woolen or fleece)

___1x spare walking trousers (NOT jeans)

___1x pair of sneakers (optional)

___1x hat (warm)

___1x pair gloves (woolen)

___1x pair shorts (in case it gets hot)

___1x sunhat & sun cream (ditto)

TEAM KIT (SHARED BETWEEN INTERMEDIARY AND MINDER)

___1x tent

___2x tarps (more, if possible)

___2x stoves (& fuel)

___2x cooking pots (2 sizes)

___2x scourers

___2x compasses

___2x towels for dishes

___7x plastic bags (for rubbish, etc.)

___food (small & lightweight)

Other items: (add to this list with your own suggestions)

Rork and Deirdre looked at each other, the enormity of the undertaking on their faces.

"Just take it an item at a time," advised the clerk. He cleared a space on the counter and set their two rucksacks on it. "You can put your things here. Give me a shout if you need help."

Rork and Deirdre shopped as if time were standing still. The pile on the counter got bigger. The clerk looked over their items one by one, smiling, refolding (as the case may be), and rearranging. After some time, he asked, "How about a cup of tea?"

"We'd love one!" Rork and Deirdre said together.

The clerk went through a door behind the counter. They heard dishes clattering. Soon he returned with three camp mugs of mottled stainless steel. He set them down carefully on the counter.

"Watch out," he said. "They're really hot."

Deirdre held hers gingerly by the handle. Rork blew on his, creating ripples across the surface. The clerk leaned on one elbow, observing them. His coarse gray hair grew riotously around his face. His beard, too, had the look of a small animal. Rork looked at the clerk askance. He knew he was somebody he had met or seen before, but who exactly remained in the foggy part of his memory.

The clerk gazed at them benevolently, comfortable in the silence as they drank their tea. Rork could hear ticking, like a clock, but couldn't locate the source.

Rork cleared his throat. "I don't see a map on the list of supplies."

"There isn't one," said the clerk. He drank the last of his tea and set his mug on the counter. "Shufftie is not a permanent place. More like an occurrence," he said, "slightly different each time a Switch is used. Every simulation has its own strange logic." He smiled tightly, his voice hoarse, as if he was out of the practice of speaking. "It will seem familiar but be wary." He grew quiet and started ringing up their items. Rork looked at Deirdre who put her palms up.

"How will we know which way to go?" asked Rork.

"Follow the path," said the clerk. He continued to move items from one side of the counter to the other.

Rork swallowed, dry-mouthed. In his mind, the journey had just gotten more daunting. He worried about money. He didn't have a lot. The cash register was old, ancient even, and he couldn't see the mounting total. He fidgeted, worrying, typing with one hand on his knee.

Deirdre observed him in her quiet way, especially the typing, with curious eyes. With only one hand, Rork could only type simple words like p-i-n or m-o-p, but for some reason he was stuck on j-o-i-n, and typed it over and over on his leg.

"Why the quantity of seven?" asked Deirdre, consulting the list again.

"It's the number of constancy," said the clerk, "not a prediction, although there is a calculated degree of asymmetry in it, too." He hung the clipboard back up on a hook. "You'll see."

Rork and Deirdre had more questions but hesitated to ask as the clerk packed up their gear, his hands folding each item carefully. They had amassed quite a pile, and the clerk placed everything in black shopping bags that read NECESSARY AND DESIRABLE SUPPLIES in an otherworldly typography. When he was done, there were five bags in a row plus their rucksacks.

"How much do we owe you?" asked Rork, reaching for his hip pocket.

The clerk eyed him humorously. "The banshee took care of everything."

"Oh," said Rork. He hadn't understood that the banshee was now his benefactor. The idea made him feel awkward. He typed emphatically, trying to adjust to a discomfort that felt like a current running through his body.

The clerk walked them to the door, letting his pale hands rest briefly on Rork's shoulders. He stared into the door pane's diffused light, his eyes filmy and far away. He had effectively supplanted Deirdre, who moved behind the two of them.

"Rork," he said, "I know a thing or two about uncharted territory." He opened the shop door. Distantly, the door chimed again. "And it took me years to learn that going out into the wilderness was really a going in. Try to remember that," added the clerk as he pushed Rork ever so slightly over the threshold.

8: Sign

"WHAT SHOULD WE be looking for?" asked Rork. He tried to whisper, but small animals scattered at his voice. He was tired, nervous, and light was beginning to drain all too quickly from the sky. If they were going to find the Switch, they needed to do it soon.

Rork and Deirdre were in a tangle of marshy woods behind the teashop's small walled sitting garden after changing into their hiking clothes in the restroom. The hiking trousers were a little stiff from the store, but he liked the many capacious pockets. Deidre kept her headband and colorful scarf, he noticed. Rork looked up. A tall oak stood sentry in the distance. They wandered aimlessly — tree to tree, tree to shrub — looking for the Sign. Their rucksacks bulged with all the new gear, and they swayed awkwardly under the top-heavy weight like overburdened ants.

"I'll know it when I see it," said Deirdre.

Rork took a deep breath, trying to rid himself of agitation. He had half a mind to fire up the computer and do a quick search for 'oscillation' or 'banshee simulation,' but he realized instantly the futility and slapped his fingers against his pants leg, keeping them limber.

There was a hushed quality to the woods, which was odd in such close proximity to the busy teashop. Deirdre put her hand on the grayish bark of a nearby aspen and stood silently. Rork wondered if she was asking the tree for help.

"Are you ready for this?" asked Deirdre, not exactly looking at him.

He could hardly hear her. Rork wasn't completely convinced she had spoken. He could almost see her anxious thoughts fluttering around behind her headband. His own thoughts behaved like erratic dive bombers, careening in his mind, soaring with excitement one minute and plummeting with fear the next. He worried about who she worried about. Him? He hesitated. The sun continued its downward trajectory, the sky turning delicate shades of pink, purple, and red-violet.

"I think so," said Rork. He stepped next to Deirdre so he could see her face. There were thumbprints of shadow beneath her eyes.

"I'm excited *and* scared," she said. "I am like my own tug of war." She smiled wanly.

"I know what you mean," said Rork. "I feel like I have a spear in my side."

The sky deepened its purpling as night descended. Birds called to each other, their cries echoing in the gathering stillness.

"Promise me," said Deirdre. "Promise me that no matter what, we stick together."

Rork heard something flap above his head. He looked up and saw a bird alighting on an aspen branch.

"I promise," he said, responding to the urgent tone in Deirdre's voice. Inching forward, his big feet tripped over a pile of stones, and he fell.

"Ouch." He got up and rubbed his knee, walking around stones dislodged from a taller tower.

"What?" asked Deirdre.

"Look."

The stones had been carefully laid, one on top of each other, in a conical spire. Rork considered the ancient stones, how long ago the spire had been built, each stone stacked with care. What had the spire withstood through the ages? The entourage of the dead inside his head whispered reverently. He asked himself silently about when he had started thinking of the voices in his head as the voices of the dead.

"What is it?" asked Rork.

"A cairn," said Deirdre.

"It memorializes the dead, right?"

"Yes," said Deirdre. "It's obviously out of place here. It must be our Sign." She reached out for the topmost stone.

"The banshee *is* only a banshee-in-training," reminded Rork.

Deirdre gave him a smile.

Suddenly, they felt a jolt beneath their feet. Rocking into each other, they noticed the faint trace of a path ribboning through the woods. They tilted their heads one way and then the other. Seen. Unseen. Seen. Rork peered unblinking ahead, the view toggling between pristine, untouched woods and woods marked by the passing of bodies with the scuffed earth and flattened grass showing the beginnings of a trail. The sun hung onto the horizon, ready to plunge the woods into darkness. The temperature dropped. The cooling night air created a low, rolling fog. Rork felt a ripple run down his spine.

Deirdre touched his arm. "Do you see?" she asked.

Following the path, they came upon a gap in the trees. The sentry oak they had seen in the far distance was now only a hundred yards ahead, tall, commanding. Even in fog they could see it was an incredible size, bigger than a house, a mansion, with a prolific network of branches reaching into the sky. The wide trunk was spliced, and the two sides of the trunk gapped and twisted but continued to grow, joining together again higher up, leaving an opening at its center.

When they got close enough, they could see letters carved into the base of the trunk in wormhole script: EYE OF THE NEEDLE.

Deirdre began to string words together under her breath, chant-like. Rork had no idea what she was saying. It sounded like a foreign language to him. Gaelic? Latin? He recognized the word "genus" and suspected the words might have something to do with Deirdre's plant knowledge.

A brilliant, egg yolk-colored light beckoned from the eye. The pressure in Rork's head increased tenfold, erupting into a chant.

> **Eye of the
> Needle.
> Eye of the
> Needle.
> Eye of the
> Needle.**

A creeping vine unfurled and wrapped itself around Deirdre's ankle, drawing her inexorably forward. "It's the Switch," she whispered, gripping Rork's wrist.

Rork heard a sound like water rushing and tried to mouth a warning to Deirdre, but it was too late. They had been captured by a forceful current, sucked towards the Eye of the

Needle. The force was incredible. Rork had visited a space museum once where they'd reconstructed how it would feel to be launched in a rocket. This was worse. He felt force sub-anatomically — in his platelets, hair follicles. He closed his eyes and felt himself being pulled through the Needle's eye.

Suddenly, all was light and sound. He was inside the tree's enormous bulge, only distantly aware of Deirdre's hand digging into his palm, refusing to let go. His body felt electrified. Powerful jolts of energy illuminated every nerve ending in a cool-tempered brightness. Like Christmas tree lights covered in snow, the snowflake crystals refracting countless points of light. As his body was suspended in this cool lightness, his mind flashed images against a background of chaotic voices, buzzing — his gran, his da, Morag, Hamish, the banshee, Deirdre — in a crazy slide show of encounters, tiny points of light beading together, connecting them, firing a rush of feelings — happy, sad, fear, anger, surprise, disgust. And a myriad more — rejected, confused, proud, lonely, disapproval, frustrated. Was he experiencing his life in reverse or fast-forward? Could he? Would he do anything differently?

Rork felt the relationship with his father as an ache in his heart, which was pounding, pounding. The energy felt like it was way too much for his body. He couldn't contain so many sensations! He would explode, vaporize into a million microscopic feeling pieces. He was leaving the plane of the living, and his body — his being — wasn't up for the job. Why had he agreed to this? Why? He was literally going to burst in some kind of cosmic implosion.

Rork somehow understood that the tiny points of light were connected to his gran, and she knew better. Rork had chosen this journey with Deirdre and Boo because he wanted to change the trajectory of his life. He wouldn't just pine away in grief and rejection. He would follow the points of light, become an intermediary between this life and the other, the voices and silence, his expectations for himself and his father's.

That is, if he lived. His body felt near collapse, on the verge of breaking apart into fragments. Shattering.

Rork desperately tried holding himself together — mentally and physically — but it was too much. It was beyond him, and he couldn't help it. He surrendered to the oscillation.

GHOST SIGNS

9: It's Just A Simulation

IN THE DARKNESS, Rork assessed himself. The insane pressure and brightness had passed. He felt somehow returned to himself, his body, his thoughts. Deirdre still had a clamp on his wrist, her nails digging into the soft pad of his palm. Apart from that, he felt no pain. He did not feel any different, and yet he felt that something had shifted. His reality was not the same as it had been moments before.

Rork opened his eyes and surveyed a landscape completely devoid of color. His nostrils flared. He smelled traces of smoke and rot and char. He could still hear the sound of water, the steady ripple of a brook or river. The voices in his head were subdued, as if they too were wary about where he suddenly was. He was afraid to breathe, and he blinked his eyes rapidly trying to make sense. Rork wondered if there was something wrong with them.

Everywhere he looked: gray. Gray, darker gray, pale gray. Gray.

Nope, there was nothing amiss with his eyes. Shufftie must eradicate red, blue, yellow, and all the other colors.

Deirdre finally unclamped her hand. Looking around, she breathed heavily through her mouth. She was her normal, eye-blinking technicolor self, but everything around her was washed out and monotone. Rork looked down at himself. He was full-color, too: khaki shorts, oatmeal wool socks, blue-green plaid button-down shirt. Rork couldn't help but sigh. At least there was that. Surely that confirmed their "virtual" status?

A mulchy path stretched in front of them, imprinted on the forest floor. Directional signposts were erected at regular intervals along its verge. On the other side of the Eye, a trailhead marker read LEVEL ONE: THE BOGS.

Deirdre nodded in the trailhead's direction. Rork dragged his feet. Was he really up to the unknown of Shufftie?

The bogpath led to an intricately wrought iron bridge, which arched over a rushing river, the source of the water noise. Entwined in the bridge railing was a weird assortment of objects: spoons, forceps, spectacles, hammers, necklaces. The bridge looked like an installation piece by some macabre artist. BRIDGE TO NOWHERE was spelled out in forks and twisted metal underneath the railing. What was it with the names of things in Shufftie? Were they supposed to help? Or were they someone's idea of a joke?

Rork heard a chorus of "oohs" and "aahs" between his ears. The voices were almost starting to make sense in his head.

Rork and Deirdre's footsteps echoed on the hollow bridge. They peered through the odd railing. Deirdre touched a spoon. In the water they could see a rivulet of letters: RIVER OF FORGETTING.

Deirdre halted, resisting, clearly reticent about proceeding across the bridge.

"Remember, it's just a simulation," Rork reminded her. "It's like a computer-generated world."

"It feels pretty real," said Deirdre.

"I know," admitted Rork.

Her bright green, curving lashes curled upwards as she stared, mesmerized by the flowing river. Her body was tense from head to toe, her bony shoulders hunched. Rork could actually see her apprehension.

"Come on," said Rork, urging her on.

Cautiously, they continued across the bridge.

Rork's body felt like hours had passed, and it was the middle of the night. Yet he had no idea of what time it really was. There was no sun, no moon. Night was not falling, just this pervading gray light, like the whole passing world was overcast. He was glad he'd brought his laptop. It had a clock at least.

Rork took a quick inventory. Not wanting to get ahead of himself, he focused on the basics. He knew they'd need rest and food. Soon. It had been the very definition of a long day. His head was groggy. His stomach grumbled. The thought of stepping off the trail and going deeper into this gray otherworld unnerved him, and he couldn't do it. Not their first day. Already he missed color.

Deirdre focused her eyes forward, screwing up her face in concentration — or pain, it was hard to tell with her — as they stepped onto the ground on the other side of the bridge. Her feet firmly on solid ground, she looked around, warily watching the wild water in the River of Forgetting.

"All I have is what I remember," she tried to explain. She flashed Rork a fleeting cryptic smile. Her shoulders momentarily unhunched. "It's what drives me, makes me an effective minder."

"What is it that you can call to mind exactly?" asked Rork.

"There is no 'exactly,'" she said. "My psyche is a pattern made up of plant knowledge, images of my family, my mother, my loneliness. The configuration gives me a certain orientation in this world. I can *feel* where we are." She looked skyward, closing her eyes as if taking inventory, and sighed, her relief palpable.

"My memories are important to me, too, you know," said Rork, feeling like he needed to explain himself. Frankly, he had no idea of what was truly at stake, having blundered into the adventure with a grief-riddled intention of reconnecting with his gran and proving himself to his father.

Deirdre did not reply. She stepped gingerly along the path, adjusting her rucksack. The track's dirt was dark, silty, and tramped down in damp patches. She stopped and muttered to herself, as if talking to the ground. "It's ash."

"What?" asked Rork.

She turned to him, her face blanched against the vibrant green of her eyelashes. "It's ash," she whispered harshly. "The path is made out of ash."

The momentary silence between them was deafening.

Rork felt queasy. He wished she hadn't put the thought in his mind. Finally, he cleared his throat. "Try not to think about it."

"We need rest," said Deirdre, shakily.

"Aye, and food," Rork said. "Before I collapse."

Deirdre looked at him, her worry obvious.

"I didn't mean it," he said, hapless. "I'm just hungry."

Deirdre reached around for a pocket in her rucksack. She handed Rork a pouch. "Here," she said.

"What is it?" he asked.

"Trail mix. My own recipe from ingredients from the supply shop."

Rork eyed the pouch suspiciously. Shufftie was making him suspicious of everything. It wasn't a place where anyone could be comfortable. "What's in it?" he asked.

"Good stuff." She gave him another cryptic smile. "It will keep you going."

He peered into the pouch, shuffling the contents. Tentatively, he grabbed a handful of nuts, seeds, and dark wrinkled berries. Some ingredients he recognized. He cupped a handful to his mouth and chewed. It was sweet, crunchy, and satisfied his stomach, at least temporarily.

Deirdre reached into the pouch for a handful of the mix for herself. She chewed meditatively, looking ahead and behind them. She held her elbows close to her body. "This gray, dismal light could get to you after a while," she said. "It's making me feel low, slightly desperate."

Rork stopped as he reached in for a second handful. "Aye," he said, acknowledging the eerie light. He felt a headache waiting behind his eyes as they strained to see. He peered closer at Deirdre. Her eyes were wide and round, pupils as dark as they could go. They made a surreal juxtaposition next to the colorful eyelashes.

Rork held out the pouch. "More?"

"No," said Deirdre. "I'm good. I'm not the gannet you are."

He took one more quick handful and motioned for Deirdre to turn around. He stuffed the pouch back into her rucksack. A few sunflower seeds littered the placket of Rork's shirt. Deirdre brushed them away. They fell to the sooty soil and disappeared, swallowed up by ash.

Back on the trail, Deirdre set the pace, and they hiked moodily for a few miles, leaving behind the River of Forgetting. The footpath took some getting used to, their hiking boots slipping in soft, silty ash. The path twisted and turned, making it impossible to see very far ahead or behind them, which added to the perplexity of the place. When they entered a tunnel of forest, tall trees arched over their heads, branches fused together unnaturally, ageless, indiscriminate. He made out their inscrutable name spelled over and over again in the crooked branches: MEMORY TREES.

Deirdre turned to him suddenly. "I'm so tired I can hardly see straight," she said, her shoulders slumping. "I think we should camp for the night. For a few hours at least."

Rork was relieved. He hadn't wanted to be the first to call it a day. It seemed like they'd just got here. But he felt so heavy and dull. All he wanted to do was put his head down and sleep. He looked uneasily into the Memory Trees' murky shadows. "Can we camp on the path? Maybe sleep on our packs?"

"Yes, let's," said Deirdre, letting her pack fall to the ground. She pulled out her rain jacket tucked between the pack's straps and spread it out on the trail. She sat down cross-legged, visibly tired. Half-heartedly, she rummaged through their food supplies. "Are you hungry?" she asked.

"I'm always hungry," said Rork, although, to tell the truth, he felt more weary than hungry.

He watched Deirdre assemble the miniature camp stove she dug out of her pack. He was glad they'd decided to carry four flasks of water. They'd worry about replenishing their water supply tomorrow. What had the clerk said again? Something about a creek? He was distracted, intent on powering up his computer, which he drew across his thighs. He needed to know normalcy existed beyond this unnatural plane of extinguished light. He adjusted the air card and muttered a curse-filled plea to the glowering trees.

"What are you doing?" asked Deirdre.

"Computer," said Rork, as if that answered the question. He fiddled with the card in the slot. "I brought an air card," he said. "I only hope it works."

Deirdre made a lot of noise with the camp stove as she rummaged around in the contents of her pack. "Maybe you need a dead card?" she said.

Rork looked at her. Was she trying to be funny? Rork couldn't be sure. He didn't really know what she was actually like, after all. He barely knew her. In fact, she seemed ticked. Her face was a mask.

His monitor chimed and filled with light, and Rork was quickly distracted. He stretched out cramped legs in front of him, balancing the illuminated laptop as best he could.

Deirdre was making dinner in a pot with boiling water, pasta, and some other ingredients. Rork smelled spices. His stomach began to growl in earnest. She passed him a couple of oatcakes with peanut butter while he tapped keys, fingers flying over the familiar keyboard. The Internet service in Shufftie was unreliable. The miracle was that the Internet existed here at all. He flickered between connected and not, an oatcake clamped between his teeth.

"Look," he said urgently, turning the monitor for Deirdre to see. On the screen, the night sky twinkled with stars.

"Where's that?" she asked.

"A weather camera on the Isle of Skye," he said.

Deirdre set down a steaming cup of tea in a tin cup. It rested precariously on the path, close to where Rork sat. "It's only powdered milk," she said.

"I'm sure it's fine," he said. "Cheers." The cup was hot. He held it tentatively by the rim. But the tea was good and strong and seeped into his bones, comforting him. Together, they gazed at the Isle of Sky's night sky on the computer screen. Rork felt a little less out of his element, his computer networked with the larger world. He was getting quite skilled at ignoring the din in his head, but he couldn't help but feel what a shame it was. All the knowledge and advice stored in generations and generations of minds lost forever, inaccessible.

Deirdre stirred the pot next to him.

A bit later, Rork was startled as Deirdre waved a steaming plate of pasta in front of him. "Sorry," he said, shaking his frizzled head. "Lost in thought." He grabbed the tin plate carefully. "That smells good. What is it?"

"Wild mushroom fettuccine."

Rork ate. Deirdre hovered on her heels, holding a plate in one hand.

"This is really good," he said, seconds later, his plate half-gone. "Where'd you get the mushrooms?"

"I foraged them in the woods," she said. "Before the Eye."

"Is there more?"

Deirdre asked, "Still hungry?"

"Aye," he said. He'd had no idea pasta could be so delicious, but it made him feel solid in a place that felt shifting.

"Are you going to want more?" he asked. Deirdre laid her fork across her plate.

"No," she said, staring at the speckles of the plate. "You can finish it."

Rork scraped the rest of the fettuccine from Deirdre's plate onto his plate. Time passed. It did not grow dark. They sat. Rork held his plate up to his chin, laptop resting on the bridge of his knees. Deirdre sat cross-legged beside him, her elbows propped on her legs, sipping her tea.

"You need to learn to prioritize," she said.

Rork set his plate to the side.

"What do you mean?" asked Rork, feeling a tug in his lower jaw at the base of his tongue where he felt weakness and insecurity, a result of his father's years of rejection. He ground his teeth thinking of it. He would show him.

"First shelter, then food, then anything else." Deirdre gestured in the direction of his computer.

Rork closed the lid of his computer. "I didn't think," he said.

"I know," said Deirdre, "and you need to. We are vulnerable here. You. Me. We need to focus as best we can."

Rork thought about what he was being told. She was right, of course. Still, the computer was his link to reality.

"I'm sorry," said Rork. "What can I do?" He scrabbled to his knees, bagging up the dishes in a mesh net. An image of the clerk, explaining that they could dunk dirty dishes in a river or lake to clean them, popped into his head.

"I think you can deal with the dishes later," offered Deirdre, conciliatory. "I'm exhausted, aren't you?"

"We've been through a lot our first day," said Rork. "I'll hang the dishes outside my pack for now." He glanced up at Deirdre. Her eyes were drifting closed, her neck starting to bob. "Hey," he said, grabbing her mug of tea. "Why don't you lay down on your pack?"

"Thank you," she mumbled, wrapping her legs around the pack, her two hands prayer-like under one cheek.

Rork finished tidying up. The light throbbed its sickly gray. The trees were deathly quiet. Rork could hear Deirdre breathe, a faint whistling in and out. Rork tapped around on his computer, checking in with his favorite web and blog sites. It took longer to load than he was used to but otherwise seemed to work fine. For now, at least.

He wasn't a big social media fan, but he liked to scan the posts. Frankly, he didn't have that much to say for himself, but he appreciated the concept. A portal for people to stay in touch and share their lives. He yawned, powering the computer down. He and Deirdre, two bumps on the trail, were enveloped in gray colorlessness.

He wrapped himself awkwardly around his pack. He knew he needed to sleep. He was desperate for sleep, but the idea of letting go made him anxious. Who knew what sleep or morning would bring? His ears strained in the silence. Wide-eyed, he scanned the ground beneath the trees for any movement in the pervading gray. He felt as if there should be wolves crying out in the distance. But he heard no sounds of wildlife at all. He should ask the banshee about that the next time they saw her. If they saw her again. So far, the banshee was rather stingy with appearances, especially considering how she had got them to go where she had wanted them to go. His head, heavy, rolled backwards on his upper arm. For sure, he'd thought she'd be available to them the minute they entered Shufftie. Maybe he was like his father said. Naïve. Rork fell fast asleep.

His sleep was driftless, strange. He wasn't at home in the comfort of his bedroom, down the short hall from his gran's old bedroom, his father's hair oil scenting his side of the house. He was far, far away, squeezed through the Eye of the Needle, processing (was that the word?) through Shufftie at the behest of a banshee, a creature that couldn't exist. Not really. His tall, angular body contorted around a lumpy rucksack. Voices of the departed muttered distractedly in his head, urging him to listen. He slept next to a lonely, green-blighted girl, haunted by loss. He did not sleep soundly. Periodically his eyes fluttered open, looking for something to help him reorient himself. His laptop. His plaid shirt. Deirdre.

He awoke fitfully to Deirdre's shaking him.

"Rork, Rork," Deirdre was whispering, alarm in her voice.

He heard a new noise. Loud. Crashing. It cut through the sound of the dead voices' agitation in his head. What? He felt moisture in the air. Water? A tidal wave?

"Rork, Rork," continued Deirdre, punching him now. Man, she was strong.

"Wha—?" said Rork.

He looked up and saw a wall of water heading towards them, roiling along the ash path with alarming deliberation. Rork clambered with Deirdre to their feet, simultaneously throwing their packs over their shoulders. They bolted off the path into the Memory Trees. They barely made it before a huge column of water coursed by them, following the trail, roaring and drowning out everything in its wake but leaving the ground below the Memory Trees dry. Inadvertently, Rork had left the mesh bag of dishes behind. It was carried off, bobbing on the water's wake. Rork's wet hair was plastered over his eyes.

Rork kept staring at the water, panting. He pushed his hair off his forehead. He gagged a little on the sea-salty dankness he felt. His clothes were drenched, heavy on his body. He shifted slightly to check on Deirdre, who had rolled onto her back beneath the canopy of trees. Rork could see her chest rise and fall, her long arms and legs a tangle of wet limbs. They had avoided the wall of water but not the wet aftermath. The curve of her green lashes blinked at the dull, gray sky, and her hair streamed across the soaked and scarred ground.

When he'd agreed to the banshee and Shufftie, Rork hadn't figured on almost getting drowned. He hadn't figured on his profound relief that Deirdre still breathed. He hadn't figured on a lot of things.

10: First Peril

RORK STRUGGLED TO HIS FEET.

"What the hell was that?" he asked. He felt for the pockets in his wet trousers. He could still feel the flash drive and sixpence. He felt a little less desperate.

"We were nearly swept away by water," panted Deirdre, rolling over, her gray eyes stormy. "Some simulation," she said, throwing Rork's earlier assurance back at him. She pushed herself up, elbows sharply hinging, and pulled her hair out from beneath the strap of her pack. It swung like limp seaweed around her face.

"If you hadn't woken up…" Rork began. He felt heavy and water-logged.

Deirdre made a determined face, putting herself back in order. She re-tied her sneakers, put her headband back in place, and rearranged her scarf. "I have nightmares about that," she said, staring at the ground.

"What?" asked Rork, puzzled by what she said and her odd expression.

"A rush of water…drowning."

Rork saw a whiteish flash in her eyes. He wasn't ready to talk about his nightmares, he thought to himself. They had just escaped a traumatic event. He kept looking at the path which swirled with backwash that could have killed them both.

"Let's get back on track," he said, not very convincingly. "There's something about these trees I don't like." He looked up into the branches. They creaked and made him feel oddly claustrophobic, as if the branches sought to draw something out of him (which was too ridiculous even to mention).

The path was washed out in the direction they'd been heading. Rork looked around for an alternative route. Deirdre, too, scouted the area for another path, careful not to get too close to the Memory Trees. Their boots squelched on the waterlogged path. Could they trust their eyes? A seam opened for them, appearing at the edge of the forest. It was a drier path, leading off to the right, although it was more of a track than a path.

Rork hung back, unsure if they should proceed. Deirdre attempted to continue along the original path but had to turn back, crouching away from the Memory Trees. Rork knew they couldn't stay put. The banshee had been very clear that the goal was to get through Shufftie, yet Rork felt less than optimistic that he had it in him to make it. He looked at Deirdre and felt ill-equipped with his computer on his back and no true sense of direction. He rubbed the flash drive in his pocket for courage.

Deirdre motioned for him to follow, holding the tree branches back in order for Rork to enter. It reminded him a little of the bog grove but less lush, if not bleaker. Rork ducked his head, turning toward Deirdre. He searched for something to say. Deirdre was looking at him in a serious way. Did she want to say something? Reprove him? He didn't know what to think or feel, so he just kept putting one foot in front of the other.

Deirdre let go of the tree branches and followed Rork on the track. "You said 'hell'," she said to his back.

Rork choked, laughed a little, and tried to keep walking. But the laughter built up and finally burst from him. He laughed hysterically for longer than was necessary. He held his stomach, gasping for air. It wasn't that funny. Still, laughing was better than crying. Or babbling in fear. He wagged his head in disbelief. After nearly being drowned, Deirdre was chastising him on his language.

The track made a loop in the denser forest and led them back to the path. Rork looked behind them back towards the spot where they'd camped and the wall of water had gathered force. Puddles shimmered in the silver light. Memory Trees creaked, their eerie branches fluttering like fingers. The deluge of water leached into the ground, absorbed by the silt.

The strangeness of Shufftie pressed in upon Rork. His boots scuffed the path and its shifting grains. None of it made any sense. Deirdre stood beside him on the original path and clenched his arm above the elbow. Rork felt foreboding and typed it haltingly on his thigh. F-o-r-e-b-o-d-i-n-g. It was the only word for it. They knew the path would lead them to more danger. Who knew what else they'd encounter in this perverse world not their own? How jeopardized would they be by their own thoughts and dreams?

Rork swallowed, his mouth dry. "Has the banshee abandoned us, do you think?" he asked.

Deirdre adjusted her pack, searching around them. "I think," she said, "we can only count on each other and our instincts."

"And keeping one step in front of the other?" asked Rork.

Deirdre looked around him warily with her tight smile. "I think these trees want our memories," she said as she directed Rork to move onward despite their uneasiness. "Do you feel it?"

He nodded, not quite able to speak.

They were back on the silt path, twisting and turning in ways that only let them see a little way ahead at a time.

Suddenly, a familiar voice spoke from behind them. "Well, I am glad to see you two haven't lost your sense of humor."

Rork and Deirdre spun around to find Boo floating in the air. The diminutive banshee hung in a halo of bright light, grayscale like the rest of the landscape.

"Boo!" said Rork, startled. Deirdre jumped, too.

"That never gets old," said the banshee, smiling her disarming gap-toothed smile. "Rork, I am glad to see you made it through your first night," she said, nodding. "Deirdre, you, too."

Deirdre dipped her head guardedly. The banshee hovered above them. Rork struggled with the mix of fear, anger, and confusion that roiled in him. He was far from amused.

"Boo, what's going on here?!" he demanded, his voice harsher than he meant it to be. "You could be looking at two bloated corpses right about now!"

"Oh," said the banshee. "Do one of you have dreams about drowning? It's amazing to me how common that is."

Rork's mouth hung agape.

"As you can imagine, dreams are very powerful here," said Boo. "Shufftie mashes them together with the landscape. Only the banshee programmers understand the formula. Some kind of otherworld algorithm. It adds," she hesitated, "to the unique experience." The banshee waved her hand expansively.

"Great," muttered Deirdre.

Rork sighed, feeling peevish. He let his pack slip to the ground so he could sit on it. "You look a little washed out," he said, uncharitably.

The banshee pulled open the full skirt of her gown. "Yes, not my best look. But I am part of this world. You are not. Which is why you look other, and I blend in."

"How are we supposed to control our dreams?" asked Deirdre. "They're dreams. You should have warned us."

"Would you have believed me?" asked the banshee.

"Probably not," said Rork.

Deirdre looked away stoically. Rork was learning how to read her and could tell she was trying to tamp down her feelings, remain in control.

Rork stood up and shouldered one strap of his pack. "What else didn't you tell us?" he demanded.

Boo smoothed back wisps of silvery hair from around her face. "I told you everything important. Shufftie is unique for me, too, you know. Otherwise it wouldn't be a challenge. You and Deirdre need to make it through all the levels of ghost experience. There are seven."

Rork exchanged a look with Deirdre. Hadn't the clerk pointed out the importance of number seven? Levels of ghost experience? Like in a computer game?

"I can appear at regulated intervals for moral support and general guidance," the banshee continued, "but I only get a predetermined allotment of time, so I have to be strategic about when I appear." She shifted her hair over one shoulder. "If we're lucky, perhaps one of you will have an epiphany —"

"A what?" interrupted Rork.

"I am *trying* to explain," said the banshee sharply. "You need to listen."

"I am, but this is all," Rork gestured at the path and the Memory Trees, "crazy!"

The irony of echoing what his father accused him about his imagination stole into his head beside the crowd of constant voices. Maybe crazy depended on context?

The banshee gave him an annoyed look. Rork tried to calm himself down.

"Explain, please," said Rork. "I'll be patient. I promise."

"As I understand it," Boo continued, "an epiphany is a showing forth that can act as a shortcut."

"Like a revelation of some kind?" asked Rork.

"Yes, it can be that, too," the banshee replied.

"What kind of revelation?" asked Deirdre.

"An insight or an 'aha' moment." The banshee peered around them, down the path. "An epiphany will release you from your current level of existence."

"Release? What does that mean? How?" asked Rork, feeling even more frustrated.

"If I knew how, it wouldn't be an epiphany, now, would it?" said Boo, visibly riled as she glanced between Rork and Deirdre. She clearly didn't relish having to account for herself.

Rork glowered at her. "Why bring it up, then?"

"You look like a mad owl," observed Deirdre, a light in her eyes.

Was she teasing him? Rork wasn't sure. He extended his glower to include her.

"You wanted to know what I know," said the banshee. "Don't get all hopeless on me. You got this far." She tapped her forefinger to her bluish lips. "It's something the others talk about, although it doesn't happen often. And I am *trying* to help. After all, I sent you the clerk," she pronounced proudly.

Deirdre plucked at the colorful scarf around her neck. "*You* sent us the clerk?"

"Yes," said the banshee. "He was my first citation."

Rork blew air through his lips, dubious. He really wasn't sure he wanted to remain in this simulated purgatory. Not if it could generate actual consequences.

Boo crossed her arms, the diaphanous sleeves of her gown hanging down. "I can make three 'special requests' for you. Citations, they're called, dead people called back to life for a specific purpose. I can cite a person with special knowledge to help you. The clerk was my first. Didn't you recognize him?" She stood up taller, proudly.

"He did look familiar," said Rork, once again beguiled by the banshee's enthusiasm and sweet smell. Could his gran be a citation?

"John Muir!" said the banshee excitedly. "One of your famous Scots ex-patriots."

"Who?" asked Rork.

The banshee pressed her lips together, clearly disappointed the name had not elicited the same level of enthusiasm from him.

"John Muir of the Wilderness Prophet?" Deirdre finally asked.

"Yes," said the banshee, clearly proud of herself. "Who better to prepare you for Shufftie, right?" She beamed at them.

"I am not saying he wasn't a help," said Rork, "but this is hardly a national park." Rork, unable to be still, paced in a small circle around both Deirdre and Boo. He tried to recall what the clerk had said about wilderness. At the time, it had struck him as significant. Something about going in. In what? But the clerk's words eluded him.

"Is there more?" he asked the banshee, suspicious.

Boo seemed to consider this. "Well," she finally said, "citations are invited ghosts. You may also," she hesitated, a small hitch in her voice, "encounter the uninvited kind."

Rork opened his mouth to speak, but words failed him, so he closed it again. He rapped on his upper thigh with his long, restless fingers, typing furiously on an imagined keyboard.

Deirdre rocked back and forth in her boots. "Aren't *you* a ghost?" she asked.

"No, banshees are *not* ghosts," said Boo, affronted. "We are fantastical beings. We herald death and move between realms."

"And ghosts are…?" began Rork.

"Dead people," said the banshee, "in various spiritual phases. Most pass over without trouble. Some attach themselves to an intermediary." She gestured toward Rork. "A few agitate. They either died unexpectedly or are seeking revenge or justice or something else." Boo shrugged. "We do our best to mediate, but…."

"There's a banshee shortage," Rork finished.

Boo narrowed her eyes at him.

"Will we be haunted?" asked Deirdre, her voice nervous. "Is that what you're trying to tell us?"

"Possibly," said the banshee. "I don't know exactly. Shufftie is new for me, too. But your dreams will influence the experience, and as you go up levels the ghosts will get more powerful. Unlike in your world, ghosts in Shufftie have a tangible presence."

Deirdre tightened her pack as Rork continued pacing. "Great," she said, saying the word in such a way that Rork couldn't tell if she was being ironic, or if she actually thought their situation was great. She was an enigma in so many ways. Rork was curious to learn more.

The banshee impassively watched them, as if letting their predicament sink in.

To Rork, the unreality of what was happening loomed dark and almost ridiculous in his head. He felt the dead stir, their voices murmuring and tugging at his consciousness.

"Who knew," he said finally, realization dawning, "that death was a user-generated experience?" He ceased his pacing and gazed past Deirdre's left ear into the endlessly reiterating gray gloom.

11: Table of Feasts

"WE NEED WATER," said Rork a few miles later, sniffing the air. The banshee had once again departed in a fanfare of comb music, zapped to heaven knew where. He hoped she was keeping an eye on them. Nervously, he ate a handful of Deirdre's trail mix. He kept the bag in a loop of his trousers for easy access. The truth was that she had been right. It was good, and it helped him feel grounded.

"Maybe on the other side of the Memory Trees," suggested Deirdre. "Did you look there?"

Rork shook himself like a scruffy dog, leftover seeds and nuts falling to the ashy ground. "I'll go check," he said and marched off in the Memory Trees' direction. Deirdre followed, her long legs high-stepping. Tall grass thatched the ground between the trees, borne down by time and transience.

Rork's head was feeling very crowded, what with the mutterers from the dead and Boo's latest bombshell. He wished he could power up his computer and record some notes. His fingers twitched to be busy, capturing his thoughts. He typed on the air in front of him, hitting an imaginary return lever for emphasis:

Control dreams. <Return>

Hope for an epiphany. <Return>

Beware of uninvited ghosts. <Return>

Rork wasn't much of a dreamer and usually didn't remember his dreams. Not really. He'd remember enough to know he'd dreamed, some lingering sense of something. A touch. A sensation. A glimpse. But not enough to put a dream story together. He did not have nightmares exactly, but he did dream a recurring feeling: getting lost. The setting might be different: the woods, a city, the seaside. But always he was lost. Lost. He could hear his father and a woman he thought must be his mother, but he couldn't figure out how to get to them. Whatever the obstacle, he couldn't get around it, couldn't find a way. He'd remain alone. Helpless. Without a clue. Each time he had the dream he'd wake up forlorn, doubting himself. He certainly didn't want to relive the lost dream in Shufftie, if he could avoid it. He was doubting himself enough already and wanted a relationship with his father that he didn't have.

Although, he had to admit that since his gran had passed, his dreaming (or not dreaming) had changed. Sometimes he found himself dreaming of her, waking up with images of her floating in his consciousness: her bracketed mouth, her scrunched up forehead, her teasing eyes. He remembered how blue her eyes were, bubbly like soda pop, especially if he said or did anything she especially fancied.

Rork's thoughts continued to stew. What was dreaming anyway? He'd always thought it was simply his brain working things out. Resetting the circuitry. Defragging all the random experiences. Now he wondered. Could dreams be more like longing, a yearning for what could be? He missed his gran. Could dreams reconnect them? Was Shufftie really an extended dream state? Why couldn't he just stop worrying and concentrate on the priorities he was facing in this strange place, clearly not a natural part of the world?

Rork heard the sound of trickling water. "Aha," he shouted, running ahead.

A creek gamboled down a jagged rock bed, water glinting dully in the dim light. Rork threw his pack to the ground and scooped up a handful from the stream.

"Wait," said Deirdre, catching up with him. She looked around cautiously. The Memory Trees cast a wide canopy over the stream and their heads. "Do you think it's safe?" she asked.

"I figure they've got to give us at least a fighting chance. We're human. Not fantastical beings." Rork drank another handful of water.

"Creek of Quenching," Deirdre read in loopy handwriting made up of small stones on the smooth bank of the creek. "I guess," said Deirdre, "so far we've found things pretty much true to their names." She slipped off her pack and from it retrieved a metal cup, which she dipped into the creek. She licked her lips. "Tastes good."

They lingered at the creek, refilling their water bottles and canteens, the trickle of water restful in the gray space. Rork still felt conspicuous when he and Deirdre were in close proximity to each other. Did he smell? Was his big body in the way? Rork felt he should be acting a certain way toward Deirdre but was uncertain how. He tried not to take up too much space, crouching near a rhododendron at the creek's edge.

Rork had never spent much time alone with a girl before. Deirdre seemed like another species. Unlike him, she took absolutely nothing for granted and seemed to evolve by the minute. Green eyelashes? Blue nails? He wondered if her quirks were the result of her near-death experience, being on her own for most of her life, or simply her Deirdre-ness. She wasn't uninteresting to be around, he realized. In fact, he liked being around her.

"Do you think dreaming in the daytime counts?" asked Deirdre.

"You mean like daydreams?" asked Rork.

"I'm famished," she said. "I can't stop thinking about food. You?"

"Haven't we covered this already?" asked Rork. "I'm always hungry." He paced beside her, walking the kinks out of his legs. "Now you've got me thinking about food."

They navigated back to the path. Deirdre was sure it was heading north. Without a directional sun, it was only logical, she said. Rork didn't argue. They left behind the Memory Trees and the River of Forgetting to the south. The Creek of Quenching flowed unevenly east and west. Or was it west and east? Rork couldn't quite get his bearings in Shufftie.

"Do you like Tomato Caprese salad?" asked Deirdre. "Juicy red tomatoes fresh from the garden. The licorice-y tang of basil. Fresh mozzarella. Drizzled all over with olive oil?" She made a vaguely Italian gesture of succulence.

"I can't help it," admitted Rork. "I am thinking about meat. Roast beef with horseradish sauce. Creamy mashed potatoes. Mushy peas."

"Pasta."

"Pork chops."

"Chocolate."

"Pie."

Rork and Deirdre continued to torture each other with thoughts of food, walking tall and lanky beside each other, naturally in step. Their boots pressed tread-shaped markings in the ashy path. After a half-mile or so of this, Rork thought he heard a bell tinkling in the distance. Curiously, he lifted his head.

"There," said Deirdre, pointing. She must have heard it, too.

Set back off the path, on a clump of low-lying moor stood a long table covered with a white tablecloth. Out of place. Out of nowhere. The cloth's whiteness looked eerie in the perennial gray light. They drew closer. The table was laid with all kinds of food on platters. A short-haired woman poured tea. Steam enveloped her ruddy cheeks and snub nose. Her short hair was light and dark, salt and pepper, her deep-lidded eyes crinkled in crow's feet. Rork could not guess how old she might be.

"Welcome," said the woman, smiling broadly, "to the Table of Feasts."

Two strands of lights crisscrossed above the table. Rork followed their filamentous bulbs with his eyes, reading TABLE OF FEASTS.

"Who are you?" he asked.

"*What* are you?" asked Deirdre.

"I think you know," said the woman. "A ghost, of course." The woman smiled at Rork. "I'm harmless."

Deirdre and Rork carefully sat on one side of the table, leaving their packs on the ground. Rork watched the woman. He was nervous despite having the advanced warning about ghosts. Would he be able to touch her? It seemed disrespectful to try. The ghost sat kitty-corner to him, her voice sounding familiar.

Deirdre was still beside him, taking stock of the food arrayed in front of them. She leaned into him. "Tomato Caprese," she whispered.

Rork's stomach growled. He kept one eye on the woman, who sipped from a china teacup. He spied roast beef on the table's far end, pink and glistening, cut to perfect thickness. His mouth started to water.

"Eat, 'Chicken,'" said the woman, smiling at Rork.

Rork, who had already helped himself, choked on a slice of tomato. He leaned forward in the chair as if to stand up but promptly sat back down again. He suddenly thought he recognized the woman's voice. "Are you the woman that was in my head?" he finally asked.

"Yes," said the woman. "I am the woman *who* was in your head."

Deirdre, sitting between them, chewed mozzarella, her eyes flicking from Rork to the woman.

"Why?" asked Rork.

"Why am I the woman? Or why was I inside your head?" The woman continued to sip tea with two hands.

"Are you trying to confuse me?" asked Rork. He reached for the roast beef.

The woman passed him a dish of horseradish. "No, but you make it easy." She smiled good-naturedly. "My name is Susan. In life I was a book editor from upstate New York before I died of breast cancer. I ignored the lump in my breast. Too busy." She shook her head. "Now I have plenty of time, and for some inexplicable reason Shufftie attached us together. I did not have children of my own."

Rork ate the beef thoughtfully, the tang of horseradish filling his nasal cavity. His head felt vacuous. "Maybe it's a random connection."

"Do you think it's random?" asked Susan. Her teacup clanked on the saucer.

"No," said Rork. "I don't think I believe in random."

"Well," said Susan, crossing her arms. "We have that in common."

Rork thought of his gran's note. "Find. A. Way. To. Connect." Was encountering Susan pointing him toward greater understanding of his gran's note? He looked closer. There was something athletic and spare about Susan. Rork guessed she played a sport. Or had played a sport. Tennis? Racquetball? Could the dead play sports? Americans always seemed to play racket games in the movies.

"Did you make all this food?" asked Deirdre.

"No," said Susan. "I'm not much of a cook. I had help. There's a lot of talent in the kitchen, and I enjoy good food." She held up a square of shortbread, eyeing it in the gray light. Large granules of sugar glimmered.

Rork took another serving of mashed potatoes, creating a small pond of gravy in the middle. "I enjoy food, too," he said.

Susan watched him eat. "So I see."

Rork grinned, his cheeks full.

"Oh, no," said Deirdre.

Rork swallowed. "What?"

"We just ate food in an Otherworld." Her eyes grew wide. There was a smidge of chocolate mousse at the corner of her mouth. "Are we going to be stuck here now? Like in the myth?"

Rork pushed away his plate, staring at it aghast. Stuck here? Like the myth? What myth?

Susan laughed. "You're safe enough. Mythology is just another way to explain the world. Shufftie has its own rules."

"Are you sure?" asked Rork. "I was saving room for pie." He eyed the pie on the other side of the table with its golden swirls of meringue.

"Go ahead," said Susan. "Have your pie." She sniffed the shortbread.

When the sweet slice of apple butterscotch pie was gone, Rork patted his stomach. "I am full," he said. "I don't like to feel empty." He could taste the richness of plum jam, a secret ingredient in his gran's pie recipe, too.

"Nobody does," said Susan.

"What kinds of books did you edit?" asked Rork.

"Self-help."

Rork chewed his lip, struggling not to laugh. But a chuckle escaped and grew. Deirdre smiled into her lap. Susan finally let out an abrupt hoot, saying, "I never realized how droll that was, what I did for a living." She poured herself more tea.

Deirdre smoothed a napkin with long fingers. Susan stirred sugar. Rork grabbed a handful of shortbread squares and placed them in a pile in front of him.

"It wasn't droll until you died," said Rork.

"True." The ghost smiled, seemingly unaffected by his statement about death.

Susan watched Rork eat shortbread, baked with buttercream and sugar. Her voice seemed to echo in his head. "Food is memory," she said.

Rork chewed slower, paying attention to the flavors and textures on his tongue. Suddenly, he was back in his gran's boarding house kitchen, in the swirl of stove heat and vanilla, watching his gran mold a mound of batter. "Food *is* memory," he agreed, polishing off the shortbread.

Susan held her teacup by its dainty handle. "Memory is the real currency in Shufftie and the world Shufftie simulates."

Rork rested his chin on the flat of his palm, listening.

"I was very content with my life," said Susan. "I wonder now if I wasn't too content."

"What do you mean?" asked Rork.

"Looking back, it seems to me like I lived in a way that avoided connection or surprise."

Rork raised his eyebrows, curious.

"Surprise can be valuable. Perhaps it's the point of Shufftie? Surprise you with your own thoughts and dreams?" Susan swirled the dregs of her tea. "Connection with other people can't help but be a surprise. Even if you think you know them. Even if they're family."

"Shall I read your cup?" asked Deirdre. Her slender arm reached out across the table.

Susan dropped the teacup into Deirdre's curled fingers. "There's only one thing my tea leaves will say."

Deirdre tipped the cup left and right. She looked up. "Death," she said. Clearly a reading she'd never given before.

Rork thought about surprise and the lack thereof. Of course the leaves read death. She was dead. She lived death. She conjured death. They were in a place of transition, permeable to death. Death got everywhere.

Susan started clearing the table. "Don't let me keep you," she said, nonchalantly waving her hand. "Since I'm attached to you, I thought I would try to aid you on your journey. I like to be busy, and it's rather quiet around here."

"No kidding," said Rork. "It's like all sound got vaporized."

Susan chuckled. "I believe it's meant to be contemplative."

"A little music couldn't hurt," muttered Rork.

"Do you have any regrets?" asked Deirdre, re-shouldering her pack.

"No, no real regrets," replied Susan. "I wish I had more memories to keep me occupied. Whoever said, 'Live every day as if it's your last' knew what they were talking about."

"Anonymous," said Rork.

"Some Roman," said Deirdre.

Susan stood. "I helped publish lots and lots of books in my short lifetime. Ultimately, all had the same message. You'd think I would have learned."

"What was the message?" asked Deirdre.

"Happiness is not a journey that happens in a straight line. There will be wrong turns, side trips, even dead ends. All you can do is begin each day — or what passes for day," Susan nodded to the gray light of Shufftie, "with your best intention, thinking of yourself and others."

"I'm not a chicken, you know," said Rork, abruptly, shouldering his pack.

Susan paused in the act of stacking dishes. "No?" she asked, a furrow appearing between her brows. "I'm not the one you need to convince."

Rork had no answer for that and was reluctant to leave the Table of Feasts. The food was excellent, and for an uninvited ghost, Susan was very encouraging. He felt he could have learned more from her. Deirdre tugged on his arm, turning him towards the trail.

The ground was spongey and thick with grass. The white tablecloth and string of lights faded behind them. Rork looked longingly over his shoulder at the leftover roast beef and pie.

Rork heard the ting of Susan's bell and liked to imagine she rang it just to hear the sound, echoing in the gray space of Shufftie. He worried about their odds of meeting another ghost as agreeable as her. How many kinds of uninvited ghosts could there be?

12: Labyrinth

"DO YOU THINK it's possible to live every day as if it's your last?" asked Deirdre, swinging her arms beside Rork, as they left the table of feasts and Susan behind and returned to the path.

"Huh?" replied Rork. He probably shouldn't have had the pie. He felt overfull, his mind foggy with food. But who knew when he'd have the chance to eat pie again? He squared his shoulders, taking a couple of deep breaths, and tried to refocus. He noticed strange boulders dotting the landscape of the bogs. Rork blinked at them, trying to make sense.

"Every day?" repeated Deirdre. "Your last?"

Rork thought he saw something move in the distance, off to his left. Were his eyes playing tricks on him? He rubbed his eyes roughly.

"Huh?" he said again.

Deirdre examined his face. "Never mind," she said, clearly irritated.

The ground rumbled, and Rork looked at Deirdre to see if she'd felt what he had.

"A mild tremor?" she suggested.

Suddenly the strange boulders multiplied and became *piles* of strange boulders. Masses. Heaps. Rocks mounded up around them, creating obstacles in every direction.

"What the-!" said Rork, jumping back as the rock mounds gave way to tall rock walls rising all around them. Looking up at the towering rock, Rork collided with Deirdre, who held out her hands to steady herself as the ground shifted below her. They clutched each other, not fathoming what was happening. The ground continued to rumble. Rocks moved. Alarm erupted in Rork's chest. His heart thundered. What he knew about Shufftie was unpredictable, reacting to unseen forces, making the unreal real. What dreamscape was Shufftie reacting to now?

The sky suddenly became dark, spotted with hulking shadows, and boulders blotted out what little light remained. Deirdre stepped away from Rork, crouching lower to the ground. Rork felt the stings of small pebbles cascading from the rock face above and wondered frantically if they were walking into an avalanche or something. But no. The moving rock walls began to marshal themselves into a kind of order, wall after wall, stepping and cross-stepping, forming a pattern, erecting a maze that forced Rork and Dierdre to move apart from each other. He wasn't sure how it happened. One minute they were near each other. The next he was looking at a crumbling wall and screaming himself hoarse. The noise of reeling rock was deafening. Reflexively Rork covered his ears. Stone debris and dust erupted into the air.

Rork was stupefied. What was happening? A wall now separated him from Deirdre. He could hear her warning cries, but he couldn't see her. More walls shunted into position, blockading them. They were caught individually inside a daunting edifice of ramparts ten feet tall, which began in the boggy hillocks and stretched into the unseen distance. The walls were ruinous, like the fortifications dotting the Highlands, walls streaked with striations of color — shell pink, peach, bone.

As the rocks ceased moving, devastating silence descended, as if they had fallen into an even more dramatic dimension of quiet. Rork could finally hear again, although sounds seemed to come from a long distance. He followed Deirdre's voice, picking a path around the half-formed stone walls until finally found his way to her. Deirdre's face was covered in a powder of abraded rock, which she had rubbed clear from around her eyes. She crouched like a dark-eyed raccoon, uncertain, looking wildly around her. He went to her side. "Are you all right?" he asked.

"Where did the rocks come from?" she asked, waving off his help. Her voice sounded panicked.

Rork tried to be calm for the both of them and climbed up a half wall to get some perspective. "Unbelievable!" he said.

"What?" asked Deirdre. Rock dust sifted down from her hair.

"It's looks like a labyrinth. It goes on and on. I can't see where it ends."

"Like a walking path? In a garden?" Deirdre pulled a compass out of her pack and consulted it, but Rork saw the magnetized needle spin and spin. Same as the last time they'd tried to look at it in Shufftie. It seemed to be a comfort maneuver for her. He didn't know why she bothered.

"Not your garden-variety labyrinth." The voices in his head concurred, and a horrible thought dawned on Rork. Had he caused this? In his pie stupor? He'd let down his guard, and a daydream had marched in. But where had the daydream come from?

"Deirdre," he said, yelling down to her. "I think this might be my fault." Why did he feel the need to confess? Shufftie, a wee shift? Ha, he thought.

Deirdre didn't respond for the longest time. Always serious, Rork knew she signaled vexation by the way she plucked at her scarf or adjusted her headband. He felt guilt-ridden and wished she'd shout at him or something.

"Can we traverse the top of the stones?" she finally asked, looking up, one palm sliding along her headband.

Rork stepped experimentally along the top of the wall. Rock crumbled in a shower of shale. "I don't think it'll hold our weight."

Underneath him the wall began to shudder. Rork teetered, leaning forward and jumping back to where Deirdre was standing. His knees buckling, he awkwardly rolled onto the crushed gravel, landing at the base of the wall he'd been standing on. A sharp stone fell, skimming the side of his face, thudding next to his ear. He rolled to his side and watched as another wall rose up, and another, and another, again cutting him off from Deirdre. This time irrevocably. They were separated by walls and walls of rock, which continued to form and divide them.

"Deirdre!" he yelled, but she had disappeared behind tall towers of rock. He struggled to his feet and lurched after where he thought she had to be. "Deirdre!" he yelled again.

"Keep moving north," Deirdre yelled from the other side. "Head north," she repeated. "Do you hear me?" There was command in her voice.

"Aye!" yelled Rork, feeling something drip down the long sides of his face. Sweat or blood, he didn't care. He was lost. L-o-s-t. He told himself to prioritize. He would focus on finding Deirdre. Finding. Deirdre. He had zero confidence in his ability to navigate without her. Why had he eaten that pie? Why? He'd eaten for other reasons besides hunger. Reasons that had created this nightmare of a daydream. How?

Desolate and alone, Rork walked and walked, turning corner after corner in the maze. He started at every skitter of stone, worried more walls would rise. The opalescent gray light never changed. It shimmered at the stark horizon's edges. How was he supposed to know which way was north? There was an eerie silence. He could hear the crunch of his boots. Perhaps the labyrinth was complete? He listened with all his attention but couldn't hear a sound of Deirdre. He knew he couldn't count on running into her. He hadn't found a single sign of her that indicated they were even going in the same direction.

The walls of the labyrinth began to look all the same. Rough stone, pocked with pebbles, laced with a network of tiny fissures, especially at the corners. Essentially, the maze was miles and miles of a crude type of cement. Just think, Rork thought ironically to himself, he had hoped to avoid hod-carrying the stuff, and here he was lost in it.

Bloody hell, his head hurt. The hair on the side of his head was stiff with dried blood. He remembered watching cartoons with his gran. Inside a character's skull would be an animated demolition crew — sawing, pounding, drilling — conveying headache, a sick head. His gran would chuckle. "Your head ever feel like that, loon?" she'd ask.

Rork plodded after where he hoped Deirdre was, thinking, Aye, gran. Aye.

The fine silt of stone got everywhere. He felt it in his mouth, in his eyelashes. It covered the tops and palms of his hands, which got gummy with sweat. He kept assessing his location. Hadn't he walked this way already? Rork didn't trust his sense of direction. Not particularly strong in the first place, it seemed to be eroding with every step into the labyrinth. He needed something more than instinct and silently thanked the clerk for making them pack a spool of twine. Like Hansel and Gretel, he unwound it behind him, leaving a trail, so he could plot a course through the labyrinth. Hopefully.

The twine gave Rork the confidence to cover new ground, becoming more familiar with the maze's mysteries. It switch-backed. It dead-ended. It formed seemingly pointless cul de sacs. It stretched into the endless distance.

He was dry, dusty, and thirsty but hoped to conserve his remaining canteen in case Deirdre would need it. The wall had divided them so suddenly he wasn't sure how much water she'd had left in her canteen. His eyes itched. He listened to the thud of his boots. Thud, thud, thud, thud. He felt more than heard a hot whisper.

"Eye of the needle. Eye of the needle."

"What the—?" Rork said aloud, swinging around.

An invisible figure bumped into him from behind and suddenly materialized beside him, keeping step with him.

Thud, thud, thud, thud.

Rork's heart jackhammered in his chest. He gulped down a scream. He considered the apparition marching beside him. It continued to mutter, "Eye of the needle. Eye of the needle." The ghost was tall and loose-limbed. His eyes vacantly slid away from Rork's eyes. Rork wondered if there was something wrong with the ghost. Some mental incapacity? Did he even know what he was saying? Susan at her table had seemed so sane.

Rork felt a breeze and smelled a buttery sweetness. All of a sudden, Boo appeared on his other side as if in a pale whirlwind. "Shoo," she said to the shuffling ghost.

The ghost shambled away, glaring over his shoulder at the banshee.

As if reading his mind, Boo said to Rork, "No, he has limited awareness." It was a little unsettling how she appeared and disappeared, each time revealing some new tidbit for him to chew on.

Rork stopped to blot his face. Sweat and grit dripped into his eyes. He watched the shooed ghost stumble off.

The banshee hovered near Rork. "He's what we call a specter. Spec for short. A dumb, insensitive kind of spirit. Very typical of T-band frequency. That's first level, you know."

"A specter?" asked Rork.

"Yes. They wander about haphazardly, without any real purpose, bumping into things, falling down. Clumsy. Always in the way."

"What? Like a vagrant?" asked Rork.

"Yes," said the banshee, "very much like a vagrant. See how our worlds parallel? But specters can be a real nuisance. Ever feel like you tripped on nothing at all? Or something was blowing on your neck?"

"Aye," said Rork.

"Well, it was probably a spec, being an annoyance. They can't help it."

"Will he ever progress to the next level?" Rork pocketed his sweaty bandana and resumed his search. Whatever the next level was, he murmured to himself.

"It's not impossible," said the banshee. "But the more evolved ghosts usually skip T-band and go to a higher level of frequency right away."

Boo's talk of levels and frequencies was crazy, as if she was caught in a computer world run amuck. Rork remained silent, imagining the lopey apparition trudging on forever, muttering to himself. Not his idea of a rewarding eternity.

"Now," said Boo, radiating a little brighter and fixing him with her clearie eyes. "What have you done with your minder?"

"We got separated. By the labyrinth." Rork's shoulders sagged.

"Hmmm." Boo tapped her upper lip with a finger.

"We were hungry and somehow conjured up a feast. The food was brilliant. I met one of the voices in my head." He pointed to his head. "Suddenly, a labyrinth rose up, surrounding us. We were separated by a rock wall. I think it came from my food coma."

Boo crossed her arms. "You're an idiot."

Rork didn't argue. Yet he didn't feel belittled like he did when his father would say the same thing. He wondered why. He knew the banshee was invested in Deirdre and him. He knew she was only commenting on his behavior, not the essence of his being. Rork could probably say the same things about his father. Still, his father had a way of making him feel judged and found wanting. His words could wound. Rork began to wonder if he was somehow *allowing* himself to be wounded. But then he didn't want to think about it anymore. He wanted to find Deirdre.

"We have to find her," said Boo. "Minders have a strong survival instinct, but they are not without their quirks. Who knows how she'll respond."

The banshee turned a corner in the labyrinth, gazing up at the walls. Rork followed. "These look rather permanent, which is unusual for a dreamscape." She looked at Rork. "Did you say you *met* a voice in your head?"

Rork nodded.

"Interesting. Usually it's just the voices."

"Deirdre," said Rork, focusing on what was important. "Help me find her." He typed on his knee 'findherfindherfindherfindher.'

Together they searched the labyrinth, the banshee gliding into every turn, occasionally looking up at the gray horizon as if following a navigational star or moon or satellite un-seeable by Rork.

Boo chattered while she searched. "We don't really know much about Deirdre. She came back from her accident only to lose her family one by one in a freakish series of events. First her sister. Then her mother. Finally, her father. I don't know all the details, but when I asked about her profile, I was told she had a 'tragic story'."

Later questions might occur to Rork, but at this precise moment the banshee's banter just added to the static of voices in his head. He hated the fact he was somehow responsible for their separation. He vowed to consider more than his stomach in the future.

After another hour of searching, they at last found Deirdre on the other side of the labyrinth, waiting for them. She had leaned against her pack just off the trail in a grassy hillock covered in rock dust. She had a gash on her forearm that she had bandaged with a tea towel.

Relieved and even joyous to see her, Rork ran to her, pack jouncing on his back. "Deirdre, are you all right?" he asked, surprising himself with the anxiety in his voice.

"I'm fine," she said. "It's nothing. Just a graze."

Boo stayed near, keeping a benevolent eye on the two of them. She sang softly, an aria to the lost and found.

Rork felt the lump of pie, which had lodged in his gut, dissolve. Around them the walls of the labyrinth started to give way, the sound of crumbling surrounding them. Stones fell to the ground like heavy hail, miraculously missing them. When the dust cleared, the viscous light of Shufftie prevailed once again on a scene that looked like a minefield with piles of rubble everywhere.

Rork dropped his pack beside Deirdre. "I can't believe we found you," he said, wanting to hug her or something. Instead, he sat beside her on the ground.

Deirdre rocked side to side, nudging him with her good arm. "You found me," she finally said. "You." Tremulous smile.

Rork handed Deirdre his canteen. She drank the rest of the water. "I've dealt with more walls than I care to for a while," she said, standing up and adjusting herself in the dust and debris. She dribbled the last few drops of water onto the parched earth.

"Perhaps I should stay away from pie," suggested Rork.

He watched the starburst in her eyes reappear. "Perhaps," she agreed.

Dandelions sprouted spontaneously around her feet, flat flower heads tufting the rubble. Their presumptuous brightness pierced the Shufftie gloom. They sprouted in a rainbow of color, connected somehow to Deirdre. She plucked a stem and placed the dandelion floweret in a grommet of Rork's pack.

"Head of a lion," she said.

"Head of a dumb lion," replied Rork. "I'm sorry about the labyrinth."

Deirdre tightened a strap on Rork's pack and zipped a pocket, fussing over him.

Feeling forgiven, he felt they were becoming a team. She wasn't just this strange being conjured out of nowhere by the banshee.

Boo flitted ahead of them, calling back. "I'm happy you found each other again, but let's not forget our goal here. We have many levels to go yet." She tapped her bare wrist as if to say tick, tock.

Rork groaned. No longer distracted by anxiety about Deirdre, the voices in his head gave him all kinds of advice he could never use or wouldn't remember when he needed it. There really ought to be a better system.

"Will I always hear voices?" he asked the banshee, exasperated and curious.

Boo stopped her hurrying for a minute. "Yes," she said. "Once an intermediary, always an intermediary. But as your life gets more full — family, friends, work, hobbies — they will observe more and say less. And what they do say you might find relevant."

Rork grunted. The prospect seemed surreal to him, a long, long way off possibility. He tried to imagine the real world, the world where he had lived with his gran and father. If he was going to be stuck with the voices, he was going to have to figure out a way to make them more useful.

"Are you sure you don't want me to cite a philosopher? Or a theologian?" asked the banshee. "Perhaps they could help with the epiphany thingy?"

"Hell no," said Rork. He helped Deirdre untrap her hair from her pack's straps. "We need someone to help us clear our minds because so far the ghosts are the least of our problems. We seem to be sabotaging ourselves."

"You said 'hell' again," whispered Deirdre, a soft censure in her voice.

Rork bumped her back with one shoulder. Crikey, he thought. He'd never done that to a girl before in his life. Boys, yes, but girls? Women? What was happening to him?

"Hmmm," said Boo, this time tapping her tiny teeth with one finger. "Good point," she said. "I'll have to think more on that before I see you next." She thumbed her buzzing comb, growing gradually less and less distinct. Finally, she vanished like spun sugar.

Rork wasn't sorry to see her go. A little of the banshee went a long way. Each appearance seemed to find them more and more enmeshed in Shufftie. He dreaded what the banshee might find them up to the next time she popped in. She seemed to be the harbinger of recurring disaster.

13: Haunting

RORK GOT SO HE could zone out while hiking. Moving his body, not worrying about where he was going or what it might mean. Discreetly, he kept an eye on Deirdre. She was quiet, focused on putting one foot in front of the other.

They needed water again, and the terrain had changed. Constantly needing to re-orient himself, Rork hoped he could find where the Creek of Quenching had meandered. The landscape had mellowed, become meadowlands, rolling and knolling as far as he could see. Still in various shades of gray but soothing in a rounded-edge, accessible kind of way. It was terrain he was more familiar with, but he didn't want to get too comfortable. Would there always be a labyrinth waiting in the wings? A morass of obstacles that needed to be dealt with?

While his brain chugged along, Rork hiked the gentle hills, Deirdre beside him, following the path. Finally, they saw another marker. LEVEL TWO: THE PASTURES.

Rork could tell Deirdre had been strongly affected in a negative way by the walls, so he didn't push her for conversation. He just kept pace with her long, strong legs. The dips and valleys seemed to make her step lighter. She held her head a little higher. She kept picking up their pace. The sky turned filmy. He could hear the eerie chirp of birds, streaking the trees and gray light, never settling. There was only Rork and Deirdre in a facsimile of walking to their next Shufftie encounter. Which hadn't materialized. Yet.

Their need for water was getting more serious. Rork was thirsty, the inside of his mouth parched and dry. "I'll be back in a minute," he said.

He jogged down the slope of the path off to their left, thinking the Creek of Quenching would be trickling just beyond the shrubbery. The trees looked familiar. Deirdre watched from the path.

Rork dropped down to his hands and knees and felt the ground. There was indeed a meager trickle, but no Creek of Quenching. His memory had failed him, or worse, the creek had evaporated, submerging beneath soft earth. He looked up and down the dry creek bed, his view obstructed by its twists and turns, surrounding bushes, and tall meadow grasses.

He returned to Deirdre, stomping his dirt-caked boots. "Not enough to fill a water bottle," he said. He wasn't sure what direction to take. Their compasses were of no help. Ever since the Eye of the Needle, the brass needles had become completely disabled, spinning uselessly.

"Look," said Deirdre. She peered intently at the ground. A small flower rosette peeped over the toe of her boot.

"What's that?" asked Rork.

"Saxifrage," said Deirdre.

"Sexy what?"

Deirdre grabbed him by the arm above the elbow and smiled. Rork felt his face grow hot.

"Sax-i-fridge," she repeated. "They like their roots to be wet."

Rork watched as more rosettes popped up in front of them. Their leaves were dark green, almost succulent, and their buds were tiny round baubles that bloomed. The saxifrage created a dotted trail around the next curve, veering off into the thicker foliage on the edge of the meadow.

"Come," said Deirdre. She grabbed Rork by the hand. "They'll help us find water." Her eyes shone in kinship with the flower bursts. Rork was glad. Glad, too, he'd had the rare sense to pick her for a minder.

Deirdre knelt down in a riot of saxifrage growing rough and tumble in the midst of green and fallen underbrush. Rork thought he heard water. Muffled. Hidden. Deirdre dug in the dirt, making a channel, pulling dried grasses and twigs towards her. Water bubbled up in the trough she'd created.

"The Creek of Quenching," she said triumphantly, sitting back on her heels.

Rork knelt down beside her with their canteens. Deirdre drank with both hands. Rork drank with his hands, too. They had to work at it, but the water tasted good — clean, clear, wet. Slightly peaty.

"Aye, aye, my lad and lassie," said a disembodied voice. "Take a good, long drink."

Deirdre yelped. Rork stumbled to his feet, hunkering inelegantly, almost frog-like, in front of her. He looked around frantically. Where was the voice coming from?

"There, there," said the voice.

They heard a rustle overhead. Looking up, they saw an opalescent ghost disentangle himself from the squat yew tree that shaded the outcropping next to what they believed was the Creek of Quenching.

"I didn't mean to scare you," said the ghost.

Rork thought it was an odd thing for a ghost to say and stood, squaring up to him, positioning Deirdre slightly behind his right shoulder. He could feel her breathing on the back of his neck.

"Really?" asked Rork.

The ghost chuckled. "Well, maybe I meant to scare you a little." He was balding, loose-lipped, and slightly tubby. Rork wondered how he had managed to get himself up in the yew tree. He looked way too heavy to easily climb up anything.

"I'm Basil," said the ghost.

Rork raised an eyebrow.

The ghost smiled readily, revealing large, buckish teeth. "You can call me Bazzie."

Rork stuck out his hand formally, wondering if the ghost would take it.

Bazzie shook it.

To his surprise, Bazzie's handshake was firm and real-feeling. Maybe Rork's hand tingled a little. Maybe it was his imagination.

"What are you?" asked Rork.

"Ain't you in an otherworld of ghosts?" asked Bazzie. He hooked a thumb along the side of his nose.

"I mean, what manner of ghost are you?" Rork clarified.

"These are the pastures, the lowlands. That would make me a low band kind of spirit. Still connected to my former life. Some folks call me a haunting."

"A haunting?" asked Deirdre. "Who are you haunting?"

"Why are you still connected to your former life?" asked Rork.

Bazzie smiled at the pair of them. "I need to help my wife and kids find something."

"What?"

"Some-thing," said the haunting cagily.

Deirdre peered over the top of Rork's shoulder. "If you tell us, perhaps we can help," she said.

"An island girl, eh?" said Bazzie, recognizing her accent. He pulled his flannel shirt away from his neck, letting yew twigs and leaves fall to the ground. "I'm considering," he said. He removed a pouch from his trouser pocket and began to roll himself a cigarette. Being a ghost, he couldn't actually ingest the nicotine, but he held it between two fingers and let the smoke drift.

Rork watched, fascinated, wondering if smoking had contributed to his demise.

Bazzie looked up and caught his eye. "In case you're interested, I dropped dead swinging an ax." He looked at them, his fat cheeks at a standstill, light eyes round as coins.

"It was sudden?" asked Deirdre.

"Dead sudden," said the haunting and laughed with a treble bass smoker's laugh. "But I was not the thoughtless lout they think me. Am not." Basil shook his head in affirmation to himself.

Cigarette smoke collected in the air, roiling around the haunting's face. It was dense, thick. It tickled the back of Rork's throat. He took a tiny step backwards, trying to clear his throat, and avoid getting cancer in his future, and scuffed the toe of Deirdre's boot.

"Who thinks you're a lout? Why?" she asked, moving out of Rork's way with a grace that Rork knew he'd never possess.

"Well, it's like this, lassie. I didn't always show my appreciation for what I had. But I felt it." Basil set his massive shoulders. His upper arms were ham hocks, and his handmade cigarette still smoked. He gazed at Deirdre with one eye screwed shut.

"And just because I was a simple man didn't mean I didn't have the finer feelings." He crushed out the cigarette between his thumb and forefinger then pocketed the butt. "I had 'em. I just didn't have the vocabulary to express 'em."

Basil slapped Rork on the back. For a haunting, he packed a hearty wallop. Rork had to catch himself from stumbling forward.

"Although I do have to confess one thing." Basil gave Deirdre an almost impish look. "I was rather fond of the pub."

"Can we help you?" asked Rork, dubious. He and Deirdre sat on their packs in a clearing, situated between the creek and the path. Basil paced between them.

"I need to help my family find something," said Basil. "They haven't found it yet. I didn't put it in the usual way."

"I don't understand," said Rork. "Can't you just reveal yourself to your wife and tell her where to look for it?"

"No, I can't just do that," said the haunting, annoyed. "There's rules and such. Protocol."

Rork couldn't help but smile at the haunting's adamancy, but he was a little tired of hearing about Shufftie's rules and protocols. Deirdre cast down her green eyelashes, trying to keep a straight face.

"Damn it, laddie. If folks understood how near at hand we was, they'd have a hard time living a life." Basil rubbed his face roughly. He had thick eyebrows with many stray hairs. Rork tried not to stare.

"What can you do?" asked Deirdre.

"For the first six months, I can only appear in their dreams." Basil's round eyes were limpid. The poor haunting really was distraught.

"Well, do that, then," said Rork.

"Do that then?!" mimicked Basil. He gave Rork a darkling look. "I'm not an actor. I'm not expressive. How do I tell 'em?" He began to pace in a square, muttering, "It's useless, useless."

"Okay, okay," said Rork. He unstrapped his computer from the exterior of his pack. He powered up, resting his computer on the bulk of his pack, his legs outstretched on either side. "Let's do a storyboard."

"A what?" asked the haunting, looking suspicious, confused, and hopeful all at the same time.

"It's how you plan a visual presentation," explained Deirdre. "Like a video or a short-short movie."

Rork looked at Deirdre incredulously. She really was full of surprises. She seemed to be up on modern technology culture. What else didn't he know about her?

"Oh," said the haunting, crouching on one knee next to Rork. He clearly hadn't understood what Deirdre had told him. Deirdre pulled her pack closer and looked on. Rork's fingers flew, pressing keys with expertise.

"What else should I know to do this?" asked Rork.

"I can't speak."

Rork made more keystrokes, opening up a text box.

"No cheating subtitles neither."

Rork sighed, sitting back, hands idle on his knees.

"I was thinking," said the haunting.

Two intent, high-color faces looked up.

"I was thinking that I might have a better shot getting through to my boy," said Basil. "He'd at least come out to the shed once in a while. Watch me work. My wife and daughter complained it was too cold and draughty out there."

"We want him to go to the shed?" asked Rork.

"Yes," said the haunting, reluctantly.

"How do you get in his dreams?" asked Deirdre.

Rork typed "Thanks" on the back of her hand. She always seemed to think of things he didn't. They were good together that way, and although she didn't look at him, he felt acknowledged.

"There's a dreamstage," said Basil. "My son's already programmed in." He stood up again, grunting, shaking out the kinks in his legs.

"Can you use props?" asked Rork.

"I'm not sure," said the haunting. "I'd have to check the handbook."

"There's a handbook?" Rork's voice got higher, broke, and for a second his thoughts were distracted, but then he shook his head and repositioned his fingers over the keyboard. "What did you used to do in your shed?"

"Whittle," the haunting's voice caught. "I used to carve small figures."

"That should be easy to mime," said Rork, growing excited. At least he had something that could be part of a message. He typed on his keyboard furiously. "And if we could find you a stool, and lighting, and some subliminal background music, I bet we'd be close. There's something in the shed you want him to find?"

"Aye, something I stashed away," said the haunting.

"Cat's in the Cradle?" asked Deirdre, naming a possible song title.

"Ugh," said Rork. "I think we can do better than that old cliché."

"I want him to know I believed in him, his future," said Basil, "that I can be there for him. When he's ready."

"There," said Rork.

Basil gave him a tortured look, afraid to hope. He squinted at the dreamscape, as if assessing whether or not his son would understand what he was trying to say beyond the grave.

Rork and Deirdre made Basil practice the dreamscene three or four times.

"Action," said Deirdre, slapping her arms together like a clapboard. It was Rork's cue to roll music.

The haunting was stiff at first, but the more Basil practiced the more fluid he got. Rork pretended to watch him through the viewfinder of a camera. "Your face," said Rork. "What kind of an expression is that?"

"Oh," said Deirdre, watching Basil closely. "There's a secret compartment in the wall."

"It must be important," said Rork. "Look at all the trouble he's going through." He looked significantly at Deirdre.

When Basil felt more comfortable with his part, Rork sent the script and background music to his phone. "Here," he said to Bazzie, handing him the phone.

"How do I get this back to you?" asked the haunting. He stared at the phone. "Shufftie is anything but predictable."

"Don't worry about it," said Rork. "Leave it somewhere. Maybe we'll stumble across it."

"I *will* leave it for you," said Basil. "Some place you're bound to find it." He looked at the phone curiously. "Does it have a beacon setting?"

Rork laughed. "No," he said. "No beacon setting."

"Well, there should be," said the haunting. He punched the buttons on Rork's phone, playing and stopping the music a few times. "This is going to work?" he asked. Then he smiled. "I don't know how to thank you."

Rork could see that words were difficult for the haunting. He looked away, powering down his computer. His backside was stiff as he crawled to his knees. He restrapped his computer to the exterior of his pack.

"Make sure your son understands what he meant to you," said Rork. His throat felt thick. He could almost see his father standing on the small hill beyond the yew tree. He pretended the smoke was still bothering him.

"I'll do that," said Basil.

"Do you know if it's night or day?" asked Deirdre a while after the haunting had left them. She was so tired, her words slurred. "Helping Basil felt almost rewarding and simple, and nothing has been simple in Shufftie yet." She laid her face on the harsh weave of her pack, her body draped across it just off the trail on softer ground.

"Mmm," agreed Rork distractedly, sitting beside her. He scanned the sky. "I have no idea." The monotone gray light was starting to make his eyes strain.

Deirdre slipped her hands beneath her cheek. "I wish we could see the haunting's dream," she said.

"Me, too," said Rork, although it came out more like one word. "I hope he could follow our script okay."

"What script?" asked Boo, popping into their tableau, sitting pretzel style on the ground between their two packs.

"Aarrgghh," said Rork. "I wish you wouldn't do that!"

The banshee smiled smugly. She steepled her fingers and asked again, "What script?"

Rork and Deirdre told her how they helped the haunting create a dream for his son.

"Dreams ordinarily belong to the dreamer and the dream-agent," said Boo after they had finished. "Your Basil. I am not supposed to give access. But you've got me curious about this low band."

"Low band?" asked Rork.

"Low band ghost. Level two. Low frequency ghost."

The banshee retrieved her comb from her gown's deepest pocket. She experimented with the tines, playing notes. "Ah, that must be him." She tugged at the tarp tied to Rork's pack. "Can you figure out a way to hang this? As a screen? I found his frequency and think I can play the dream for you."

Rork threw a long rope over a branch of a Memory Tree. The creepy things seemed to follow them wherever they went, unaccountably popping up. The trees unnerved Deirdre. He threaded the rope through two grommet holes in the tarp and hoisted it high in the air. The tarp rippled but hung smooth enough.

Rork and Deirdre huddled close to Boo who projected beams of dreamography through her clearie eyes. They saw Basil in a spotlight in a dusty shed, sitting on a stool. Music began to play, and he bowed his head, carving a block of wood with a pocketknife. There was a split screen to a boy — a young man, really — asleep in a homemade box bed. The case and sash of his bedroom window was wide open. A waning crescent moon was visible through spindly trees. Deirdre made a noise deep in her throat and pressed her fist to her mouth.

Basil mimed the completion of his figurine. He blew dust away from it and kissed it ever so tenderly. Rork was impressed. Basil walked to the far wall and dramatically counted two by four's, pounding on the wall with each count. 1, 2, 3. Basil's son moved in his sleep, rolling onto his back, flinging his arms wide. Basil found a cabinet set into the recess of the wall. He pushed on a small panel, and a door popped open. Lovingly, Basil placed the new figurine on a shelf with others. He resumed his seat on the stool while the song's ending melody played out. Rork was über-pleased with himself about the song choice. Although he wasn't a huge Phil Collins fan, the singer was tough to beat when he was being balladic, and the ending refrain was perfect:

If you look behind you, I will be there.

Back to the split screen: Basil's son's eyes opened. He lay in his bed, eyes blinking. Finally, he sat up. He stood at the end of his bed, peering out the window. The slate roof of the shed gleamed in moonlight. They watched him feel his way through the shadowy back garden to the shed. He held the padlock in his hand, momentarily leaning into the shed door with his forehead. Rork inhaled sharply.

Basil's son tugged on the padlock, and miraculously, it came open. He unlooped it from the big eyehook and opened the door. He stood in the corner, walking in the footsteps of his father in the dream and counted two by four's. 1, 2, 3. He found the cabinet. He laid his open palm on its smooth surface. Then, he pushed. The magnetic closure gave way, and inside the cabinet he found figures of himself at various stages of his life: a baby, a toddler, an adolescent. There was even a figure of himself as an adult. A professional. In a carefully carved suit, carrying a briefcase. The son sniffed, drawing his forearm across his nose. He felt deeper inside the cabinet and pulled out a metal box. Opening the box, the son found banknotes — a sizeable stack of them. The son clutched a figurine and the stack of banknotes to his chest. He watched motes of dust circulate above his head. Tears coursed down either cheek. Basil reached from his side of the split screen towards his son.

The dreamscene flickered and went black. Rork squeezed Deirdre's hand. The banshee blinked rapidly, pretending there was something in her eyes.

"Are you okay?" asked Rork.

"Don't you worry about me," said Boo. There was a quiver in her voice.

"You did good," said Deirdre, squeezing Rork's hand back.

"*We* did good," said Rork. His fingers did a little keystroke flourish over his knees. He scrunched lower on his pack, stretching out his legs in their own waning semicircle. "Now I need to sleep." His eyes were half-mast, oblivious to the banshee. "Why is it," he said, thick-tongued, "that I always seem to attract the needy spirits?"

Deirdre followed suit, sliding down into a prone position, eyelashes stuttering against pale cheeks.

"You're an intermediary, silly," said the banshee. "It's kind of the point."

The last thing Rork heard was Boo's tinny comb music.

14: Ambushed

THE PLINK PLINK of comb song gave way to the sound of wings, moving parchment-like, paper whispering. Something about the movement of air made Rork's mind leap. Half asleep, he was seeing in color. He was also afraid to move. Splotches of color. Daubs of moving, abstract color. Surreal color. Fretting, flickering, fluttering.

Rork lifted his head and looked down the length of his body. He was covered in butterflies. Hundreds of butterflies. Their tiny feet moved like whispers all over his skin. He stirred, raising himself on his hands. A blanket of butterflies moved with him. Butterflies opened and closed wings on his cheeks, his forehead, his ears. He saw spots. Tiger-inspired light and dark spots. The drama of sudden color made him giddy.

He heard Deirdre giggle, and a moving mass of monarchs heaved next to him. The butterflies burrowed in her long, wavy hair. Deirdre turned to face him wearing a helmet of flying insects.

"There are so many," said Deirdre. "Where do you think they came from?"

"I have no idea," said Rork.

Deirdre held up a finger, which held a butterfly, sidestepping with tendril feet. "I like this dream," she said.

Moving all together, the butterflies lifted off and suspended in the air around their shoulders. After hovering, they drifted back down to the ground, the grass, Rork and Deirdre's bodies. The butterflies seemed especially attracted to the orbits of their eyes. Rork cupped his hands to his temples, watching the butterflies assemble, preparing to lift off again. The pattern repeated itself — lift off, land, lift off.

"I think they want us to follow them," Rork said.

Deirdre got quickly to her feet, a butterfly perched on her shoulder.

"Let's take our gear with us," said Rork. "We don't know where they might lead us."

The butterflies moved in a swarm of chitinous wings. The sun shone high in the sky, a ball of brightness. Rork felt butterflies flutter against his ribs. It felt so real. How could this be a dream?

The butterflies cast a lacey shadow. Rork felt herded by the butterflies. He snorted.

"What?" asked Deirdre.

"Nothing," said Rork. Thinking they were being herded by butterflies was too ludicrous to share.

Rork wasn't sure if he had slept or not. His skin still felt sandpapery with weariness, but he must have gotten some sleep. Deirdre, too, seemed sprier. The landscape continued to be kind to them, declining hill-ward in its curvy way. He felt respite between his ears. It seemed the chatter of the dead were not averse to taking a break now and again.

They reached the bottom of a dip. The butterflies caught an air current and swooped left and right, freewheeling en masse. Deirdre inhaled sharply. Ahead of them, broad patches of daisies and showy milkweed grew. A DALE OF DAISIES. (Or so Rork read the writing in the wispy clouds above their heads.) The milkweed turned their sticky starlets in Deirdre's direction. The daisies bobbed their small heads.

"Oh!" said Deirdre in delight.

Overwhelmed, she couldn't say more. She ran into the dale with her arms outstretched. She seemed to float.

"What the...dell?" said Rork, adjusting the straps of his pack. He raced after her, catapulting his tall body through the meadow, his arms extended like wings.

In the middle of the dale Deirdre dropped to the ground, panting. Rork collapsed next to her. The sky was baby bunting blue. Daisies swathed the hillside with their penny hearts. A teasing breeze lapped at the beads of sweat on Rork's forehead. The sun was warm on his face, the inside of his eyelids absorbing its orange glow. His stomach growled. Loudly.

"That was my stomach," he said.

Deirdre laughed and rolled onto her side. Rork liked her laugh. It caused a strange flip-flop thing in his chest. She looked completely at home in the grass under a canopy of daisies and milkweed, her green eyelashes the color of foliage.

"You really are hungry all the time," said Deirdre.

Rork propped up his head on one arm and shrugged. "I warned you."

"Daisies make a good salad."

Rork raised one expressive eyebrow doubtfully.

"You will see."

After eating three helpings of creamy risotto and a daisy salad, Rork lay back in the grass and watched the butterflies flit about.

"I'll help you clean up in a minute," he said dozily, sprawling in the grass.

"I will hold you to that," said Deirdre, stretching out next to him. Their two long bodies made an equal sign in the tamped down meadow.

"Ah," sighed Rork. He turned his head and smiled at Deirdre. His hair formed a ginger halo in the sunlight.

"Aye," said Deirdre. "Everybody gets an idyl or two in their lifetime. At least that's what my auntie says."

"What's an 'idyl'?" asked Rork.

"A moment of complete alignment with the universe."

"Your auntie?"

"Aye," said Deirdre, eyes closed. "She mostly raised me."

"I'll have to Google it," said Rork, wanting to ask more but not wanting to push. He liked it better when Deirdre shared on her own without his prompting.

"You do that."

Seemingly of its own accord, Rork's hand inched closer to Deirdre's. Like one of those creeping vines that couldn't help gravitating towards her. Not that he thought of himself as a creeping vine. More like a sturdy sapling. His hand got close enough for him to feel the energy between them. In fact, he was hyper-aware. Marveling, he pretended to be asleep, his mouth open.

A sound interrupted their reverie. Rork tried to ignore it, but it persisted like the buzzing in his head. He scowled. He couldn't quite place the noise. It sounded like a lighter. Or blowtorch? Could it be? He smelled burning plastic: acrid, false, piercing. He felt the idyl folding up on itself, shrinking.

"Damn," muttered Rork.

"What?" asked Deirdre, sleepy.

"Get your pack," said Rork. "I hear something. I don't like it."

There was no place to hide in the dale. All Rork and Deirdre could do was crouch on the ground, trying not to move too much. They could hear voices now, brash and argumentative.

"Watch what you're doing," said a terse voice. Rork had heard that voice before. Deirdre squeezed his arm. She recognized it, too.

The burning plastic smell intensified. Rork put a hand over his mouth and nose. He could practically feel the radicalization of molecules. A jagged manhole of atmosphere lifted and slid open in front of them. A head and shoulders emerged.

Charboy!

Rork ducked deeper into the daisies, dragging Deirdre with him.

Charboy's angry piercings glinted as he stepped fully into the dale. He smoothed the black leather of his gloves, flexing his fingers. Beck, the banshee that had earlier argued with Boo, stepped out behind him, freshly-shirted and stone-colored against the dale's vibrant colors. He poked about the dale with a walking stick nobbled like the hunk of a root. Finally, a young man, dressed all in black, followed, wearing a zippered hoodie, hands clenched inside his front pockets. He hung behind the other two, looking around. The hood slipped from his head, and Rork recognized him instantly. It was Hamish, his poor, lost former friend. He sure had a knack for falling in with the wrong crowd.

"Hah!" said Charboy, aiming his gloved hand at a cluster of butterflies. Fire blazed from the ends of his fingers, ripping a seam in the tranquil sky and incinerating a flotilla of butterflies. Smoldering butterflies dropped to the ground in ashy clumps.

"No," whispered Deirdre beside Rork.

Rork placed his forefinger over her lips. They didn't want to be seen, especially by this group of misfits.

The remaining butterflies swooped and turned, leaving the dale abruptly in a dart shape. Air swirled with their lustrous wingbeats, pounding a rhythm in Rork's head. Not good. Not good. Not good. He continued pushing his body backwards, mimicking Deirdre's movements, knowing they were vulnerable. There was no way to avoid the swish of plants as they wiggled their way through the undergrowth. He did not trust Charboy, Beck, or Hamish. What an unholy trio! Where was the banshee when they needed her?

"I don't see anybody," said Charboy.

"They're here. Or will be here," said Beck.

"How do you know?"

"One of the programmers sent me a text," said Beck. "They can hack into any dreamscape if properly motivated."

"Why do you want to find them so bad?" asked Hamish.

Beck drove his walking stick into the ground. The impact created a tremor in the ground that rippled outwardly. "I want them to fail," said Beck. "To disgrace Bryonna and her mother who will then be forced to step down as Chairman of the Board. And then a real leader can take over."

"Like your brother," said Charboy, breathing smoke into the air.

Rork felt trapped. He didn't know how the formula worked. His dream, Deirdre's dream, and Shufftie added up to make this idyl. But how to change the configuration? It was a code he couldn't break. Deirdre worked with the daisies, doing their best to keep them hidden, weaving together a flower shield that moved along with them as they elbowed their retreat. Rork was assessing whether or not they could make a break for it when he smelled smoke. A roiling cloud of it. The ground became hot, unbearably so. He felt his nose hairs singe. The ground boiled beneath their feet. Rork and Deirdre were forced to give themselves up or be burned. So, they stood with their arms raised.

Beck, Charboy, and Hamish surrounded them and had them cornered. Flames blazed through the idyllic dale. Rork stepped in front of Deirdre, protecting her from the scorch.

"Damn you, Beck," said Boo, slipping into the scene just in time, as if she'd been observing from the wings. "You know you're not supposed to interfere. You have your own assignment to worry about." She held out her arms and began to turn in a circle, gradually twirling faster and faster. Like a dervish, she created a vacuum of pressure that squeezed the air, feeding the fire. It sputtered, gasped, and went out.

"I want your revelation!" shouted Beck at Rork.

Rork looked at him blankly. Even if he had a revelation (which he didn't), Beck was the last banshee he'd tell. His eyes questioned Hamish who shuffled in the background. *What are you doing with this crazy fantastical being?* he asked without words.

Hamish shrugged. *I knew you were up to something,* he mouthed back.

Beck shouted again. "I want it now!"

Boo stuck out her chin and stomped to within swinging distance of Beck.

"This is so typical of you, Beck. Always looking for the shortcut, thinking you can demand whatever you want. As if it was that easy. As if it worked that way. You will never understand anything."

Beck raised a fist towards Boo, his flat face looking as hard as cement.

Rork covered his ears, expecting Boo to retaliate with her banshee-pitched wailing. But no sounds erupted. Indeed, it was deathly quiet. Unnerving. Rork lowered his hands. The silence hurt his ears.

Boo narrowed her eyes at Beck, her face tense. Rork could see her clenched jaw moving. The air seethed with whatever was happening between the two of them, taking place at a threshold of time and space, separate and subhuman, available only to the banshees.

Pressure mounted, contracting and distending the air. Rork surreptitiously assessed their situation. He smelled of smoke, but he didn't find any burns anywhere. He had all his supplies. His pack was intact. He gestured for Deirdre to give herself the once-over, look for her things. If by chance Boo created an opportunity for them to bolt, he wanted to be sure they were ready.

The air bubbled up distress, taking place on the other side of the immediate layers of what they understood to be atmosphere. Boo was such a small banshee, Rork wondered how she could withstand the brute strength of Beck. Nervously, he typed her name over and over against the denim of his thighs. "Boo. Boo. Boo."

Deirdre inched her pack upwards to her shoulders. Concentrating, she bumped into Rork. He steadied her, a look of anguish in her eyes. No more idyl. The plant wreckage was heart-breaking, even to Rork. Deirdre kept turning her palms as if entreating the daisies to revive, but their life-sap was gone, leaving the landscape littered with singed husks of dead flowers.

Boo came back to the present, suddenly shrieking at Beck. "You are an idiot! A poor excuse for a banshee!"

In a flash, Beck had his hands around her throat, his knuckles a whiteout of frustration. Despite the throat-hold, Boo didn't take her eyes off him. Her clearie eyes seemed to bore right through him.

Beck suddenly yelped in pain and let her go. He stared at his hands. "I hate you. I hate you," he said.

"Well, good," said Boo, rubbing her neck. "Maybe you'll stay out of my way."

"Let's get out of here," said Beck, nodding angrily to Charboy and Hamish.

Beck hacked his way out of the dream with two dastardly slashes of his walking stick. He and his two companions disappeared through a jagged black hole in the dreamscape that stitched itself up in slow motion, leaving only the ghost of a trace and the lingering smell of char. The sky soon was blue again.

Rork, relieved, stared at the trace marks. Good dreams turned out bad. Bad dreams turned out worse. And now Hamish was involved. What was Shufftie conjuring?

15: Algorithm

"WAKE UP," SAID BOO. "Wake up!"

Rork and Deirdre lay curled back to back, sleeping. Boo stood in the "V" of their sloping bodies and shoved. Their bodies rocked side to side. The banshee was stronger than she looked.

Rork roused, half-dreaming. Images shuttered behind his eyes. He felt a tickle building in his nose, a sneeze created by the acrid pall of burned daisies, incinerated butterflies. The gut-punch look in Deirdre's eyes.

He opened his eyes a crack, squinting through the sleep gum. For a minute, he couldn't remember where he was. He sneezed violently, and his eyes sprung open.

Rork found Boo gazing at him, her eyes effervescent with worry. "Are you okay?" she asked.

He blinked, weirdly soothed by the dull gray landscape. "I think so," he said. "Where's Deirdre?"

The banshee nodded over his shoulder. "Behind you."

He scooted to a sitting position, holding his head. It felt dull, heavy. As if parts of his brain had moved around in his sleep like furniture inside a moving van. Deirdre rolled over and blinked vacantly at the gray sky.

"You were in my dream," she said. "You, too." She looked at the banshee standing over her. "There was color and butterflies and meadow," she continued, her voice rather wistful.

Rork snapped his head. "I had the same dream!" he said.

"I tried to explain," the banshee pouted, "about the algorithm. How your hopes, memories, even fears get all shuffled together. It is unique to each team. But the more memories you share, the more cross-overs occur."

"Beck was there," said Rork.

Boo made a 'tsk' noise with her tiny teeth.

"All that destruction," sighed Deirdre, sitting up, her green lashes downcast.

"I'm sorry," said the banshee.

"Was it real?" asked Rork.

Boo shrugged, noncommittal.

"What do we do now?" Rork sighed.

The banshee looked at him sympathetically. "You keep going."

Rork got to his feet and gave Deirdre a hand.

Boo stared down at her gray gown. Rork noticed that today she smelled faintly of fondant. "I wish we could figure out how this epiphany thing works," she said.

"Isn't there a festival day called Epiphany?" asked Deirdre.

"Yes," said the banshee.

"Wait," said Rork. "I thought it was a revelation or something."

"Divine insight," sighed the banshee. "Yes, it's both."

"What? How can it be both?" asked Rork. "Do we have to come up with our own meaning?"

"Yes," said Boo, already starting to disintegrate.

"You just got here!" Rork objected. He'd worry about an epiphany later.

"I know, but when I go second dimension like I did with Beck, it costs me." Boo made a half-hearted attempt to pull back her shoulders, buck up.

Rork had to admit she looked spent. "Hey," he said, "I wanted to ask you something."

"What?" asked the banshee, barely visible against the Shufftie gray.

"Is there really a ghost handbook?"

"More like a white paper," she said, dimpling.

Rork was hungry. And thirsty. And hot. He couldn't seem to get rid of the fire-scorched taste in his mouth. They were back on the path, attempting to keep close to the Creek of Quenching. The path didn't always cooperate, veering off in different directions as they ventured farther into LEVEL THREE: THE MOORLANDS.

Rork was feeling a little deflated after the experience with Beck and Hamish but kept walking. Deirdre walked as if overcome with plant grief. Walking for the sake of walking seemed to fulfill their imminent purpose. They "kept going," as the banshee advised. They chalked up miles. Rork's fingers tapped on the cushioned strap of his rucksack. He thought about how Shufftie jumbled his understanding of the meaning of algorithm. He'd always thought an algorithm was devising a set of rules for a problem that ultimately lead to a solution. Rork was comforted by this idea. It had clarity. It had logic. It had order. Three things his father appreciated, so Rork supposed he wasn't as *unlike* his father as he thought.

Rork remembered his A-levels project and his last consultation with his instructor. The idea was to create a macro or other application that simplified an everyday activity. At the time, he hadn't known his gran was sick, but she had grown forgetful. She'd wander the house with her freckled hands deep in the pockets of her pinny, chastising herself for laying aside one thing or another, forlorn that she couldn't remember. Rork always knew her as a compendium of practical, useful (and to him, secret) knowledge. It had been alarming to him to witness her diminishing mental abilities.

Some provident genius inside him prompted him to create a computer flip-file for his A-levels project that would capture most of what his gran knew. For one whole term, Rork shadowed her while she gardened or cooked or sent messages or cleaned or visited with her few (and getting fewer) friends and neighbors, including Morag. Gah, she'd made him feel ill at ease, but the project had been more important to him. He was creating the flip-file to help the person he most adored.

He took pictures. He made short videos. He recorded and documented what his gran said and did. Then he assembled all the pieces into a Java-driven application he called "Pinny-Full" with a shortcut on his laptop that looked like an animated pinny, or housecoat. He even made an app-version for his mobile phone. His gran had bounced on her small, furry-slippered feet when he'd demonstrated his work, thinking it a clever trick. Towards the end she had even consulted it, getting past her wariness of machine language and computers. His father, of course, thought it was a huge waste of time, although he did have to acknowledge his mother's joy in it as she insisted his father download the app to his phone, so she could borrow it when he was home and Rork was at school.

Rork's instructor had been impressed to the point of disbelief and had clicked on the "pinny" repeatedly, shuffling between entries. "Rork," he'd said finally, shaking his head as he read about the medicinal properties of basil and how to release its essential oils. "This is far beyond what I would have expected from an upper sixth final project. You have a real, real gift." He clicked again, landing on his gran's instructions for drying and preserving forget-me-nots.

Pinny-Full had required Rork to create an algorithm to solve the problem of his gran's lapsing memory. Shufftie turned algorithm on its head, treating unpredictability as the solution. There were no rules, and everything was open source — dreams, memories, desires, thoughts — which meant Shufftie was all about ambiguity, all about unreasonableness, and all about disorder.

Rork tugged on the straps of his pack, raising it higher on his back in an effort to adjust the dis-ease he felt. He flexed his fingers but couldn't seem to access any words to type. In one pocket of his trousers, he felt for the sixpence. Somehow in his mind the sixpence had become a token for his father's acceptance and inarguable common sense.

In his other pocket, he felt for the flash drive. On it Rork had stored his "Pinny-Full" project and all his working files and notes. The flash drive had become a memento of his gran's love and foreknowledge, her intuition.

Rork knew he needed both.

16: Possession

SUNK IN HIS OWN THOUGHTS, Rork looked up finally and took in the vast stretches of treeless wasteland that surrounded them on all sides. He and Deirdre were completely and utterly alone. He felt exposed, and he didn't like it. Walking dispelled the feeling of vulnerability a little. At least he was doing something active.

"How're you doing?" he asked Deirdre.

"Fine," she said. She watched the ground, looking up reluctantly. "You know the moors when the heather's fairly blooming? Great swathes of purple flowers? As far as the eye can see?"

"Aye," said Rork. "This looks a little different."

"Aye," said Deirdre, tucking her chin.

Rork noticed Deirdre held her hands together in front of her, as if protecting something. He thought he caught a glimpse of color.

"What do you have there?" He motioned with his head.

"Nothing," said Deirdre.

"It looks like something," insisted Rork.

Deirdre didn't answer him, and Rork let it go. Certainly, they had enough to contend with without him prying deeper than was acceptable to Deirdre.

Companionably silent, they continued to walk the lonely, sweeping landscape, the wind whistling through the weedy heaths. Peaty soil muffled the sound of their boots.

They stopped for water, Deirdre handicapped by her two already occupied hands. At last she looked at Rork.

"I have a stowaway," she confessed, opening her hands to reveal a bedraggled daisy, still thriving coin-eyed in the palm of her hand.

"Oh," said Rork, dribbling water down the front of his shirt. "How are you doing that?"

"As long as it remains in contact with me, it will survive. At least for a while." Deirdre smiled like the Flower Girl he'd first encountered.

"That's quite a trick," said Rork.

Deirdre touched the daisy's petals. "I have a memory of my mother with daisies in her hair. She had long, wavy hair like me."

He thought she was looking for something from him. Understanding? Compassion?

"I don't know what the occasion was, but I can still see her. Vaguely. Her face creased. Smiling into the sun. Daisies tucked in her hair." Deirdre placed the daisy carefully behind her ear. "Eventually it will need more nutrients than I can provide." She took a gulp of water from her canteen and wiped her mouth with the back of her hand. "Don't tell me when it dies."

The moorland waited for them, unrelenting into the distance. Rork had no idea how many days they'd been hiking. If it even had been days. Increments of time didn't feel the same in Shufftie. He'd figured at least that much out about where they were. He wondered what kept the banshee. Should they stop for the night? Or would-be night? He reached for the bag of Deirdre's trail mix he'd looped on his belt. Suddenly, he felt strange all over. His heart began to beat rapidly. His skin tingled. Supernatural feelings were beginning to feel all too common to him.

"What the…*tell?*" he said, explosively, trying to avoid again offending Deirdre.

An uncanny cackle reverberated in the air around him, through him. It seemed to be emanating from him, but it wasn't him.

He began to hyperventilate.

Deirdre looked at him, concerned.

The cackle grew louder. "I am you, and you are me!"

Rork's chest rose and fell, rose and fell. He clawed at himself. "Get out of me!" he yelled again. "Deirdre!" he yelled, simultaneously a cry for help and a warning.

Deirdre took a wary step towards him.

"No!" he commanded.

Deirdre backed away, moving closer to the ground, crouching as small as possible.

Rork contorted in the throes of his backpack. "Off, off!" he cried. He threw his backpack to the ground. It kicked up gray dust, but still he struggled, seemingly at war with himself. He felt like he had a fever, a tightness in his chest, a heavy binding. "Get. Out." The words were strangled, tortured.

The cackle filled the whole of his skull. "We are one. I squat on your bones! I feel what you feel."

"No!"

"Yes!"

Rork threw himself to the ground and rolled back and forth as if possessed, continuing to slap at himself.

"I love your granny. Maybe I will meet her. Yum. Yum."

"Shut. Up!" Rork could feel thoughts he didn't recognize, strange, dark thoughts lurking, as if he were being taunted, stalked. He felt like ripping the heads off dolls, chickens. Doing damage.

"And you feel something for this one. Yes?" That infernal cackle! It was an assault to his ears.

G-a-a-a-h, Rork thought, rolling into a clump of vicious-looking scrub. He'd rather feel anything — discomfort, pain. Any. Thing. But. This.

Distantly he felt the jagged slicing of skin, the stinging of nettles, pickers, the air-wrapped coolness of many small wounds.

"Stop that," said the ghost, an edge of annoyance creeping into his voice. "No pain! Pain, I've had enough of! I want your other thoughts."

Rork rolled deeper into the scrub, protecting his face with his forearms. He didn't think. He tried not to regard the piercing into his flesh. Thorns, sharp edges seemed to find him. His clothes bunched up, exposing his shins, stomach, lower back. The scrub lacerated him. Now in his head the sound of ripping, small tears.

"Nononononononononononononononono," whined the voice.

A ghostly head erupted out of Rork's chest. Rork paused in his self-immolation.

"Why'd you have to do that?" the ghost asked Rork, nose to nose. "I want my fun."

"I don't want *your* fun!" gasped Rork, dripping blood from countless small cuts crisscrossing his forearms, hands, neck.

The rest of the ghost emerged from Rork, a short, dumpy man with waxy skin and a sparse comb-over. He had a large belly and short, fleshy arms.

"I want my fun," he continued to pout, the shadow of whiskers darkening the loose folds of his neck. His pants were too short, revealing pale ankles, incongruously manicured feet in walking sandals. "Fun, fun, fun is what I'm about."

He spied Deirdre, kneeling in the moorland, limp daisy petals drooping from behind her ear. Her eyes were huge, cumulus, but she seemed frozen in place as the ghost parasite almost skipped towards her.

Rork panted on the ground, watching in dread as the ghost closed the distance between them. "Come back!" he shouted, trying desperately to disentangle from the scrub.

But it was too late.

The ghost chanted. "Fun, fun, I will have my fun. Get ready, because here I come."

With that, the ghost pinched his nose and dove feet first into Deirdre.

"N-o-o-o-o-o!" said Rork, renting the open sky of the vast, open moorlands with his shout.

Deirdre's arms buckled, and she sunk lower to the ground, absorbing the ghost's impact. She began to breathe fast, shallow breaths through her nose. Like the Little Engine That Could. Or couldn't. Rork dragged himself out of the scrub, watching her anxiously. How would she react to the ghost's invasion?

Deirdre got up hesitantly, unfurling upwards, as if testing her limbs.

"Ooo, ooo," squealed the ghost. "Lots of room. Such tidy thoughts!"

She turned almost coyly and looked at Rork. Something Deirdre in her storm cloud eyes. Something not.

"Not immune to you either, the Fergus." The ghost's godforsaken cackle rang in the air.

Rork had managed to haul himself to a standing position. His skin was starting to welt and throb, but he ignored it. He took a few cautious steps towards Deirdre, thinking that perhaps he could wring the ghost out of her.

"No, no, loonie," said the ghost. "I am not such a fool."

Deirdre closed her eyes, facing what would have been the sun. She bunched her hair in a makeshift ponytail, letting the bulk of her hair remain in a loop. It was a uniquely Deirdre gesture. As well as the squaring of her packless shoulders. That was Deirdre all over. Her quiet resolve.

"What are you thinking, my girl?" said the ghost, a note of concern creeping into his voice.

Deirdre took off running, her long legs churning across the moorlands. She didn't seem to care where she went. She just ran. Forging forward. Like a deer or gazelle. As if speed and distance and sheer propulsion could rid her of the cackling menace.

Rork took off after her, doing his best to keep up, but he was tired and sore, and his clothes rubbed against his poor, abraded skin. It took everything he had to keep her in view.

She was so fast. He'd had no clue of the ground she could cover.

She raced through LEVEL FOUR: THE MEADOWS, the dry grasses waving as she sped past, the rushes, too. Flowering marsh plants seemed to perk up and pay attention, Eyebright, blue-white in the gray light, but distinctively striped, with leaves like parsley, and hairy lousewort with their waxy, flowering tubers.

There was static in Rork's head. Was it exhaustion? Fury? Had the voices in his head changed channels? Rork inhaled a ragged breath and tried to close the ever-widening gap between him and Deirdre. Whenever his gran had needed to cajole him — to try something new, to expend a little more effort — she got round him by calling him her pet name, "the Fergus."

"Come now, the Fergus."

"You can do it, the Fergus."

It was part of the shared lexicon between he and his gran. Private.

Rork growled at the thought of a ghost violating this revered space and got a spurt of energy. Up ahead, Deirdre's legs flashed on the trail, gleaming in the gray glow. Rork hoped the ghost would find all the exertion upsetting. He looked like a particularly indolent sort of ghost to Rork.

Deirdre galloped past the trailhead to LEVEL FIVE: THE LOCHS, and then they overlooked a valley of glistening tarns, reflecting silver-glint in the overcast sky. The lochs were movingly beautiful but shadowed by looming mountain precipices on all sides, hinting at more treacherous terrain to come.

Rork stopped for breath, clutching his side. He took in great lungfuls of air, the static in his head continuing its white noise distraction. The dead chorus was on hiatus, and it worried him. Like something bad was about to happen. The calm before all-hell-broke-loose.

He watched Deirdre continue to run, her legs rippling with muscle, grit, sweat. Unable to stop. Desperate. And so far, the ghost was unshakeable. Rork could hear its cries echoing back to him.

"Giddy-up, young lassie!"

As if Deirdre was a wild mustang for the breaking.

Even the water plants, the ones that liked their roots wet, water lobelia and water plantain, shook their lush abundance with worry.

The white noise began to gather, getting louder in his head. Rush. A premonition of fear gripped him. Rork ran and hobbled, ran and hobbled. A strange sound came out of him as he tried to catch Deirdre. He hissed to himself. "Keep up, the Fergus. Keep up."

Deirdre's desperate run dead-ended at a bluff. There was nowhere for her to go. A raging river coursed below, agitated by the fall of water from above them. The waterfall dropped from the jagged foothills of the mountain summits.

Deirdre stomped around the bluff's edge, snorting through her nostrils.

The crash of water filled Rork's skull, building pressure behind his cheekbones. It appeared to be the source of all the static he had been feeling. If only he'd known.

Deirdre paused to look back at Rork who was hurtling towards her, streaked with blood and sweat and grime.

For a moment it was really Deirdre. Rork was close enough to see it in the flash of starburst in her eyes. She moved her lips, trying to say something.

The damned ghost cackled.

Deirdre gave him her version of a smile and turned back to the bluff. Then she long-jumped into the rampant river, hanging purposefully in the air, surrounded by the thunderous sound of white water.

"Deirdre!" yelled Rork. He bent over at the edge of the bluff, panting, and saw Deirdre's boots disappear in a sweeping wave of water. The ghost pulled out just before Deirdre plunged below the surface.

"What have you done?" gasped Rork.

"And so, we become our fears," said the ghost. He waggled his eyebrows, and the scant pelt on the top of his head moved up and down.

"I could kill you," said Rork, through clenched teeth.

The ghost cackled. "Already been done, dear boy. Already been done."

Rork could not even feel relief when the ghost took off into the sky. He watched Deirdre struggle to keep her head above water as she was carried relentlessly downriver, telltale letters following her: RIVER OF FORGETTING.

17: River of Forgetting

RORK DREAMED he jumped into the water, his body buffeted between wave and boulder and current. He dream-yelled for Deirdre, but all he got was a wall of water down his gullet and up his nostrils. He choked. His eyes rolled in his head. His clothes dragged on him. He clamped his mouth shut. Maybe he dreamed. Maybe he was wide awake.

The water was cold. His limbs felt stunned. He had no idea how banged up he was getting. He dog-paddled. He treaded water, spinning in the river, trying to catch sight of her, a part of her, any indication of her continued existence. How could she be gone? Just like that?

He was nothing to the river.

The river must flow. That was its nature.

Rork tried not to despair. He kept in his mind the possibility — the real hope — of finding Deirdre. Images of her flashed behind his eyes, warped and distorted with water. He had to keep blinking to see past them, sodden hair clinging to the sides of his face like seaweed.

Images continued to shutter. More images than he could ever have amassed in a lifetime. Were they sharing this dream, too?

What was this river?

He stopped moving against his clothes. It was just easier. He didn't fight the current either. He went where the river wanted to go. He bent his legs to avoid getting clipped by underwater shoals of rock.

He dreamed he found her, snagged on a branch of a fallen oak tree, submerged branches slick with moss and life. The tree seemed to be cradling her.

He dreamed he summoned the strength of his great-great-great-grandfather to pull her ashore. Gently, gently, he carried her, thankful at last for his overgrown size, past rocks and snaggletooth debris forgotten along the river's edges. Objects misplaced, accidentally left behind or intentionally disregarded.

Rork found her pulse on the ribbed column of her neck. It beat beneath his fingers. Her chest rose and fell, her lungs working their bellows action. Rork's ears popped, and he felt a whoosh of air, of breath, a collective inhalation, exhalation. Relief exchanged through time, generations of daisy-wearers. A daisy chain.

The only thing.

She wasn't conscious.

Was she concussed? In shock? Exhausted?

Rork dreamed it wasn't possible to know. He thought — briefly — about kissing her. But knew if he ever did kiss her, he wanted her to know what was happening. He lay down beside her. Deep, deep in the recesses of his brain some deceased person soothed him. With singing. And a harpsichord.

He dreamed the lingering reverberation of notes was the barest touch of their bodies, beckoning a closeness, inching them nearer to each other. His dream logic urged him to keep her warm. He snaked an arm beneath her neck and head, aligned himself along the length of her. Her body responded imperceptibly. He felt the soft chug of her breath against his brow. It made him glad, happy. He could let the dreamsleep take him. Maybe he had found her. Maybe he only dreamed he did.

18: Out of Sync

RORK STIRRED. He was conscious of being observed, eyes trained on him, taking in the fact of him, their close proximity, starburst centers subdued.

Here he was awake. Here he was battered and bruised. He looked at Deirdre who had a flickering light of recognition in her eyes.

He remembered everything.

"Hi," he said.

"Hi," she replied.

He let his head fall back, staring at the gray, featureless sky, and tracked the clues, bit by bit assembling the reality of the moment — if such a thing truly existed in Shufftie. He was damp, but only where his body came into contact with Deirdre. He was a very weak swimmer. Graceless. Could he have jumped in after her? Would he have? Desperation didn't always bring out his best thinking. Still, he was learning. Still, they both could have drowned.

Feeling was returning to his feet. His drenched, sodden feet. He remembered wading out into the river, slipping on slick roots, their treacherous feel defying the grooves of his hiking boots. He couldn't get to Deirdre fast enough. The fallen tree held her face above water. Thank goodness. But he'd had to really work to disentangle her. The tree wouldn't let her go. It had cast off a sheaf of bark in the process. Her hair had cascaded across his shoulder and forearm. He remembered how scared he had been carrying her. The weight of her.

Rork turned back to Deirdre. She laid perfectly tranquil, hands splayed across her ribs, blinking at the gray dome of sky. Tears seeped out of her eyes, moving in slow motion, hanging on the curve of her cheek, finally disappearing into her hair.

"Deirdre, Deirdre," Rork said, putting his face next to hers. "What's wrong?"

Her eyes followed his voice, wet eyelashes glittering green with tears.

"Do you remember anything?" asked Rork.

"I feel so…so empty. I remember I am Deirdre. I remember shadows. I'm cold." Deirdre turned on her side, arms and legs drawn close. Her hair streamed in wet clumps around her face.

"I have no idea where our packs are," said Rork. "I think we lost them a couple levels ago. What do we do? Go forward? Go back?" Absently, he rubbed Deirdre's shoulder, trying to keep her warm. He removed his flannel shirt and draped it over her. It was damp and badly snagged with pickers from his run-in with the thornbush but would offer some warmth. She pulled it around herself.

She watched him curiously. "Thank you," she said. "I know you?" It was half a question.

Rork ducked his head, smiling crookedly. "Yes, you've been saving me from myself in this wilderness for days. At least I think it's been days. It's hard to keep track."

"Who needs saving now?" she asked, the taste of bitter fruit in the tone of her voice.

Rork noticed the synchrony of her words was off, sound slightly delayed from the movement of her lips, but he didn't say anything. Hopefully it was a temporary symptom of what she had just gone through. "You don't need saving," he said. "You need help remembering."

Deirdre gave him a smile, and his heart wrenched. She was still inside the girl lying on the ground, washed up on the shore of the River of Forgetting.

"Where was Boo?" he wondered aloud.

"Who?" asked Deirdre.

Rork stared at her mouth, the eerie lip-synching.

"Are you hurt?" he asked, changing the topic, standing, reaching for her. The question was not the brightest one he had ever asked. She'd almost drowned in a raging river after all.

Deirdre looked at him, thinking. Her mouth muscles worked first. "No, I don't think so." She pulled on his hand and started to get up. Slowly. She held her head as if it was imperfectly attached. Finally, she was upright and at eye level with him, troubled gray eyes expectant on his.

"I think we should find shelter," said Rork. "Rest until you feel stronger."

Cryptic-smile.

Rork watched Deirdre warily. Physically she didn't seem impaired, even though that was some kind of miracle.

In front of them was a series of lochs leading away from the river. Were they north? South? East? Rork wasn't sure of anything at this point. The path cutting through the lochs was wide and open, making it possible for them to walk side by side. It was odd to be hiking without packs. Rork let his arms dangle. Deirdre hugged herself. Around them was the silvery shimmer of lochs connected in a chain, rippling gun metal.

Rork worried about what kind of ghost haunted this level, but he was more preoccupied with Deirdre's mental state. Where had her mind gone? Could he help her remember? She was acting like she couldn't remember anything, not Shufftie, not him, not Boo. He kicked a stone. It skipped across the surface of a small tarn, creating ripples that lapped the shoreline, causing the many plants in the water to bob. Deirdre was arrested by one plant in particular. Leaflets clustered on a spike that drooped over the water. They almost looked like hands in prayer. Dotted amongst the leaflets, rising on their own stalks, were constellations of starry flowers, wildly inflorescent.

Deirdre stepped closer. Water seeped around her boots. The flower cluster was hairy with filaments, antlers cockeyed, with a pearlized brightness. "Bogbean," she whispered.

Rork bit his tongue, unwilling to break the spell of the moment.

She smiled at him, walking next to him, her hands floating out into the air. "I haven't forgotten everything," she said proudly.

Rork's brain revved. Some of what she knew was there. If only he could help her reconnect, build on what remained.

They found a water cave, a rock cavity where the cascade of water changed directions, flowing from loch to loch. It was a decent size. Rork paced off four strides. The transfer of water from the higher loch to the lower was soothing, a sheath of sound surrounding them. Light got into the cave from a natural skylight, casting a gradient of gray, depending on where they stood or sat in the cave. Pewter. Smoke. Wrought iron.

Deirdre stood in a dark corner, a sheen on her skin from the exertion after her ordeal in the river. "Do you think we can manage anything to eat?" she asked, her voice husky in the gloam. She visibly shivered.

"I have a little trail mix left," offered Rork. He dug out the plastic pouch from his trouser pocket, mawled and mangled from the river and the battering. He gave it to Deidre, who took some and began to chew it slowly. He patted down the large pockets of his trousers for other supplies and laid out on the ground a small torch, a foil-sealed pack of hardtack, a water bottle with a carabiner clip, and a tube of peanut butter.

"What do you have in your pockets?" asked Rork.

Deirdre stopped chewing and stared at him nervously.

"Sorry," said Rork. "That didn't come out right." He ran a hand through his coarsely matted hair. "I was just wondering what we might have for supplies between us. I was hoping you might have stashed a few things in the pockets of your hiking trousers." He pointed at the small pile he'd made with his rummaging.

Deirdre patted the pockets of her trousers, as curious, it seemed, as Rork to discover what she might find. She pulled out a pocketknife, her compass, a top-coil notebook, damp with curled edges, a stub of a pencil, and a screw-top cannister with two dry matches.

They assessed the stash between them. It was better than nothing, but it wouldn't keep them going for long.

"I need to sit down," sighed Deirdre, holding her forehead. She reached for the ground.

Rork crouched, rearranging his shirt around her shoulders, and handed her the trail mix. She shook it, assessing the remaining contents.

"Are there any plants we can eat?" asked Rork.

"Aye," said Deirdre. "Dandelion, nettles, cattails —. I might think of more."

Rork cheered silently, once again, thanking the moon, stars, and banshee impatience for the brilliance of picking Deirdre as a minder. Her knowledge and memories were not all lost, just scrambled. He typed a quick riff of "yes, yes, yes" on his pant leg with his fingers.

"Should I go forage? Or should I stay?" asked Rork. He rattled the cannister with the two stick matches.

Deirdre looked up wistfully. "Could we start a small fire?" she asked. "I know it's an extravagance, but I can't seem to stop shivering." The word 'shivering' was wrecked by her asynchronous lip movements.

Two matches, thought Rork, missing the cook stove. "Could we cook something, too?" he asked. His belly also had ideas. Cattails would go down easier as a side dish.

"Like what?" asked Deirdre.

"Squirrel?" asked Rork without a single strategy about how to catch one.

Deidre made a face of horror.

"Fish?" His father had ruined him for the pastime, but local fish were one of his favorites, and they *were* surrounded by lochs.

"How will you catch it?" asked Deirdre.

"Think I could use my T-shirt as a net?"

"Take the torch," said Deidre, nodding to their stockpile. "If you shine on the water's surface, they'll swim up to the light." She huddled in his flannel shirt. "I'll be all right," she added, "if only I can get warm."

Outside the cave, trees grew alpine, deciduous and sappy. The wood would be harder to light but hopefully would burn without too much tending. Rork wished he had an axe. He scavenged for fallen and almost-fallen timbers. It wasn't long before he had an armful.

He returned to Deirdre and let the wood fall to the ground. She had dug a shallow hole for him to start the fire. He pulled out a handful of tinder from his back pocket and started to arrange the fire in teepee fashion.

Deirdre kneeled beside him. "The fire will be more stable if you do it like this." She leaned forward to rearrange the wood back and forth in the shape of a log cabin.

Rork reveled in her knowing things. "I could kiss you," he said without thinking. He lurched forward to light the fire, knocking down one side of the log construction.

Deirdre righted the wood. "Could you?" she asked, studiously looking at the would-be fire.

Rork paused mid-strike and looked at her profile, half in shadow. Was she asking seriously? Daring him? The wide and wet yellow headband was a sharp contrast to her riotous hair. The old hanging-back Deirdre would not have asked such a question. He smiled somewhere between his lips and brain and struck their second-to-last match.

Maybe forgetting wasn't *all* bad.

Rork left the cave and clambered to the higher loch and circumnavigated its shoreline, thick with cattails, flipping the torchlight on and off. Biology was not his strong suit. He'd struggled with it at school because it wasn't intuitive to him like computer science was. He wondered why motherboards and circuitry were much more natural to him. Yet gene code and computer code weren't that different. Rork thought ruefully he could have had some insightful breakthrough with Deirdre if only his belly hadn't decided to stage a coup, demanding attention and f-o-o-d. He squared his shoulders, resolving not to go back to the cave empty-handed.

Rork found a promontory that didn't sink under his weight and sidestepped out over the water. His thumb worried the sliding switch of the torch. He peered over the edge. The water was dark, mysterious, and it looked deep enough. For what kind of fish, he wasn't sure. Perch? Pike? His father's mates were anglers for trout and salmon, and he knew enough to know they ran in the rivers and not the lochs. Other breeds swam the stiller waters.

He turned the torchlight on and off. Assuming Deidre was right, and fish would be attracted to the light, he considered how to make his shirt more net-like. Rork set the torch down gently on the flat plain of pocked stone and slipped out of his T-shirt, knotting the arms. All alone in the middle of Shufftie, he still felt self-conscious bare-chested. The word *naked* made him nervous. Certainly, a part of him desired it, a deep, subterranean part of him, the part that also imagined spontaneous stripping and rounded breasts like magical spheres and endless bronzed legs squeezing the very breath out of him. But the brainiac, thinking part of him couldn't even think through how to get naked, the logistical steps, the small increments of clothing removal.

"Foo," he said out loud, his upper teeth creating a ridge on his lower lip.

The plane of rock tipped slightly, dislodging the torch. which began to roll towards the water. "Stop!" shouted Rork, placing his big foot between the torch and the rock's edge, almost tipping himself into the loch. He managed to maintain his balance — just barely. He bent over, breathing heavily, trying to steady himself, his two straight arms clamped to his knees. Just when he was beginning to build some confidence in himself and his survival abilities, life, not life (whatever this was), taught him a lesson or two. His clumsiness was something he would need to come to grips with, probably chronic, his mind always two or three steps ahead.

Well, he'd have to learn to live with that.

Rork got back into position, clicked on the torch, and waited. At first the water looked amorphous and black, with no fish visible. But gradually his eyes adjusted, and he was able to discern movement in the murky depths. He could see/sense the back and forth wavering of fish swimming, shadows in the water, venturing ever closer to the torch's light. He held his breath, looking for patterns.

He moved the torch to his left hand and lowered the T-shirt into the water, tugging it to make it balloon. The fish retreated from the shadow he'd made. He was careful not to move. The knit fabric of the T-shirt hung suspended in the water. The fish resumed their forward and back sashay with the light. One daring fish broke the water's surface with its fin. Rork swooped the T-shirt. The weight of the water slowed him down, the fish half in, half out of the T-shirt net. The outcome weighed in the balance for tense seconds. Rork hadn't reacted fast enough, and the fish wriggled away, splashing frantically across the loch.

"Damn."

Rork tried again.

And again.

He kneeled down on the jagged peninsula, simultaneously chilled and sweaty from effort. He tucked the torch under his chin and maneuvered the knotted T-shirt with fingers of both hands. Finally, he was able to close his makeshift net around a fish. A good size, too. He pulled it out of the water, and it flopped desperately inside the shirt. He tucked it under his arm. It was cold and slimy, but he didn't care. He felt charged, empowered. He grinned from ear to ear. Me, angler. You, dinner. He remembered the dazzled look on his gran's face when he'd made her proud.

Well done, the Fergus.

After gutting the fish with the pocketknife, Rork returned to Deirdre. He stepped through the cave's mouth and held up his wet T-shirt/fish combination triumphantly. His bare chest gleamed in the fireglow of a neat fire in the floor's hollow.

"You caught a fish!" said Deirdre, sitting cross-legged near the fire. Her hand quickly covered a ripped sheet of paper from the notebook. She tucked the pencil behind her ear. "I'm glad." The rest of the notebook was by the fire, pages fanned out.

"I have cattails, too," said Rork, showing her the green spikes.

"Good. I'm perished," she said., taking one and eating it like a carrot.

"What were you doing?" asked Rork.

Deirdre hesitated. She looked down at her flat hand. "Drawing."

Rork could see fine lines, crosshatching, and shading through the open spaces of her fingers. It looked like a botanical drawing, intricate, detailed.

"I didn't know you could draw."

Rork noticed her eyes flick across his chest. She noticed he noticed. Some kind of atmospheric pressure started to build between them. It spilled over into the cave. Flushed, Deirdre looked away.

"Any idea how we're going to cook this thing?" asked Rork.

"Here, have your shirt back." She threw his plaid, button-down at him.

Rork caught it in his fish-free hand. He set the fish down next to the fire and put on the shirt but didn't button it.

Deirdre busied herself around the fire. A quick flick of her eyes. Rork tried not to smile. She placed a flat rock in the center of the flames, creating a makeshift griddle for the fish.

"Is there any water left?" he asked, leaning towards her for the water bottle, sucking in his stomach, glad he didn't have the pelt of hair on his chest like his father, just a neat arrow of darker hair between his naval and pectoral muscles.

"Save me some," said Deirdre.

Rork handed her the bottle, and Deirdre poured a quick dollop of water on the smooth part of the rock. It sizzled. She unwrapped the fish from the T-shirt. Deirdre ran her fingers up and down the ribbed cavity. "Good work," she said.

"Thanks." Rork sat down next to her by the fire.

Deirdre placed the fish cavity-side down, spreading the two fileted sides. "It shouldn't take long," she said.

"Brilliant," said Rork. He saw she thought he wasn't looking. Flick. Longer this time, lingering. What a way to pass the time, he thought, fun and maddening. What was she thinking? he wondered.

The fish crackled and spit, collapsing onto one side. Rork could see the skin pulling back from flesh as it lost its raw translucency. The smell of it was delicious. His mouth watered.

They used a sleeve of bark and skimmed off the cooked fish, seesawing back and forth. Deirdre quickly stacked hunks of fish meat sideways on the bark, blowing on her fingers. They set it down carefully. It steamed between them.

"That looks good," said Rork.

"Yes," said Deirdre. Ghost of a smile. Flick. She hugged both shins, perching her chin on one kneecap.

"I can't wait anymore," said Rork. He shoveled fish onto three fingers and dropped it into his mouth. "Mmmmmm."

Deirdre let her legs sweep to the ground. Dropping her knees to one side, she pinched off some fish to eat. "Mmmmmm," she said.

Rork ate more fish. "This would be really good with lemon," he said.

"And pepper," said Deirdre, licking fish off her fingers.

"And chips."

They both laughed but continued eating, pulling small bones out of their mouths, until the fish was gone. Rork ate a corner of crisped fish skin but decided it was too inky tasting, even as hungry as he was.

"Have a cattail," suggested Deidre.

Rork took a tentative bite. It tasted a little like celery. "Can I see what you drew?" he asked.

Flick. Flick. Rork watched her gaze scatter, not knowing where to look. She looked from the ground to the corner of paper tucked beneath her thigh. Finally, reluctantly, she held out the sheet of paper, dimpled by water stain and pencil, for him to see.

Rork peered closer. "Is that the bogbean?" he asked.

She nodded.

"It's like I can touch it. It looks so real." He tugged on the paper, wanting a better look.

Deirdre held firm. Her face got that stubborn look he recognized.

"Come on," he teased. "Let me get a better look."

Deirdre let go of the paper and wrapped her arms around herself, hands tucked away. "It's the plants," she said. "They are so present to me."

They sat next to each other by the fire, long legs pretzeled like wings, a knees' breath away.

Rork held the sheet of paper up to the light of the fire. "Deirdre," he said. "This is amazing. Really good."

She shrugged with the barest of smiles.

Rork placed the paper back in her lap. His hand brushed her leg for a millisecond.

The distinctive pressure between them increased.

They ignored it, watching the fire smolder and shift.

Rork typed distractedly on his thigh, humming. A line of poetry scritched across his mind:

I sing the body electric.

Maybe, he thought, with true attraction there wasn't any orchestration. Maybe there was only current. Positive. Negative. The pull between two forces.

In the cave's gloom Rork didn't notice so much the asynchronization between Deirdre's lips and words, but he was hyper aware of her.

Rork's fingers moved, telegraphing the building pressure, emotions that roiled over him. What to do? What to do?

Suddenly, Deirdre leaned over to him and put her cool hand in his, stilling its frantic keystroking.

He wondered for a minute if she wanted to sketch him. Some diversion in this cave of nothing-to-do.

But no.

She took his hands and placed them on either side of her face.

"Your hands are warm," she said.

He threaded his fingers through hers.

And then he kissed her. Without thinking about it at all.

She smelled like sunshine and brine and mulch.

He was awkwardly perched on one buttock, but he used all his strength to maintain his closeness to her.

It was a long kiss.

His lips lightly grazed hers.

She closed her eyes. Her forehead was smooth.

He closed his eyes, too.

He felt the heat of her in the tingle of his lips, down the bone of his nose, the indentation of his chin. He could feel his heartbeat in the ends of his fingers.

He pressed a little more, moved his lips shyly, exploring. A longer hello-what-is-this kiss. He liked it. He could almost sense her mind responding to his, space narrowing between his thoughts and hers. He had always assumed intimacy was a euphemism for sex, but he now thought this — closeness, openness — was perhaps a better definition.

The fire crackled and spit. Flames cast a two-headed shadow high up on the uneven surface of the cave. They hardly noticed, every touch, smell, and small movement amplified between them.

Rork got a cramp in his right side. It was awkward sitting on the ground. The walls of the cave were dank and chill. He swung his legs around and lowered himself to the ground, his arms maintaining his embrace of Deirdre, bringing her with him, somehow entangled and wondering, eyes reflecting the many flickers of flame. They lay side by side on the ground, facing each other. Deirdre had her back to the fire, her face in beautiful eclipse.

"Will you help me remember?" she asked.

"Aye," said Rork. He leaned forward on one elbow and kissed her again.

She smiled sleepily, murmuring. "It's nicer than I thought. Lips touching."

Her eyes closed, and Rork watched her face relax — forehead, cheeks, jaw. Her breath got slower, more resonant.

The rhythm of her breath lulled Rork. Exhausted, his muscles replayed every tense moment of the day. Two days? How many had it been since the River of Forgetting? He wasn't sure. Time blurred in Shufftie, a blending of awake and not.

His eyes returned to Deirdre, the subtle shift of shadow on her face. She stirred, her hands clenched in front of her as if she were still chilled, head oddly angled. Rork pulled her closer, sliding one arm beneath the column of her neck until she rested comfortably (he hoped) on one shoulder, his two arms enveloping her, holding in the heat between them.

She was right, he thought. Kissing was nice. More than nice. He even liked the word. Kiss. K-i-s-s. Hard 'k,' short 'i' and sibilant 's's.'" He began typing the word on the smooth plane of her upper back. Kiss. Kiss. Kiss.

After a while, adjectives began to occur to him. Soft kisses, hard kisses, fun kisses, serious kisses, quick kisses, slow kisses. He typed those, too.

Then his mind began to embellish further. This was how it worked. He would start with a seemingly simple thing, idea, or random thought. And his brain would add to it, layer upon layer, node upon node, like a budding tree, like circuitry, interconnecting, adding more and more and more, an endless web.

Kissing in the fire-lit shadows. Kissing in sunshine. Kissing in rain. Kissing on rooftops. Kissing in the garden. Kissing in the living room. Kissing in the kitchen. The back hall. He typed all the possibilities.

Rork, thinking all this hopefully, opened his eyes to look at Deirdre again. She was such a presence in his arms. She filled them — lush, plush — capturing the essence of soft and solid. Watching her, he was surprised to see the wild movement of her eyes behind her thin-skinned lids, the movement fast, frenzied, beyond anything Rork had ever seen before. Charged. He wondered what she was dreaming about.

"Keep typing," he heard in his head, a woman's voice, coming forward in the cavern of his head, very clear.

"What?" Rork said aloud. He didn't know if he'd ever become blasé about hearing the voices. No matter what Boo said. He looked at his hands, firelight streaming between his fingers.

"Keep typing," the voice repeated. "Something's happening." The woman's voice was musical, lilting, despite being dead. Rork had a flash of long blonde hair, flowing scarves.

"What should I type?" he asked.

"Images, memories," said the voice. The dead woman began to recite in her singsong voice. Rork typed as fast as he could, transcribing what she was saying:

"Her mother Maggie liked to hillwalk the ancient pine forests of the Highlands, the smell of sun, pine, and cedar making a fragrant tea of the air, crunch of needles underfoot. Maggie felt alone, not alone — the scurry of small animals all around, chirping of birds overhead. She felt her skin wake up, each pore opening like a flower petal, the ever-present Wood Sorrel. She liked knowing the names of things.

'Hello, Wood Sorrel.'

'Hello, Yellow Pimpernel.'

"She would watch the sky turn from a crystalline azure to an angry, roiling gray. She felt the prickle of rain on her face and made a dash for shelter at the summit of the trail, a half-sided structure with a slatted wood roof. She huddled inside, slightly cold but exhilarated, surveying the flash storm's escalation along the horizon, from one side of the lookout to the other, like a sliding panel. Behind the storm, the sun returned to the sky, dotted with clouds, puffy, as whorled by a whiskbroom. Yet the storm left its pigments behind. Sun and storm intermingled, creating orange-blue-purple, a fireball agate sky. Beautiful, unanticipated.

"It's what she thinks of whenever there's bad weather…"

There was a long pause, the woman lost in her reverie. Was she Deirdre's mother? Someone who knew Deirdre or her mother? At the very least, she was someone important to Deirdre's history.

"Keep going," the woman said gruffly. "I'll find more."

Then there was silence. Signal out of range.

Rork cast about in his memories. Those he remembered with the most fondness were bound up with his grandmother: working with her in the kitchen, the garden, their long walks harvesting whatever was in season. He typed, trying to recapture these moments. He wasn't a bad storyteller, although he wouldn't vouch for his spelling.

"We're back," said the woman. She was out of breath, buffeted by a procession of departed noisy souls, who crowded from behind.

"Can I be first?"

"No, me."

"Me."

"Hey!"

Deirdre slept on, eyeballs in motion behind their waxy lids.

Rork worked all night, typing whispered stories and memories onto Deirdre. He had this idea that the site on which he typed could somehow help her partition the memories in a way that might feel organized to her later, in recollection, so he varied where he typed on her body — her knees, her back, her abdomen. Each memory seemed to belong to a different part of her anatomy, and he cached them accordingly.

A queue of dead relatives waited patiently for Rork's channeling fingers. Nobody wanted to be forgotten. Each wanted to contribute and give Deirdre a piece, a fragment, something she could remember, hang onto.

As Rork typed into the night, he felt something in the ends of his fingers. A tingling? There was sensation to it, yes, but there was also a light, a fledgling shining forth that pulsed around his hands, as if his fingers knew a truth his brain could not comprehend. The dead jostled in the recesses of his mind, eager to come forward — the soft pads of his fingers, a rhythm primordial. Was it really that simple?

M-e-m-o-r-i-e-s w-e-r-e l-o-v-e.

The dead and their memories came to him with an order, it seemed, as efficient a system as take-a-number. Or maybe the mind was more pliable than he thought. Or maybe he was just tired and lacked any critical ability. The dead volunteered their memories, and Rork memory-typed until his hands began to cramp.

Hours later, he ached in every joint of his body, especially his wrists and knuckles. A sharp pain throbbed in the knob at the back of his neck. Deirdre moved restlessly in her sleep. He took a break from the voices in his head and lay next to her, his fingers fluttering reflexively.

D-e-i-r-d-r-e.

It was night. It was not night. It was in between.

19: Memory-Typing

"RORK! DEIRDRE!"

"Rork! Deirdre!"

Rork heard someone calling him in his sleep. It was a voice he knew he should recognize but couldn't place. He was so tired. He didn't want to wake yet. He was getting quite good at ignoring voices he didn't want to deal with.

"Rork! Deirdre!"

The pitch was intensifying. Rork rolled away from Deirdre and covered his ears with his arms.

"Rork! Deirdre!"

The voice grew louder, more piercing; it shot straight to his brain stem. Rork stumbled toward the cave's opening, his eyes bleary. He steadied himself against the cave wall. He found it difficult to move. His muscles and tendons — the very sinews of his body — were sore. As if he'd been digging in the garden (a task he'd hated), sent out in the dripping spring with a heavy spade by his gran. Digging was alien to his everyday range of motion, and it caused a kinetic kind of pain. He could feel the blazing of new synapses. The memory-typing he'd been doing on Deirdre had taken a similar toll on his body.

Deirdre woke, her eyes calm, steady, considering him across the cave. She swept her loose hair behind an ear while she lay on her side, her other arm pillowing her head. The gaze connecting them was a live, vibrant thing.

He couldn't see Boo, although he could certainly hear her.

"I'll go tell her where we are," he said to Deirdre, ducking out of the cave.

The landscape was still, the ever-present gray light shimmering on the loch. Rork surveyed the scene, trying to locate the banshee, knowing she liked an entrance.

"Rork! Deirdre!"

Earsplitting, the voice exploded in his brain cavity. Rork's legs buckled, and he sunk to his knees on the sandy shore of the loch, holding his head.

"I'm here! I'm here!" He held up one hand helplessly. The voice needed to stop.

"Thank betweenness!" said Boo breathlessly.

Her slippers glided into Rork's view, and he smelled her sweet butterscotch smell. "Please…don't…yell for me…anymore," he said, panting in the wake of her shrillness.

"I found you, silly," said Boo. "I don't need to call you anymore."

"Just. Don't." Rork dragged himself to standing and glowered down at her.

"Don't scowl at me," she said. "A banshee needs range." She pushed out her lower lip mulishly. "Hopefully, I'll get to be one." She hovered above the uneven shoreline, her gown billowing out like a bell. "What happened?" she asked.

Rork felt like he had crushed iced in his head. Her flitting about aggravated him. He wished she'd settle on the ground where he could get a fix on her.

"What do you mean?" he asked, standing up and brushing the sharp pebbles from his knees.

"Something had to have happened. Shufftie went down and had to be reset. We don't know how much disruption took place. We couldn't find your coordinates for the longest time." The sweet-sugar smell of the banshee intensified. "It seemed an eternity!" she said dramatically.

Rork flashed back on Deirdre's wild-eyed tear through the forest, the jumper goading her with his bald-faced taunts. The banshee's melodrama seemed appropriate. "Deirdre fell into the River of Forgetting," he finally said.

"N-o-o-o," mouthed Boo.

"Aye."

"Is she —? Is she okay?"

Rork tried to parse out the meaning of the question. Was Deirdre okay? It struck him as totally inadequate. But then the last time they'd seen Boo — he couldn't remember. Level Three? Four? A schism loomed inside his brain: before he kissed Deirdre and after. And there was no going back. They were facing new emotional terrain — new territory inside new territory inside new territory. What were those Russian nesting dolls called? Matroshka? He wondered vaguely, massaging his temples. They had been the inspiration for an early design paradigm that organized web content streams. At the moment, he felt very much outside the design paradigm, making things up as he went.

"Is she okay?" asked Boo again, her face very close to his, hovering, exuding a maddening scent of burnt sugar.

Rork recognized her tone of exasperation. She wasn't the most patient of banshees.

"Aye," he said. "Sort of."

"What do you mean, 'sort of'?" Boo stepped back, eyeing him head to toe.

Rork recalled his shirt was unbuttoned. The chill air and scrutiny made his bare skin pucker with goosepimples. Self-consciously, he buttoned. "She wasn't hurt, no sprained ankles or gashes from the rocks, which was amazing really, considering she leapt into the river."

"She *leapt* into the River of Forgetting?" asked Boo. She looked distraught. "But why?"

"A damn jumper took her over. He got into her head and wouldn't get out."

The banshee shook her head. "Poor Deirdre. I've heard that lower level ghosts can be a real nuisance."

"Aye, she is feeling a little done-in and complains of a headache. But there's hope, I think."

"Can you take me to her?"

"Aye," said Rork, glancing at her sideways. "But first I have to tell you something."

"What?" asked Boo, warily. She alighted on the ground in her slight slippers.

Rork felt nervous. Excited. "I learned something about being an intermediary. Not only can I hear the dead's chatter, it seems I can also channel their memories." He held up his hands and rippled his fingers in the air like a surgeon. "I've been typing all night!"

"Typing?" Boo echoed faintly. She wore a puzzled expression. Air whistled in and out through the gap in her teeth.

"Aye," said Rork, "typing." He bobbed his head, the knob of bone creaking between his shoulders. He moved his head around in a circle, stretching his neck. "Imprinting letters… keystroking…creating words…."

"I know what typing is," interrupted the banshee.

"But this is a new kind of typing," exclaimed Rork. "Memory-typing."

"Memory-typing?" Boo licked her lips. "I've never heard of such a thing."

"I know," said Rork. "I think I might have discovered it. Amazing, right?"

"Yes, amazing," said the banshee, tilting her head to the side, as if to get a new angle on the situation. "I need to see Deirdre."

Rork had hoped for a better reaction from Boo. She seemed almost put out, but he took her back to the cave, stepping out of the way to let her enter first. They found Deirdre awake, sitting cross-legged on the hard cave floor. Her eyes were closed. She hummed softly.

"Deirdre," whispered Rork

Boo hung back, observing.

Deirdre's eyes opened, their dark centers dilating on Rork's towering height. "Hi," she smiled.

"Hi," he smiled back. "Are you meditating?"

"Did I not do that…before?" asked Deirdre.

"You chanted us into Shufftie," said Rork. "If it helps, I think you should keep doing it."

Deirdre's eyes slid closed again as she returned to meditating. "I find when I'm quiet the memories don't jostle around so much, and I can remember some. They feel like dreams. I never noticed that before."

The banshee whispered to Rork behind her hand, "Why are her words and mouth not lining up?"

Rork aimed his ear closer. "What did you say?"

"What's wrong with the way she talks?" asked Boo in a slightly louder whisper.

"I don't know," Rork whispered back. "She's been like this since the River of Forgetting. Any idea how to get her back in sync?"

Boo scrolled her forehead, thinking. "Not at the moment." She paced the cave, her slippers slapping the packed earth, her silhouette giving off a grayish glow in the gloomy cave.

"What do we do now?" asked Rork. He leaned against the cave's wall. The chill of the rock felt good on his bony spine. His stomach growled. He thought about the hardtack and peanut butter.

Boo's head snapped at him. "Where are your supplies? Your packs?"

Rork looked at his feet, not answering. The banshee had sharp points in her eyes that gave him pause. He noticed it when she was tired or annoyed or both. They must have really given her a fright.

"Well?" she asked again.

"I don't know," said Rork. "We had them before the jumper. But afterwards, all I could think about was Deirdre…fishing her out of the river…getting her to safety. It happened so fast I hardly remember. I thought I'd lost her."

Boo set her jaw. "I could scream," she said.

"Please don't," said Rork, his ears still ringing.

The banshee made a fidgety face. "Shufftie was only supposed to be a mock shuttle. I did not expect so many…obstacles, dead-ends."

"You said dead-ends," said Rork.

Fidgety, *un*smiling face.

"Well, on the good news front, we're already at Level Six," said Rork.

"But you have no supplies, and I don't know how useful your minder will be. Can she even lead you out of here?" Boo wrung her small hands.

"Don't give up on us yet," said Rork. He pushed off the wall and began to pace opposite the banshee. "Is there any way you can get us more supplies?" he asked.

"No," said Boo. "Banshees do not shuttle supplies. Especially banshees-*in-training*."

"And it probably doesn't make sense to go back..."

Extreme fidgety face.

Rork held up his hands. "Okay, okay. I was just trying to assess all the options." He paced across the cave in three strides, his fingers flexing. Distractedly, he typed on his lower abdomen, through his damp, wrinkled T-shirt. W-h-a-t t-o d-o. Deirdre was tougher than she looked, he knew, but he thought their current situation — especially in her rather overwhelmed state — was a bit of a challenge. Also, he would need more than cattails to thrive. What did that leave?

Seeking some of his gran's insight, Rork felt for the flash drive in his pocket and touched its familiar, rectangular shape. But when he reflexively felt for the sixpence in his other pocket, all he found was empty fabric. His heart thudded with dread. How had he not noticed? His father's sixpence was missing! He'd been too worried about Deirdre and surviving. How could he get it back? He *needed* to bring it home. Just like his father had. It was an imperative. Now he, too, had lost something meaningful in the River of Forgetting or its rocky shoals. D-e-f-e-n-d-e-r o-f t-h-e-f-a-i-t-h, he typed.

The banshee tapped her slipper impatiently, but Rork refused to believe the sixpence was gone forever. He'd figure out a way to recover it. Just like he'd figured out a way to recover Deirdre's memories. Somehow.

"If we can't go back," he said, "and we can't get more, then we'll just have to ask Beck to lend us some gear."

Boo looked at him like he was insane and groaned in frustration.

"Or," said Deirdre from the other side of the cave. "We could borrow some gear *without* asking."

Rork echoed, "Borrow some gear without asking?" He didn't exactly comprehend. What was she suggesting?

"Yes!" crowed the banshee. "That's a brilliant idea. Borrow from Beck without his knowing!"

Rork looked at Deirdre searchingly.

"We sneak into their camp," she explained, "and scrounge some gear. Just what we need, of course."

"Sneak into their camp? Borrow their gear?" Rork knew he sounded like an imbecile, but where had this new boldness in Deirdre come from? He didn't know what surprised him most. The idea of sneaking into their camp? Or that Deirdre had come up with it?

"Take what you need from Beck and that friend of yours," reasserted Boo.

"He's not my friend anymore," said Rork.

"Friend, not friend, what do you say about the idea?" asked the banshee.

"I'm in." Rork feigned an assurance he couldn't quite summon. He was distracted by the missing sixpence. He wanted to hug Deirdre and her new boldness, but he held back because of Boo, not wanting to risk any more of her irritation. He just smiled stupidly at Deirdre (as if that wasn't a dead giveaway). He hoped Deirdre would inspire him with her new-found boldness.

"Maybe *I* should meditate?" He turned to the banshee. "Maybe it will help me locate them?"

A slow smile crept across the Boo's face, revealing her gap-teeth. "No need," she said. She really didn't like Beck. It was apparent all over her face. "I know exactly where they are."

Rork raised an eyebrow.

"When I couldn't find you, I called BT — Banshee Technology. They were struggling to reset Shufftie, but they let me watch. When Shufftie came back online, I was able to locate you with the heat map interface. Well, your general location."

"Heat map interface?"

"Yes, it's the latest in banshee technology."

"You also saw the others?" asked Deirdre. She'd given up meditating but continued to sit cross-legged on the other side of the cave.

"Yes," said Boo. "They're a level behind you. Their progress has been more erratic. It seems Beck can't always get his team to cooperate." She couldn't resist a smug expression. "Last I saw they were halfway through the Meadows."

"Should we leave now?" asked Rork.

"We can make up for lost time and slow them down at the same time," said Boo, getting excited.

"No time like the present," said Deirdre. "Charboy and Hamish have to rest. We'll just wait for them to fall asleep and sneak in then."

Rork had a moment of misgiving. His father used to say Rork made the noise of an elephant in the woods, but Deirdre looked so confident, asynchronism and all, that he pushed aside any uncertainty. "If you think it'll work," said Rork. "I'm game."

The banshee's comb buzzed in vibration. "I have to go," she sighed in exasperation. "Dispatch gave me extra bandwidth because of the disturbance. But just for today. Please be careful," she entreated as she began to fade. "We can't afford any more delays."

Rork had his own worries. He was thankful he hadn't lost his gran's flash drive, but he knew he couldn't go home without his father's sixpence.

20: Replenishing

RORK AND DEIRDRE returned to the path, walking single file, Deirdre setting the pace. The landscape of the lochs was open and strangely serene, dotted with loch-side trees and shrubbery. He would never get used to the perpetually overcast sky of Shufftie. It was downright unnerving how the two of them stood out in full-color, their outlines sharp against the gray background, Deirdre especially, punctuated with color—headband, eyelashes, nails, scarf. After the dankness of the cave, the contrast was a lot for his eyes to take in.

The plan was simple but not simple, and as usual Rork was ravenously hungry. Why did his hunger dominate his thoughts so much? Especially in Shufftie? He gave Deirdre side glances, but she seemed unperturbed. Calm even. He wondered how she was faring with her new memories but was afraid to ask. Now that there was "something" between them, conversation seemed riskier, more constrained. Rork wondered at the contradiction. He worried about the flash drive in his pocket and wished desperately he had the sixpence. And, complicating matters, he wasn't convinced they could take the supplies they needed without a confrontation with the other team. Rork picked up his pace. He did not like confrontation.

"Don't worry," said Deirdre, a furrow across her brow. "We'll figure it out."

"How?" Rork asked. Another side glance. Wait a minute. He thought he saw something new and different about Deirdre. A marking of some kind. He caught a glimpse of it as she swung her arms, straining her camp shirt. But then it was gone, vanishing up her sleeve.

"They are a volatile team," said Deirdre. "You will find their weakness, vulnerability. They will give us an opportunity."

Rork's stomach growled in response.

"Would you like me to forage for something?"

"No, thanks," said Rork. "But I sure wish I had some of your trail mix."

She looked at him quizzically.

"Trail mix?" he prompted. "Your very own recipe?"

"I have a recipe for trail mix?" she wondered. "In my mind I can see hands stirring ingredients together, a smudged notecard, but the memory doesn't seem to belong to me."

They slowed, Rork not wanting to stir up anything more. The fact that she was who she was, but was still disjointed somehow, disconcerted him. Perhaps the memory-typing had jostled her memories?

"Do you suppose," asked Deirdre, "that remembering might be as simple as claiming what is meaningful to you?" She was obviously thinking about her experience.

Rork would like to claim the sixpence. He cleared his throat, thinking he should tell her about the memory-typing. It was one thing confiding in the banshee, but he wasn't sure how Deirdre would react. Would she be grateful? Or resentful? He did not want to slow her recovery. "I don't think memory is the finite thing we think it is," he said. "I remember stories my gran told me as if they were my own memories. The few stories I have from my father, too. Do you think sharing memories is a way for us to connect?"

"Aye," she answered. "Memories are the foundation for every emotion. As young bairns, we have to remember faces we can trust."

Was his a face she could trust? Rork remembered the Wood Sorrel woman.

"Deirdre, I —" he began.

"Aye?" she asked.

Rork couldn't tell her. Not yet. His stomach rumbled again, and he thought of the many recipes of his gran's saved on the flash drive. "You can see how to make the trail mix, right? On the notecard? In this memory that doesn't exactly belong to you?"

Deirdre laughed spontaneously. "You really *are* a gannet," she said.

Rork smiled to himself. Deirdre would come around. He was convinced of it.

As they came within sight of the trailhead marking the transition between Levels Five and Six, they heard voices. Rork motioned to Deirdre, and they crouched lower, searching the area for a place to take cover. Deirdre tugged on his sleeve, and he followed her. She kept low, picking her way towards a grassy berm overlooking the Meadows. They rolled to its far side just as Beck, Charboy, and Hamish emerged from the tall meadowland grasses scattered with cockscomb.

"Level Six," said Beck, gloating, rubbing his hands together. His bare arms bulged with muscle. His dusky-colored sweatshirt was sheared off at the arms and belly ribbing, revealing a glimpse of banshee abdomen. Rork was jealous for a split second. Charboy and Hamish jockeyed for position behind him, pushing and shoving each other, Hamish's wallet chain jingling in the echoing space.

Beck consulted a large-faced watch on his wrist, which seemed to be emitting some kind of alarm. "Boys, I am going to have to leave you now," said Beck, kicking rocks and small stones out of his way. "Make camp and try not to cock things up too bad." Beck began to do pushups, moving briskly up and down, his body a stiff plank, air snorting in and out of his nose, wristwatch flashing a beacon of light onto his face. Gradually he disappeared, leaving Charboy and Hamish alone and staring at each other uneasily.

"Come on," said Charboy. "This looks good enough." He dumped his pack a good distance from the trail where tall grasses lay flattened and ox-eye daisies stood sentinel. He pulled out a tent. Hamish set his pack down more gently and jangled over to help. His grimy trousers kept slipping down, showing a squint-half-moon of upper buttock. He had to stop repeatedly and pull up his trousers by the belt-loops.

Rork shook his head and slid farther down the berm. Beneath him, Deirdre carefully rearranged the grasses to create a cushion for herself. The meadow fescue was tall and stiff but not uncomfortable. Rork figured there was maybe a hundred feet between them, divided by the trail. If they could remain unnoticed, the berm offered protection and a good perspective on their quarry.

"Grab an end already," sniped Charboy. Hamish sighed heavily and grabbed one end of a modular tent pole, doing a quick hop-a-long skip with a belt loop and lifted leg. Charboy roughly clipped the tent to the overarching tent poles, his movement abrupt, charred clothes giving off snaky tendrils of smoke and ash. At the back of his bald-head two rolls of neck flesh created a visible ledge.

Despite the discordant exchange between them, the tent went up. Charboy dug a sandy hole and scythed grass away with his switchblade to start a fire. Hamish collected firewood, but he didn't venture too far from the campsite, keeping a wary eye on Charboy.

"Here," said Hamish, dumping an armful of wood behind Charboy's feet and tugging up his pants.

They seemed to be speaking only to give each other commands. The fire crackled and guttered as Charboy fed it broken twigs and branches with his black-lacquered fingers. He was an efficient fire starter, and the fire soon licked the monochrome sky with searing flames that were much higher than they needed to be for a two-person campfire. They didn't seem to regard the wastefulness. Hamish dragged his pack to one side of the fire and sat down next to it, unzipping a flask from an outer pocket. He pulled meditatively on the flask's contents while inhaling deeply on a cigarette.

Charboy made a derisive sound with his thin lips.

"Want some?" asked Hamish.

"Yeah, right," said Charboy, crouched by the fire, staring into its burnished coals.

Hamish tamped out the end of his cigarette and stowed away the butt end in his shirt pocket. He leaned the flask against his pack.

"Throw me some food," he said to Charboy.

"Help yourself," said Charboy, kicking his pack nearer Hamish and the fire.

Hamish rummaged inside to retrieve food packets and a collapsible pot for cooking. Measuring water from his canteen, he stirred together the lumpy powder from one of his food packets.

"Here," he said, handing the pot to Charboy. "Can you heat this up?"

Charboy grunted and took the pot, setting it in the nest of coals.

The smell of cooking wafted over to Rork. He groaned softly and rolled onto his back, feeling swoonish. The horizon swirled. It must be the lack of sleep and limited food. They'd eaten the hardtack and peanut butter hours ago.

"Are you all right?" asked Deirdre.

"I'll be fine," he said, feeling a glimmer of hope. Hamish's drinking might actually give them a chance.

Rork heard the clatter of dishes as Charboy and Hamish finished off their camp meal. He sensed more than saw what was occurring in the camp. A muted silence prevailed as Hamish and Charboy took to their opposing campsite positions. Charboy stirred the fire broodily. Hamish smoked an endless series of cigarettes while he scratched in his sketchpad, occasionally drinking from the flask tucked between his legs.

Rork squinted at the horizon. Gray, darker gray, pale gray. Gray. He rolled onto his forearms and found Deirdre blinking her green eyelashes at him. He made a sign to indicate he was good. Her face relaxed. He attempted to adjust the creep-up of his pant legs and felt something crawling on him. He didn't have time to investigate as his attention was brought back to the campsite by the sound of harsh words.

"What you drawing?"

"None of your f—ing business."

Charboy grabbed Hamish's sketchbook. Hamish lunged for him, and they rolled around on the fire's periphery, kicking dirt into it and causing smoke.

"F— you!"

"F— you!"

Rork guessed this was a regular occurrence. Maybe this was how they were ending each of their evenings together. Or maybe "rest sessions" would be more accurate since he had no idea if it was night or not. Then a flash of insight dawned on him. Hamish must be the intermediary, which meant, like Rork, he could commune with the dead. How? he wondered. He watched Hamish fight to keep his sketchbook out of Charboy's reach, despite a bloody nose and scraped back, and then suddenly Rork realized the sketchbook must be how Hamish communicated with the dead.

Charboy lost interest in the fight and stepped out of the skirmish, shoving Hamish to his knees.

"What do I care what you're drawing?" he said. Pushing Hamish with the flat of his boot, he left tread marks on the cotton of Hamish's exposed underwear.

Hamish grappled with his sketchbook in one hand and tugged at his belt loop with the other.

Charboy sneered and shoved him again with his boot. Off-balance, Hamish fell onto one shoulder and scrabbled to get back up.

"I'll be glad when this farce is over," said Charboy, disappearing into the dark meadow, his bald-head bobbing like a wayward moon.

Rork looked at Deirdre meaningfully. She shook her head, *not yet*, resting her chin on her hands next to him on the berm's slope, her bright blue nails motionless. Rork sighed into his crossed arms, trying to be patient.

Temporarily, Hamish was alone.

He leaned against his backpack, unscrewed the flask top, and drank deeply. His head drooped. Lengths of wood in the fire shifted, resettling, sending up sparks. He traced what he'd drawn in the sketchbook, his face smoothed of its ever-present snarl.

Charboy returned, snuffling. "I'm taking the tent," he barked to Hamish.

"Sod off," said Hamish, as the flap of the tent swiped closed behind Charboy.

Hamish stared out gloomily at the perennial dusk. Rork wondered how he'd gotten dragged into Shufftie.

The fire crackled and sifted. Hamish slid down his backpack until he was curled up on the ground, breathing heavily. Rork waited for a signal from Deirdre. When the fire died down to embers, she stirred.

"Sssshhhh," she said, leaving the berm and nodding for him to follow. Her boots hardly made a sound, as if the grasses made way for her as she moved seamlessly through the night. She moved like poetry, thought Rork. His fingers twitched. If he ever found his laptop or phone, he would make another slideshow inspired by her movement. He started to imagine the frames. Pictures of her. Superimposed over botanical photos — plants, flowers, trees. Music. Voice-over verses. *O, my luve is like a red, red rose...*

"Ooof," said Rork under his breath, colliding with Deirdre as she crouched outside the glow of the dying fire. He cursed himself for his clumsiness. If he could only stay in the present! "My loonie with his head in the clouds," his gran used to say. He tried to shake himself out of his reverie, touching Deirdre on her shoulder to focus. She signaled for him to stay put.

Deirdre crept low to the ground, giving the fire a wide berth. Hamish thrashed in his sleep. Deirdre crawled the last few feet and grabbed each backpack by a strap. She drew them towards her, backing away from the fire. Rork inched his way towards the trail, watching his feet, alert to her every move. Deirdre quickly assessed and selected contents of each backpack, combining them into one, leaving behind a backpack and enough essentials, along with Hamish's sketchbook, flask, and pack of cigarettes. Rork was glad, although he was curious what might be drawn in the sketchbook. He had voices. Hamish must have images.

After two long (mostly soundless) strides, Rork and Deirdre were on the trail moving swiftly back the way they'd come through the lochs. They didn't dare stop for fear of being followed. Rork kept looking behind him but didn't hear any movement from Hamish or Charboy. He wore the pack and typed on the air with his left hand s-a-f-e.

"Do we dare stop?" asked Deirdre, leaning over to rest.

They'd re-entered the braes of Level Six, hiking at a faster clip than their normal pace in an effort to put as much distance as possible between them and Charboy or Hamish. The braes towered above them, a windswept mountainside of rock, heaths, and scree.

Rork looked up, around, and behind them. "How about we go a little farther?" He wasn't comfortable stopping yet. He felt oppressed by the sky, and he didn't understand why. Was it the aftermath of fear? Apprehension? Was he feeling guilty? Hamish had once been his friend. Was it getting darker?

He wished there'd been another solution to taking supplies from the other camp. Hamish had looked so forlorn. Rork thought about taking. And giving. And losing. The dimensions of each. Taking somehow made him feel less. Losing was devastating. Shufftie was littered with his losses. First his phone. Then his computer. And now the sixpence.

Rork sighed, trying to shake off the feeling of oppression. He regretted the labyrinth. He regretted the River of Forgetting. He wished he could have predicted what might happen and reacted... better? Faster? More competently? Yet there really was no predicting in Shufftie. It was as volatile as — he didn't even know.

"Ouch," Rork stumbled on a pile of rocks on the trail.

Deirdre turned at his voice. Her face looked pale and pinched, still recovering from everything she'd been through.

"Should we stop?" he asked. The ground sloped off to the left. Rork followed it, hoping for a spot hidden from the trail.

Deirdre drank the last dregs of water from her canteen.

Rork dropped the pack and focused on being useful. Perhaps he could work off this feeling of oppression. He found a tarp and rigged it up beneath a scrub tree. The ground was broken with exposed roots, but he staked a relatively clear area. He batted the tarp's edge as he ducked back out.

"Does the sky seem darker to you?" he asked, kneeling next to Deirdre as she dumped out the backpack.

"I'm not sure," she said. "Maybe."

Rork examined the contents of the pack. In addition to the tarp, there was a small sterno stove, a few packets of dehydrated food, fruit bars, socks, T-shirts, a sweatshirt, camp kit with mugs and a sleeping bag that looked like it had put on some miles. It wasn't much, but it might be enough to keep them going.

Rork shook the empty pack and felt something rattle at the bottom. He pulled out a drawing pencil, embossed with a name in gold. HAMISH. Rork remembered the pencils. He was at the birthday party. Hamish's mother had been so pleased with herself, ordering the specialty pencils from L. Cornelissen & Son's in London.

"Beautiful pencil," said Deirdre.

"Yes," said Rork. The noises in his head chattered. Rork ran his finger over the embossing. Hamish's mother had given Hamish a part of herself with this gift. A part that withstood everything. Her death. Hamish's defiance. Something sacred happened in the giving and receiving of the pencil.

Rork returned the pencil to the backpack and sat down cross-legged behind Deirdre. What was it about Shufftie? He pulled Deirdre against him and wrapped his arms around her. "How do you feel?" he asked. He felt gravel dig into the undersides of his legs.

She resisted at first, holding a food packet in her hand, her resistance like a thin veneer of ice on the surface of milk in winter's pantry. After a few beats she let herself relax against his chest. Rork was relieved because a part of him believed that what had happened between them was more dream than reality.

"Tired. Hungry. Like I have secret rooms in my head I need to explore." She looked at him over her shoulder.

Rork pressed his cheek to the side of her neck, the soft skin hidden by her hair, the smell of her like summer. D-e-i-r-d-e, he typed on her upper arm. Once again, he noticed a faint tracery of lines disappearing into the collar of her shirt. "What's this?" he asked.

"What?"

He pulled at her collar to get a better look. The pattern continued down her back.

"What are you doing?!" Deirdre leaned away from him, the asyncronization of her lips and words very noticeable.

"There's a pattern on your neck, your back. Look!"

Deirdre twisted around, trying to see. She unbuttoned her shirt and peered over one shoulder. Finally, she took the shirt off and underneath she wore a thin, ribbed undershirt, what his gran would call a semmit. She pulled the semmit up, contorting for a look at the small of her back.

Rork couldn't help himself. He whistled.

"Tell me," said Deirdre.

"It's a tattoo of some kind, I think. The design looks like a vine with trailing stems and bright blue, star-shaped flowers. But what's most remarkable is it seems to be responsive. The vine draws and undraws. Then a curlicue appears. Then a bud or a bloom. Then shades of color and shadow. And then the actions happen in reverse, blooming and fading, blooming and fading. I don't know what to make of it."

"I wish I could see it," said Deirdre.

"Watch," said Rork, turning her slightly. His hand held the curve of her waist. "It's coming around your hip."

Deirdre watched the pattern unfurl on the skin above her trousers. "Forget-me-not," she said.

"What did you say?" asked Rork.

"*Myosotis sylvatica*. The flower is Forget-me-not. Some say, in the creation of the world, it was the last to be named. 'Forget me not.' See?" Deirdre traced the outline of a flower with one finger.

"Does it hurt?" asked Rork.

"No," said Deirdre.

Rork moved so they faced each other. He rested his hands on her shoulders, and the forget-me-nots reacted by flowering up her arms. "I have to tell you something," he said.

"Yes?" she asked, lifting her eyes to his face.

"Last night, I was so desperate to help you, I learned how to memory-type."

The starbursts at the centers of Deirdre's eyes flared.

Rork stuttered a little. "Voice c-came forward with stories and memories, and I typed them onto your skin. A woman, especially, wouldn't let me stop. Something happened to you, your body as I typed. I memory-typed all night, until I collapsed."

Deirdre spoke finally. "I had the most vivid dreams of her."

"Your mother?" Rork asked.

"Aye," said Deirdre.

"Maybe the forget-me-not tattoo is a sign from her?" asked Rork.

"Or a sign of something else?" Deirdre smiled her enigmatic smile.

Rork could not trust himself to speak. His heart erupted in his ears as Deirdre leaned back against his chest. He counted the seconds, feeling a fullness that began to dispel the sting of his father's rejection. He hoped Deirdre felt it, too.

"Let me see if I can get the sterno to work," said Deirdre, disentangling and rolling to her knees. "I could really use a cup of tea. There's macaroni and cheese, too."

Rork unzipped the sleeping bag, intending to air it out. He still felt uneasy, that vague sense of oppression nagging, and he was so hungry his stomach was past growling.

"Let's try not to make too much noise," he said. "We don't want Hamish and Charboy to know where we are."

Rork flung the sleeping bag over a sturdy bush. He wondered at the determination of the dead. Their gifts. Their acts of service. What had Boo said about Shufftie? A small oscillation? A wee shift? Did that mean some wavelength of Shufftie traveled along beside them? Always? The dead trying and trying in their myriad ways to communicate?

He believed that the memory-typing was a breakthrough of some kind. Perhaps not an epiphany. But something.

And then Rork found his phone, stuck in the vee of a nearby tree. It smelled like Woodbine cigarettes.

21: Pests

THE PHONE WAS DEAD, of course, but Rork was glad to have the blank screen back in his possession.

He felt there was hope for the other objects he'd lost.

After washing the dishes, it wasn't long before Rork was asleep. His heart *and* stomach were full, and he'd only snatched at sleep during the long vigil of memory-typing. Boo had woken him before he was even half-rested. Now he slept like the dead. If he'd been awake, he would have thought that funny. As it was, he slept in a dreamless black hole. He, Deirdre, and all the pilfered gear were tucked out of sight beneath the tarp's thick plastic. The ground was rough and uneven. Rork had sacrificed comfort to stay close to Deirdre, his hip and shoulder jammed painfully against the stippled dirt, growing numb. In the sleep-scuttled corners of his mind he heard a scratching, an irritating sound, like the rubbing together of two dissonant materials — silk and barbed wire? Sandpaper and sateen?

Rork twitched in his sleep, the scratching materializing in the forms of a creepy-crawlies, insects hideously beetling, scritching over the bare skin of his exposed ankle. He could feel a bug's awkward waddling on the bone of his shin. It felt huge, larger than a normal beetle, bigger than a cockroach. He felt another one on the back of his arm. He twitched some more. Soon he was covered with beetles, too many to count, slip-sliding over his skin, his trousers, his flannel shirt. He didn't want to open his eyes. His gran would say insects were necessary creatures — pollinators and waste recyclers — but bugs of any kind creeped him out. Hesitantly, he opened his eyes and peered between cracked eyelids. On Deirdre's rounded shoulder he saw the most gruesomely tentacled bug he'd ever seen. It was as large as a computer mouse, with a sheen on its pitch-black cantilevered shell-like bug spew, and a tiny, old woman's chiseled face. He recoiled, a shriek lodging in his windpipe. Soon he and Deirdre both were covered by the slimy things.

Rork saw Deirdre's mouth work as she too choked on a scream she was too horrified to utter. Her large gray eyes pleaded with his. Help!

Even worse than the big beetles' physical ugliness was the emotions Rork felt. A horrible sense of oppression emanated from the hag beetles. As they settled on his body, heavy in their repulsive armor, he felt himself go into shock. His skin felt clammy. His chest hurt. He heard himself pant but couldn't get enough air. He was dizzy and confused, his eyes rolling in their sockets, not knowing where to look. Deirdre's pupils were dark and spreading with panic. Her lips were blue, and her skin ashen.

Rork felt a crushing weight, a heavy burden of misgiving. Hopelessness. All he wanted to do was succumb. The oppressiveness overwhelmed him. He didn't feel worth the one life he'd been given. He was as inadequate as he'd always been told and secretly suspected. He felt less consequential than an insect. Miniscule. Nothing.

Yet Rork refused to give up. Despite his lack of confidence, despite his father's lack of faith, he wouldn't let his gran down, he wouldn't let the banshee down, and he definitely wouldn't let Deirdre down. One side of him argued with the other while his body lay frozen, covered by crawling hag beetles.

Where had the beetles come from? Had they skulked out of the strange ecosystem of Shufftie? Had they crept out of some dark corner of Rork's mind? Rork shuddered at the thought.

The hag beetles shifted their hard-shell bodies along his arms, legs, and backbone. He felt their menace, their sticky feet stirring up every negative emotion he'd ever felt, paralyzing him with depression and despair. One side of him flashed alarm. Do something! The other side was caught in a thrall. Deirdre's upper body began to tremor, quivering with the same terror. Rork could hear the clicking of eyes. His? Hers? He had to do something. Deirdre was still getting used to her gifts of memory, and she was vulnerable with her out of sync speech. *He had to do something.*

Rork held his upper body rigid and inched his hands along the ground until he was able to position them beneath his shoulders. He thought if he could concentrate enough, he could winch his body upwards in a push-up maneuver. He was stronger than he looked, thanks to his gran and her apprenticeship. He typed into the ground with his right hand: u-p, u-p, u-p, avoiding direct eye contact with the hag beetles, which made him feel weak and overcome, although he couldn't escape the feeling of dread that clung to him like a trap. Rork strained, grunted and hyperventilated until beads of sweat broke out on his forehead, but the bugs continued to bear down on him like a black boot, driving him down, down, down. His brain fogged over.

No, thought Rork.

He couldn't believe, after everything they'd been through, that bugs would shut them down. His vision started going dark, and he reached for Deirdre's hand. D-e-i-r-d-r-e. He wanted her to remember the promise of her name. Deirdre, who outlasted the raging waters, the sorrows, the forgetting, who lived.

Rork wondered how many levels of consciousness he could survive. This entombment in his own body was worse than rejection. It was *de*jection. An evacuation of his very spirit.

Rork blacked out.

22: Lady's Maid

"BAH," SAID A VOICE. "BAH!"

Barely hanging on, smothered by hag beetles, Rork could smell smoke, a fragrant, incense-thick smoke.

"Get ye gone, ya buggers." It was a woman's voice, bold and brassy, in a regional dialect that sounded familiar.

Smoke swirled at the back of Rork's throat. He wanted to cough to clear it but couldn't. The hag beetles waggled in agitation across his body, moving like they were under attack. Rork kept his face forward as if his eyes were blinkered, not wanting to catch sight of a hag beetle and its withered little face. They made his stomach turn. They were hellish looking.

The mound of beetles next to him stirred. Underneath was Deirdre, doing her best to endure, too.

Rork opened a bleary eye and could sense the person, a woman he guessed by the sound of her voice, stepping around them, waving her bundle of burning herbs. Her efforts were accompanied by a looping litany of: "take that," "bah," and "away with ya." The smoke was sharp in his nostrils, but he could feel it loosening the terrible oppression of the hag beetles. He began to feel lighter somehow, and — dare he think it? — hopeful. He wondered who the woman was and where she'd come from. He thought he recognized the herb smells. Mugwort or perhaps Sweet Cicely? His gran used to burn a small twist of herbs in a stoneware saucer when she was feeling "lowlie," as she put it.

When Rork was able, he turned more fully towards Deirdre. His hand had not quite found hers, stranded a wrist's width away, typing without purpose. Her eyes were screwed closed as she deep-breathed the herb smoke. He could see her chest rise and fall. She was very pale. He watched the hag beetles skeeter off her in a cavalcade.

The incense's intensity gathered strength. Rork blinked through a cloud of it. He didn't know if he should try and get up and help. He didn't know if he could.

The woman continued to command, "Away, scourge. Away."

Rork could see the woman's well-worn and sturdy leather-flap shoes advance on the hag beetles over and over again. She kept moving back and forth, first toward Rork and then toward Deirdre. She was very determined. He'd give her that. Thankfully, the hag beetles retreated in a swarm, disappearing in all directions to unseen crevices. Had he and Deirdre been easy prey in this half-dead place? Could he have better protected them? Rork had no easy answers. Some things were unforeseen.

His feelings of foreboding began to disperse. Rork inhaled the pungent sweet-herb scent. Deirdre moved beside him. He felt the black boot of despair lift off his chest. He raised himself up on his elbows. Deirdre's eyes opened.

"What was that?" she asked, her words haltingly out of sync.

"I'm sorry," Rork mouthed, feeling responsible, protective.

"Bah, bah, bah," said the woman. She jabbed about with her burning bundle. The last flank of hag beetles waddled off down the trail. The bundle smoldered, and the woman blew gently on its embers, reigniting the herbs. The woman propped it carefully next to the small ring of stones Rork had created, in which she set a small fire lit by her bundle. She rattled a kettle, and Rork could hear the slosh of water.

"Hrrmmph," said the woman.

Sitting, Rork wondered who the woman was. She wore a mobcap and petticoats. He could hear the ruffles swish beneath her frock with its tiny, covered buttons. Not from this century, surely. He stood up groggily. His head felt like half-churned butter.

"Should you be making a fire?" he asked hoarsely, stumbling closer.

The woman took him in, a long gaze up and down the great length of him. "You're a mighty lad, eh?" she said. She wiped her hands on the bell of her dress, stuck out her hand. "Fit like?" she said. "I'm Maggie."

Rork reached for her hand and pressed his into it. "Fit like yourself," he said. "Rork." He dipped his chin. Maggie's curly hair threatened to escape the mobcap. Ringlets clustered around her small face. She was scrubbed clean and had a sprinkling of freckles across her nose and apple cheeks. In Shufftie she appeared in shades of gray, and Rork wondered what color her eyes were in life. Her eyelashes were dark, furling like the ends of fern.

"I know there's bad ones after you, but I'll only make a small fire. My special tea will help get rid of the infestation. Hag beetles indeed," she said, turning back to the fire. "Bah," she added, for emphasis. "You'll feel better in yourself in no time."

Behind him, Deirdre stood shakily. She squeezed Rork's arm, steadying herself. Rork looked around, smiling crookedly. He was glad to see her up, although next to brisk Maggie she looked listless with her worried eyes and tattered trousers.

"Who are you, Maggie?" Deirdre asked in her typically direct style.

Maggie considered Deirdre, a flash of something in her eyes. "Ask me that again, lassie."

"Who are you, Maggie?"

Maggie stood up proudly. "I'm Maggie, maidservant of the Duchess of Gordon." She created a billow with her trousers. The kettle began to clatter with rising heat. "Never mind me, lassie. You are a wee bit out of step with the reel, I see. Let me think how we can fix you up."

"Gordon?" asked Rork. "Of Castle Farm?"

"Aye, laddie, the very same."

"Are you –?"

"Och," said Maggie. "You've seen me haunting the tower, have you?"

Rork gawked. The stories were true?

"I do it to please my Missus, God bless her. The Duke was fairly prejudiced against her. Do him and his ancestors good to think the tower's possessed by ghosts. Bah," she said again for emphasis.

Upon steeping, Maggie poured the tea and handed each of them a cup. Rork sniffed suspiciously, holding the camp mug carefully by the handle. The mug was hot to the touch. The tea smelled floral, not its usual smell. Rork scowled.

"Drink, drink," motioned Maggie extravagantly with her arms. She snuffed out the fire with a few handfuls of sand she scuffed from the ground with her pointy-toed boots.

Rork took an experimental sip. The tea was scalding and tart-tasting. It tasted strange on his tongue.

"I like it," said Deirdre. "It tastes like meadow."

"Fanciful," said Maggie, appreciatively. "You have something of the Missus about you, lassie. Aye, the tea brews up dried petals of wildflowers, and a few other herbs and oils my mother taught me. And her mother before her. The missus hired me special for my ways."

"Your missus lived at Gordon Castle?" asked Rork.

"Aye," said Maggie. "For many years while her children were young. She was very knowledgeable about farming, but she was most famous for her parties. Och, they were loud, lavish affairs, with hundreds of people coming from miles around. Important people, too. The sky fairly lit up with the candles and torches we'd burn. Politicians and scientists came to converse with my missus. And the dancing!" Maggie held up her skirts and made a quick hop step. "My missus loved to dance. She invented a reel, ya know."

"You would help in the preparations?" asked Deirdre. Her tea half-gone, she looked a little less shook despite the lip sync issue.

"Aye," said Maggie. "I had a particular responsibility. Before every one of her grand shindigs, I'd clear out the rooms first with my wee burning bundles. I'd tailor them to each occasion. My missus couldn't abide negative energy or bad spirits."

"Do the plants call to you?" asked Deirdre quietly.

"Well, lassie," said Maggie, "they don't exactly 'call' to me, but they do present themselves to me based on a distinct problem or challenge, along with extracts and other tinctures. I was my mother's apprentice for many years, cataloging and cross-referencing her notes in wooden boxes she stored under her bed." Maggie sighed wistfully. "They are all I have of her, the boxes with their worn lids and clever clasps. Inside they smell like my memories of her. Och," she tsked, "now who's sounding fanciful?"

"I get the solving problems part," said Rork, squeezing the flash drive in his pocket.

Maggie picked up and set down the kettle. She felt its base. "Still warm," she said. "Good." She fixed Deirdre with a determined eye. "Now we're going to do something about this speech discord of yours, my fine dree lassie."

"What speech discord?" asked Deirdre.

Maggie paused only infinitesimally. "Never you mind." She collected their tea mugs, emptying the dregs into the ash of the fire.

"Your words and lips don't always match up," explained Rork to Deirdre, pacing in the background. "I didn't want to worry you."

"Don't you go far," Maggie said to Rork. "I might be needing your help."

"I'm not going anywhere," said Rork.

"Has she had a shock?" asked Maggie.

"You could say that," said Rork. "She fell into the River of Forgetting."

Maggie clicked with her tongue. "That doesna sound good," she said. Crouching, she poured the still-warm kettle water into a bowl. Into it she pinched some flower petals and some drops from a vial, both retrieved from leather pouches hung around her neck and tucked inside her bodice.

"Have you a flannel? A cloth?" asked Maggie.

Rork looked to Deirdre. Where was the backpack? Once again, he allowed himself to be distracted. Why couldn't he keep it together? A more practical man would never have lost sight of the essentials. Like supplies. Or backpack. As his father would always say, "A wing and a prayer only gets you so far, son."

Deirdre dragged the backpack out from their sad lean-to, still half-covered by the tarp, which looked bedraggled. The backpack, too, looked a little worse for wear.

"Let me look," said Deirdre. "There might be something you could use. What's it for?"

"I'm making you a compress, lass." Maggie smiled broadly. "You'll be as right as rain in no time."

"Will a T-shirt do?" asked Deirdre.

"Aye," said Maggie. "Looks like it will do nicely."

Maggie put the T-shirt into the bowl to steep and motioned Rork to help her with the tarp. They made a cover for the rough ground, folding it so Deirdre could lie down.

Deirdre did as she was bid, lying on one hip, alert, anxious.

"Relax, lass," said Maggie. "Would you mind lifting up your blouse and semmit? The compress will work faster on your bare skin."

Deirdre lay down on the tarp on her stomach with her shirt unbuttoned and undershirt bunched under her armpits. She rested her chin on her two stacked hands.

"Och," said Maggie, stopping midway between the kettle and Deirdre with the compress-T-shirt held in her hands. She inhaled, making an animal-sounding yip at the back of her throat. "That's special," she said, eyeing the tattoo and watching it animate. "Such an interesting lassie you are."

Maggie kneeled beside Deirdre, swishing her underskirt out of the way, and placed the compress along the bony ridge of Deirdre's spine. Maggie moved her hands up the center of Deirdre's back, pressing the compress into her skin. "Relax, lassie," she said, gently pushing between Deirdre's shoulder blades.

Deirdre let her head drop, resting her cheek against the back of her hand. "It smells good," she murmured.

Maggie stayed by her side, shushing her and singing softly to herself, long notes with a warble of vibrato. A pretty melody really. Rork could pick out the words: "O, can you sense. O, can you see." He could also smell the compress, or at least the stronger herbs, tangy, green and fragrant like wild heather. He could feel the combination of scents inside his nostrils, sharp like tonic. He was on the verge of a sneeze, mesmerized by Maggie's low singing and Deirdre's deep, murmurous breathing.

"Aye, lassie. Settle down. Settle."

Rork smiled to himself. Maggie pronounced "down" like his gran. *Settle doon.*

Shrubby plants of heather, thriving between the rocky braes, breached the ruin of their lean-to to stretch and grow toward Deirdre. Their bell-shaped flowers and scale-like leaves trembled in rhythm with Deirdre's breath. Rork could empathize. He also felt himself drawn to Deirdre in an elemental way.

"Well, I never," said Maggie, with another yip-like intake of breath. She eyed the migration of plants. "Wild heather," she said wonderingly. "Magical."

"She's had the affinity since a child," said Rork in a hush, looking on. "I don't think she knows what to do with it."

"Imagine once she understands it better. Oh la."

Maggie resumed her singing, shifting onto one hip. She lightly touched her fingertips to Deirdre's skin, running up either side of her back, stirring up forget-me-nots, which bloomed on contact. The pitch of her voice grew higher, warbly with age, but she continued her singsong.

Awa' we long, awa' we see,
wildest heather sweeping the lee,
blooming together in complete harmony
with woodland sage and
forget-me-not, so sweet.

Awa' we long, awa' we see,
wildest heather rippling the breeze,
blooming together in complete harmony
with woodland sage and
forget-me-not, so sweet.

"Sing, laddie," said Maggie.

Rork knew the song, a local ballad. How his gran loved a singsong. He vaguely knew the words but was only sure of the chorus. "Awa' we long, awa' we see."

Maggie wrung out the T-shirt and reapplied the compress. The forget-me-not tattoo rippled up and down Deirdre's body. It was an amazing sight. Rork wondered if it was some kind of sign from the other side. That woman intervening? Her mother?

Maggie pressed the refreshed compress to Deirdre's back. Wild heather proliferated, its tiny bells and leaf spires growing thicker and thicker around Deirdre, entangling with other wildflowers — sweet woodruff, wood sage, and woodland forget-me-not.

Awa' we long, awa' we see,
wildest heather sweeping the lee,
blooming together in complete harmony

Rork's voice grew louder, singing the ballad with Maggie.

Deirdre wriggled as the carpet of woodland plants grew lush, shrouding her body. Rork's last glimpse of the tattoo flashed at a rapid pace, the back of her arms, shoulders, zipping down her spine. "Awa' we long, awa' we see." His voice resounded in his ears. Deirdre was completely cocooned in plants. Maggie sprinkled the remaining drops of the steeping water. The smell was powerful.

Maggie finished another chorus, holding the last note. "Now we wait," she said.

Rork started to get impatient, worried about time and enemies. Not wanting to disrupt the spell Maggie cast, he backtracked alone on the trail to make sure Hamish and Charboy weren't closing in on them. He didn't know why suddenly he'd become so anxious. The sensation of passing time? Or maybe he was finally developing *some* awareness?

He missed the routine of the trail, and his legs twitched to get moving again, especially since he still felt creepy crawly from the hag beetles. The compass's herbal blend had opened up his nasal cavities. His thigh muscles were strong, his step sure-footed. Rork felt very much alive and alert, despite the washed-out scenery. If Hamish and Charboy were stalking them, they would be very noticeable against the dull, gray tones.

He didn't go far — just around a few turns — in case the women might need him. He didn't notice anything. No movement or color or sound. Still, he worried. Apprehension might be his strongest defense mechanism. Not quite the survival instinct he'd hoped for, but he'd take it if it gave them any kind of edge.

Rork returned to camp as the mound that was Deirdre began to stir.

"Blooming together in complete harmony," Maggie sang under her breath, watching Deirdre, absent-mindedly rearranging the herb pouches across her body.

The wild heather quivered with Deirdre's movement and disentangled from her body, as if a blanket were lifting. Sprigs of heather and other wildflowers caught in Deirdre's hair and clothes. She pushed herself off the ground, and Rork could no longer see the erratic rippling of the tattoo. He only saw the cream of her skin. The T-shirt compress slipped to the ground. Maggie retrieved it and inhaled the scent.

Deirdre sat cross-legged on the tarp, which crinkled. "What's blooming?" she asked, her words and lips in perfect synchrony.

Maggie smiled broadly at Rork.

"It worked," cheered Rork.

Deirdre buttoned her shirt and gave him a smile. An unequivocal smile with upcurved lips. Helpless as the wild heather, Rork grinned back at her.

Maggie chuckled. "You, two," she said. "I know young love. I used to help my missus keep her trysts with her true love. Och, so tragic. She thought he'd died in the war, but on the night of her wedding to the Duke — the *very* night — she received a letter from him. He'd only been sorely injured in some infantry hospital. She fainted clean away. The only time I ever seen her faint in my long years of service. She tried to be a good wife to the Duke. But the Duke had his mistress. That common woman. Bah." She shook out the compress-T-shirt rather violently. "Here, lass," she said, handing it to Deirdre.

"Keep this with you. The herbs will keep their strength for a wee while yet. Just moisten the shirt."

"I don't know how to thank you," said Deirdre, her words and lips in unison.

"Och," said Maggie. "It was just a wee crookedness a'tween your body and spirit. It can happen. No doubt this is a strange, strange place." She looked around her, at the skirt of her gown and her tiny-button shoes. "I'm looking a wee peely-wally myself." She chuckled again.

As Deirdre stood, Rork said, "Look." He turned up her wrists, and on their insides were two bunches of forget-me-nots impressed on her skin — at rest — five blue petals with dainty yellow centers.

"So I'll always remember," said Deirdre, following the lines of a flower with her forefinger.

Overcome, Deirdre grabbed Maggie in an awkward hug.

"There, there," said Maggie, patting her back soothingly, as if she were a small child.

Deirdre was so much taller, usually so aloof. She engulfed the smaller Maggie, who had been caught momentarily off-guard.

"Now that I think on it," said Maggie, muffled in Deirdre's long-armed clasp, spying the tendrils of forget-me-nots on her wrist. "My missus used to embroider forget-me-nots. She stitched them into tapestries, on handkerchiefs, on napkins, even her undergarments. The king at the time was one of her admirers. He used to call her the 'Flower of Galloway.' My missus loved a ballad, the power they had from the retelling, but I always thought she was the flower of yearning, more like, for her lost love and her homesickness for Scotland. Aye, aye," sighed Maggie, as Deirdre released her.

Maggie busied herself around the campsite. "Let's get you lot sorted," she said. "They'll be ringing for me soon."

"Ringing?" asked Rork.

"Aye," said Maggie. "A sound they thought I'd be familiar with. I've been listening for the bell my whole life." She chuckled to herself as if it were a private joke.

Deirdre refolded the tarp tightly and strapped it to Hamish's backpack. Rork looked wistfully at it, wishing he had his laptop. He felt incomplete without it. More lost? Was that even possible? What a topsy-turvy place Shufftie was. There was so much he wanted to record. He knelt inside the ramshackle lean-to to make sure they hadn't left anything. It didn't take them long to re-pack.

"This has been grand," said Maggie, tugging on her gown, tucking the stray curls back inside her mobcap. "Meeting up with you two, getting a break from the tower. Make sure to give me a wave if you see me." She wagged a finger at Rork.

Rork agreed to give Maggie a wave in her tower but wondered when he'd be home to walk Angus again.

"Och," said Maggie, "there goes the bell."

23: Pall

RORK AND DEIRDRE switched off carrying the pack on the relentless climb that started the next level. Even the name was grim. LEVEL SEVEN: SUMMITS OF NO RETURN. The landscape itself was forbidding, great hulking bluffs of rock with very little vegetation. Only the hardiest moss, rockfoil, and white gentian could withstand the extreme temperatures, arid conditions, and harsh winds. In the perennial twilight, weather cues were difficult to decipher.

Rork got his wish. They were moving again, but his breath was labored, going in and out in ragged gasps. His lungs burned. Their boots kicked loose rocks and stones that rolled, gathering speed in tiny avalanches on either side of them.

"Careful," said Rork, sliding backwards. It was his turn with the pack.

Deirdre steadied him with her hand in the small of his back.

"You okay?" Rork asked her.

"You?" she answered.

"Aye." He stopped to rest, leaning over with the pack, bracing himself with his arms. "This is going to be a slow slog."

"Are you in a hurry?" asked Deirdre.

"To reach the Summits of No Return?" he drawled. "No, I guess not."

Up seemed to go on forever. Their progress was discouragingly slow. Rork kept his eyes focused on the trail. He was aware of Deirdre's every movement behind him. Had she fully recovered from her time in the River of Forgetting? He would try and carry the pack as long as he could.

They reached a slight plateau, and Rork was relieved to drop the pack and perch on a rock, dribbling a little water into his mouth. He could hardly swallow he was panting so hard. His legs were on fire. Deirdre perched, too, leaning against his back. She was in much better shape than he was, he decided, but he could hear her breathe, too, in long, measured breaths. He tried to follow her example, timing his breath with the cadence of hers, but he soon gave up, sucking in air haphazardly.

Rork looked ahead of them and behind. More hardscrabble terrain rose above them in both directions. He sighed, trying to reign in his frustration. He was tired of Shufftie. A wee shift? Hah! He was tired of colorlessness, of gray. He was tired of the banshee and her comings and goings. And he still missed his gran. His heart felt like one of those stress balls. It squeezed whenever he thought of her, a hard knot of rubber. Only Deirdre's presence gave him any kind of relief. He thought how much his gran would have liked her.

He stood and repositioned himself on the rock so that his legs were on either side of Deirdre's, and she leaned into his chest.

"I could sure use some of your trail mix right about now," he said. He felt the reverberation of his own words in his chest. His stomach flipped with hunger.

"Hamish has more hardtack and a tube of peanut butter in his pack," said Deirdre.

"Really? Must have been on special."

Deirdre shook her head. Her hair tickled his throat. "Your gran is *so* right. You are such a gannet."

"I warned you," he said, squeezing her. He went to the pack on the ground and started to rummage around in it.

"Let me find it," said Deirdre.

Rork ate. The ground was hard. The wind howled. Deirdre closed her eyes, sitting in her contemplative pose. Eating made Rork feel more fueled, capable. He made a cracker for Deirdre.

"Here," he said, "have one."

Uncertain smile.

"You know you need it."

She nibbled. Her eyes couldn't help but flit upwards. The wind didn't just howl, it whined, moaned, yowled. As if it was a real-life being straining at a leash.

"My vocabulary of gray will never be the same," she said. "Before Shufftie, I never realized how many shades there were between black and white."

"I know what you mean," said Rork.

"Pearl," she said, "for that shade just above the horizon." She drank a little water. The peanut butter was dense and tacky, not the best quality. She continued. "Abalone, a deeper gray, around the edges of trees and other brush. Remember the Memory Trees?"

"Yes, I remember the Memory Trees," said Rork. "I remember how creepy they were. 'Abalone,' that's a good word."

Deirdre dipped her head, acknowledging.

"How about pewter?" said Rork. "For the color of the rocks."

"Aye," said Deirdre. "And steel wool for the color of the trees."

"How about silver? For the tips of the grasses?"

"Aye, good," said Deirdre, wistfully. "Like them — fleeting, illusive."

Rork took a bow from his sitting position. "Thunder?"

"Is that a color?"

"For the roof of the sky?"

Deirdre looked up. "Aye, I can see that now." She rubbed her hands on the legs of her trousers. "Smoke is the color of everything else. It gets in my eyes."

He couldn't think of anything encouraging, so Rork said nothing more, eating more peanut butter and hardtack.

Deirdre fell quiet, meditating from her perch on the rock. Rork replayed in his head the words for gray, typing them on his trousers, now stiff with dust and wear. He wasn't sure of his judgment of distance in the high altitudes. Maybe they had another day to climb upward. Maybe two. But he was more worried about what would happen when they made it to the high summits. What then? It seemed they were truly reaching a point of no return, and now that he knew something about the nature of Shufftie he didn't like it. And where was the banshee? She'd last appeared forever ago. What was keeping her?

With his thoughts cycling in a pointless loop, he didn't notice at first the vague muddying of the sky, but he did notice the change in smell.

"What the —?"

The air suddenly smelled like the worst kind of flatulence. His eyes flitted to Deirdre, but there was no way that odor was coming from her. Rot. Decay. Offal. Rork could hardly stand it. He held his nose.

Deirdre stirred from her lotus position. "Do you smell that?"

"Aye," said Rork, "and it seems to be getting stronger."

"Look!" said Deirdre.

Above them, the sky roiled like a cauldron, swirling, steaming, boiling with bile.

"That's not gray," said Rork, gutpunched with fear.

"Blackest black," murmured Deirdre, moving closer to Rork.

"It's moving," said Rork, trying hard to swallow. The black cloud shape-shifted across the sky. Now a crow. Now a bat. Now a cat. Now a colossus in a cape. Horrifically, the cape furled open, whipping up the wind, grit, and other rubble. Sharp stones pelted them from all directions. The hardtack and tube of peanut butter began to elevate from the ground. "The pack!" yelled Rork, diving on it.

A squall swirled around them. Rork and the pack began to rise from the ground, lifted by an unseen force. He grasped for something to hold onto. Deirdre's sun-gold hair lashed around her face. She clung to the shirttail of Rork's shirt. "I can't lose you again," she said. "I can't lose myself."

"You won't!" he said as loud as he could, trying to convince himself. With Deirdre's help, he contorted himself back to the ground, although he disbelieved what was happening and his abilities. It all felt surreal, a dream within a dream.

They were engulfed by black noise, the antithesis of white noise. Whereas white noise filled space, comforting, relaxing and domestic, black noise was a roaring nothingness, emptied of feeling. Like extinction. The blackness was a pall, a vast, accumulating cloud of would-be extermination. It was nullifying. Everything Rork thought he knew or felt or sensed or intuited was without value. Worthless. Rork knew they had to get out of range of this thing, this pall, this devourer of good and light and joyousness.

"Stay with me!" Rork yelled. Scrambling to his feet, he clutched the backpack to his chest.

The pall whipped away Deirdre's words, but he felt her tug at his trousers, so he had to trust she would hold tight. The colossus moved like a nightmare, flinging its cape-like shroud. It hulked above them, around them, kicking up a windstorm, a sandstorm, a shitstorm. Pervading everything was that god-awful stench, a smell like the excrement of death. The reek made Rork's eyes water. With one hand he covered his mouth with his shirt's collar and breathed through the cotton's weave. He still gagged.

Rork operated by instinct and hope, his feet finding a path or what passed for a path, up and around to the steepest side of the summit they were climbing, wish-wish-wishing for a cave, a declivity, an overhang, for bloody's sake, some sort of shelter that would enable them to get out of the presence of this p-a-l-l.

"Ow!" said Rork, swapping arms. One forearm protected his face as shrapnel of rocks, scrub, and shale hurled against him. He was hardly aware he spoke, except for the parched tautness in his throat. The black noise was insidious. Pressure built. Rork felt like he was a plug wrenched from both sides. The world tilted, the plane beneath his feet gave away, threatening a slow slide into loss, destruction, annihilation. He couldn't stay on his feet. He half-crawled like an over-burdened ant. He felt Deirdre bump him from behind. Sand was in his eyes, his mouth, his nose. An inexplicable memory from Hamish's art history textbook of the color plate for *The Sleep of Reason Produces Monsters* popped into his mind, the clawing, gnawing, depressing otherness writ large in oil on canvas.

After his parents were killed, Hamish had been obsessed with the painting and began to paint his own versions, the beginning of the bad in their friendship. Hamish could have chosen any painting to mimic, but anguish made him gravitate to de Goya's blackest paintings. Rork remembered the shock of coming face to face with one of these paintings, how a cold, finger-tingling panic had come over him. How dark his friend was, how talented, how he'd confronted a despair Rork didn't want to acknowledge, bubbling beneath the surface, an unavoidable ingredient, it seemed, in the soup of his soul.

Reaching, Rork's hand met a prickly bush, and the sharp thorns made him stop suddenly. Deirdre expelled "oomph" into the small of his back. Jagged barbs pierced the ends of his fingers. His mouth made an agonizing "O," but no sounds came out. His eyes streamed, leaving tracks of sad smears down the sides of his cheek. He felt a gust of air like a belch pouring out from somewhere ahead, and despite the piercing pain in his fingers from the thorns, his hands inched further. The thornbush was in front of an opening in the rock. Rork squeezed forward, unseeing, angling his body, one hand as support, the other probing forward, into he-didn't-know-what.

Overhead, Rork heard a horrible creak. Around them the pall was agitating: the sky, the horizon, the whole scene it overshadowed, including the immediate vicinity and the sharp spires of the summits in the distance. More pressure built, as if the pall was tightening a ratchet. Rork could hear the skitter of rock giving way, the pall a faceless force all around him. Without mercy. Without an ounce of humanity. Without. It was the worst kind of ghost, seeking only destruction, carnage. Did it collect black souls into its swirling mass? Like an anti-nemesis? The pall did not speak, but black noise pricked Rork's forehead with grit, stinging with its black bile. Beads of sweat and blood erupted on his skin. I. don't. matter. I. don't. matter. He thought he heard Deirdre moan, but he couldn't be certain. The pall spread its poison, suffocating the gray light.

The obliteration was extreme. Far, far worse than anything Rork had ever experienced or witnessed. His father's rejection, as much as he had felt annihilated by it, was nothing in comparison. Nothing. The pall was different from the hag beetles, too. Their creepy-crawliness had produced a kind of apathy, a shutting down, but behind the feelings they generated, reality had felt intact. But all sense was ripped away by the pall. It wiped out everything, a complete and utter system swipe. Rork strained and grunted in the fissure of rock, resolve surging up, echoing, "N-O." He jolted himself forward, jamming himself deeper into the rock gap.

No, not after all the levels and dreamwork he and Deirdre had done rebuilding memories.

No, not after the well-meaning and gracious dead had come forward with the best of what they could offer: their memories. True, not all the memories had been undiluted happy memories, but they were meaningful memories, a part of the shared memory pool, their DNA, their circuitry, and this thing, this pall would not eradicate it!

Desperately, Rork dragged the pack behind him in order to wedge his body through the crack in the rock, but it would require Deirdre to let go of his beltloop.

"No," she whispered, clutching at his foot, hobbling on hands and knees after him.

The pall pulled at them like a siphon, drawing, trying to extract. Rork felt his skin move with the suction. In the depths of the black noise, he could hear — torment was the only way Rork could describe it to himself — a cacophony of despair.

Deirdre practically twisted his ankle with her grip. She clasped his foot to her chest as he crawled one-handed upward. They were a strange, four-legged, four-armed creature, slithering along. They moved awkwardly, but Rork was relieved to feel evidence of Deirdre's presence. He did not know what he would do if either of them succumbed to the pall or were separated.

N-O. As soon as the gap in the rock widened enough, he pushed the pack in front of him and gave Deirdre a hand up until she was only slightly lower than him.

The pall whipped up its furor. A fracturing resounded inside the rock's mass. Rork could feel a vibration in the rough shale under his hands and knees. His forward palm and elbow were scraped, but he pressed his eyes shut and pushed on. It wasn't like he could see anything anyway. The blackness was impenetrable. But the more they burrowed the less he felt the pall's sick sucking. He concentrated on the feeling of less. Pain, he would worry about later.

Rork and Deirdre kept crawling. First, he'd push the backpack forward. Then he'd pull himself along by elbow, knee, or hip, or some combination of all three, and then he pulled Deirdre towards him, trying not to drag her, but frequently having little recourse but to skud her along. He felt like they were tunneling to the center of the summits above them.

In his head he heard his father's gruff command: *Action is better than inaction.* Keep moving. He kept moving. The movement was a strange comfort.

They wriggled deeper, deeper into the rock mass until they heard less and less black noise. Until they could progress without feeling the immense pull of pressure from the pall. Rork wondered where the pall went when it was not wreaking havoc. Did it furl up on itself, waiting and lurking until the next hapless hikers came climbing the Shufftie summits?

Rork pushed the backpack, and it slipped over the lip of an edge. He could hear it thud on the other side. When he reached the lip himself, he found there was enough space to swing his legs around and sit. He exhaled a sigh. It felt good-bad to move with more range. He slid down the small decline on the butt of his trousers. He felt around with his hands and found they were in a widening seam of the rock mass that had probably been caused by the trickle of water dribbling down one wall. Rork could feel Deirdre following close behind, clawing forward, breath ragged, every sound amplified in the rock crevice.

"Deirdre, Deirdre," said Rork, making his way to her by touch. He could half-stand in the widening.

"I'm okay," she said, clearly trying to convince herself and Rork that she was.

"Just a little farther," said Rork. "I think I found a place for us to hole up."

"Thank you."

"I mean it literally. I'm afraid."

"Hole… hollow… pit. I don't care," said Deirdre. "As long as I don't have to look at that… thing or hear…"

She didn't finish.

LAST CITATION

24: Crevice

RORK AND DEIRDRE crouched, concealed from the pall. Deirdre patted blindly until she found Rork's hand, which she then sandwiched between her palms.

"There's not a lot of room," said Rork. He turned their hands until he was holding hers. "But there's water. Of sorts. We'll probably have to lap it off the wall." He snorted. He'd done worse, he guessed. "The crack seems to continue there," he said, pointing ahead with their clasped hands.

Deirdre inched deeper inside the cavern. "How about we rest here?" she asked. Rork felt her tug on his arm. "Is there enough room for you?"

Rork moved next to her. The wall was mostly dry. More crushed shale beneath them. "It's fine," he said. All he cared about was staying out of the way of the pall. He stretched out his legs. "I'll get the tarp." He rummaged in the darkness.

They spread out the tarp, letting it lap up the wall behind their backs. The ripple of plastic sounded loud in the tight space. Water dripped at the bottom of a nearby wall. Drip. Drip. Rork leaned against the rock, trying to stay alert. In his mind he could still hear the pall's ravages. He shivered, feeling a sharp bump between his shoulder blades. Deirdre was restless, trying to get comfortable. Rork could hear the crinkle of tarp beneath her. She lay down with her back against the wall, her head butting his thigh. He reached out in the darkness and soothed her shoulders, her back. For a tall girl, she could sure get into a tight ball. He was glad when he felt her breathing get slower, sonorous. He was lulled by the sound. Drip. Drip.

His ears continued to strain for signs of the pall. Inside the cave felt like a vacuum. Quiet. Except for the drip, drip. But he didn't trust the pall, the blackness. He feared it would infiltrate the rock, compromise their refuge. He tried to reason with himself, but it just led him in an endless circle of self-doubt. The pall was like a virus, replicating its bad code, looking for a way in.

Deirdre squeezed him above the knee. "Sleep," she said.

Yes, sleep, he thought, unable to let go. Rork's mind was a jumble, stuck in overdrive. He didn't know where his memories ended and Deirdre's began. Is that what a relationship was all about? A merging of memories? He was exhausted, his soul shattered, but still he remained tethered to Deirdre in some fundamental way. She was the light in his darkness. He would concentrate on that: Deirdre, in technicolor.

They'd never really gotten a chance to discuss his memory-typing, how he had mediated memories of her dead ancestors. Vestiges of memory still clung to his fingertips like meta tags. Family. Home. Grandparents. Meals. At the time, he had felt their urgency and continued to get flashbacks of a stark seascape, snippets of conversation he couldn't understand. Deirdre's ancestors were for sure from the islands, raised on isolation, a survivalist's resourcefulness. He saw her bent over a task with an old woman, the old woman's hair streaked with silver, their voices united in song. Water, water everywhere.

The old had a way of laughing, he thought. It took a lifetime to acquire that. Something in the way their heads dropped back. Unreservedly.

Rork slid down the wall, trying to find a more comfortable position. His arm pillowed his head, his other arm draped Deirdre. He dreamed the horror of the pall, groaning distress. Behind his eyes swirled psychedelic color, neon yellows, greens, blues, and reddish pinks. If he were making this web show, a track of Fifth Dimension would be playing in the background. His hands typed on shadow. Ghostly. The pall had known his weakness.

"D-e-i-r-d-r-e," called a woman as she danced in a grassy clearing with a toddler in her arms. She twirled the toddler in a circle, the sun high in the sky. The woman wore a blouse that swirled out from her body. Sunshine, out-of-breath laughter, and the dry, green smell of grass in the moment. With her flyaway hair, the toddler ducked, aiming for the area beneath the woman's chin, tucking in against her breastbone, already the stiffness in her shoulders, cowed by the wind in her face, the light-shadow, light-shadow circumnavigation. In the distance was the roar of surf, sea crashing on a cliff of rock, stair-stepping to the sky.

The woman flopped to the ground on a bunched-up blanket and ate a section of orange upside-down, orange peeled and sectioned on a picnic plate. The toddler rested on her knees, watching. The mother rolled closer to the toddler, licking her fingers. The two gazed at each other, letting sunshine in, beaming love. The mother touched the toddler's cheek with the front knuckles of one outstretched hand. The toddler didn't move, her fair hair haloing around her face. The mother rolled to her stomach, and the toddler played with strands of her streaming hair. The woman dashed to the edge of the grass where she plucked daisies. She sat cross-legged on the blanket, wrapping her long legs around the toddler. She did not wear shoes, and her bare feet were like poetry. The toddler leaned forward on locked arms, letting the mother put flowers in her hair, the daisies pushed into the thickest hair around the crown of her head. The mother smiled, trimming daisies for her own hair. The toddler helped, bare legs straddling her mother's lap, already depleted of baby fat, showing signs of muscle. The toddler wore shoes, sockless. With her head wreathed in daisies, the mother lay back to look at the sky, making room for the toddler under her arm. Clouds moved across the blue expanse, wind rustling the grass, the edge of the blanket rippling, blond-tipped eyelashes screening the brightness. There was a sense of falling up, deep peace.

Drip. Drip. Rork rearranged his face in the dim crevice. His arm was numb, but he hung onto the feeling of the memory of the woman and child as long as he could. Deirdre's memory of her and her mother, the continuum of Deirdre.

"I dreamed about my mother," said Deirdre in the darkness.

"Yes," said Rork.

"It was so vivid."

"She was the first to come forward." Rork reached for her hand again. "I just knew she had to be your mother."

"What do you mean?"

He linked his fingers in hers. "It's hard to explain. Something in her voice. The crooning way she told her stories, the words skipping off my fingers. The joy."

"Joy?"

"Aye, the joy of you."

Deirdre fell silent. Soon she fell asleep again. Beside her, Rork's eyes closed against the blackness. It wasn't like he even had any kind of choice.

They slept in fits and starts, cocooned in the rock. The pall was high-powered negative energy, negating, taking away, so sleep was necessary, restorative. Rork felt the husk of who he was, used, despondent. Voices of the dead rushed in, the melancholy attracted by the depressed, compelled by the rankest odor. But he realized Deirdre had discovered a secret. Being quiet helped him handle the pall. He imagined himself a small pond, a blue-green pool of water in an open meadow, a grassy clearing. He concentrated on behaving as if he was in fact a tarn and tried not to ripple. He was algae-spiked water, burgeoning with microscopic cell-life. He was water that gradually sloped deeper, the change in light saturation altering shades of blue-green: here dark as hidden cloud, there light as trapped starshine. He experienced the weight of water at the center — buoyancy, emerging bubbles —. It hardly mattered. He felt cradled, super-cooled. His hair floated around his head like orange-y seaweed. Time rewound.

A small woman walked the bluffs overlooking the North Sea, wild, vast and choppy. He knew these people. She wore the boots of house help, worn leather, with tiny eyelets. She skipped along the gravel path, her hands scooped inside the pockets of her pinny, white as the foam washed up by waves. There was the scrim of trail, earth turned over by wind and water. A man in a farm vest walked beside her, self-consciously tall, his upper back stooped. The sea took their laughter. The man walked closer to the woman, who kept her line, eyeing him sideways. Their clothes were threadbare, lived in, the colors of the landscape: gray, shale, cream. The man wore a flat cap, the woman a tight bun with escaping ringlets whipped free by the wind.

The man looped his arm through the woman's. She stopped skipping, enfolding his arm against her chest. In the distance they could see an ocean-going barge, departing the port at Peterhead. A smile tugged the corner of the man's mouth. Beneath the cap he had a high forehead, blue eyes like a streak in the sky, dark lashes. Her eyes were blue, too, improbable like the rock sweeties she loved. When their gazes connected, their lives and their children's lives were decided. The man swept her off her feet, embracing her easily against his chest as if he were hay-baling.

"You have to marry me now, quinie, or I'm going to throw you into the sea," said the man, flat cap knocked to one side rakishly.

Rork knew this story. But whose memory was it? His gran's? His father's father? Did it matter?

"Aye, aye," said his gran, kicking her feet flirtatiously. She liked where she was. "Aye, I will. I will marry you." Waves crashed. At his grandfather's back a plume of sea wind pushed them inexorably into the future.

25: Wonder

THE VOICES IN RORK'S HEAD muttered, reemerging after the pall had unexpectedly disappeared inside the rock fissure. "Did you sleep?" Rork asked Deirdre, gulping too fast, choking. His stomach growled, hungry, hungry, hungry.

"Yes," said Deirdre. "The sounds of your stomach lulled me to sleep. Like gurgling. Like the sea foaming against a rocky shore."

Grunting, Rork sat back up, leaning against the rock wall, his legs stretched out in front of him. Deirdre repositioned her head on his thigh. Rork smoothed her hair away from her forehead.

Deirdre's headband slipped, so she pulled it off. Their hands brushed for an instant. Together they lingered on the seascape dream, hearing the sound of waves. Rork had heard the story of his grandfather's proposal to his gran so often it had become like his own memory. Now Deirdre's, too. This sharing of dreams was becoming a powerful bond between the two of them. Born of the dream's moment, Rork bent down and kissed Deirdre on the lips. He did not move his mouth; he just pressed his parted lips to hers, wondering what she would do. The action made him feel less bleak.

Deirdre reached up and touched his cheek. His beard was sparse but coarse; he could use a shave, his jaw itchy with stubble. It seemed like forever ago when he'd last used a razor. Was it days? A week? Shufftie had clouded his understanding of time. The emotional and physical exertion had also compounded, stacking up, confusing the stamp of time even further.

Deirdre's lips were loamy as a garden. She kissed him back.

Outside the cave was annihilation. Inside the cave was Deirdre and her soft lips.

Rork felt his edges blur, losing distinctness, like he was some new being. The starburst of Deirdre's eyes was a lightshow behind his closed eyelids. They shared puffs of breath. Rork pulled Deirdre up, wrapping his arms around her, and kissed her more. She sat between his legs, so tall in the body they were nose-to-nose. He knew she would always be separate, her own being, but he decided he could spend a lifetime learning more about her. She smelled of sun, new-mown grass, and the tang of sap. He felt wild, kissing her lips, ears, and neck. Her fingers entangled in his hair. He felt her tug.

Rork's body was hot-cold. Holed up in a dank and chill rock space, heat was trapped beneath his skin. There was something starting to happen to Deirdre, too. She was incandescent. Not like he could see in the dark. But it was as if he could see with his other senses, like a starfish with canals of sensation along rays, inching tube feet. There wasn't enough closeness, as his rays, his arms and legs, enfolded Deirdre, rushing in his ears, the heat, bursting from within. He liked kissing, smiled his shadow self, braver than his light-of-day self. Or rather, his half-light-of-Shufftie self.

Rork was dizzy with Deirdre's scent, dispelling the pall's offal stench. His nose was a new kind of organ, ruddering his every gasp. An odyssey within an odyssey, this first love a boat, poised and adrift. He squeezed her tighter. His chest was a secret compartment Deirdre could fit inside. She, too, seemed to be consumed with the fitting. She shed layers of extra clothes, peeling away the nonessential so they could be closer. He sensed the unwinding of scarf, kaleidoscope of whirling color, Deirdre's sharp elbows. He was loath to let her go even for a milli-second. His arms felt lost. But then he felt Deirdre pull at his shirt, untucking it from his trousers. He inhaled sharply with surprise, something else. Rork felt he was reaching the very edge of what language was capable of. He could no longer speak.

Rork's shirt dropped away, was forgotten. He felt different. His lips pressed to Deirdre's. He could not deny biology, but there was also this burning, pressing desire to fit, to match body-to-body, urge-to-urge, skin to skin. C-o-n-n-e-c-t. Rork typed on Deirdre's back, each figurative key flashing a spark in his mind, flinting.

He cared about Deirdre with a capital "C," what she was thinking, what this would mean. But she seemed as propelled as he, the two of them separated by only the thin cotton of his T-shirt and her semmit. Her arms were bare, presenting more skin for him to explore. He wondered about the forget-me-not tattoos, centered on her pulse points.

Oh, oh, oh. Oh, the sensations. Oh, the nearness of her. Oh, he hoped their kissing would go on forever. Oh, if he could only describe what he was feeling.

Now. He had never had such a sense of being in the moment. He was fat in the moment of kissing Deirdre, holding her shoulders, caressing her face, smoothing her hair.

Nearness. The pure, unadulterated elixir of Deirdre: her smell, her touch, her small mammal sounds.

Ears. He heard everything. His heartbeat. Hers. Tremulousness was a silvery ripple down his spine — excruciating, delicious.

Carried away, Deirdre pulled harder on his T-shirt. Rork helped her take it off. Then they worked together on hers. Flesh of his flesh. Gorgeousness was her skin. He couldn't see, but she shivered at the touch of his shadow self.

Tantalizing. Minutes stretched in possibility. Their T-shirts were gone, melted away. Deirdre's long fingers memorized his chest, shoulders, abdomen. He could feel her bare breasts pressed to his chest, the heat of her skin. Deirdre was her shadow-self, too. She peeled him like a plum. They heard the drip of the cave. Drip. Drip. The awfulness hardly mattered. Rork thought of doors opening, creating a new and vibrant world together. Find. A. Way. To. Connect. His gran had said.

Later, cold, Rork's arm half-numb, Deirdre lifted her head, and something unspoken and expansive passed between them.

He pressed his lips lightly to the side of her face, that soft downy spot next to her ear. "You make me possible," he said.

Dierdre turned her face and kissed him once. Hard. Her fingers held his head at the at the nape of his neck. "We make us both possible," she answered, her eyes shuttering.

Every nerve in Rork's body felt energized, aware. He considered his nervous system, his textbook understanding of it, a complex system of sensory information and actions, creating signals between his body and brain.

Rork had a nervous system. Deirdre had a nervous system. His gran. His father. The banshee. Shufftie itself was a kind of nervous system. All interaction with each other in a beautiful, complex network. It was too big a concept for Rork to contain in his mind for long. It slipped, jostling with the voices, leaving Rork to stare at Deirdre's collarbone, which he thought supremely beautiful for some reason. He could create a web show to that collarbone, the way the curves of the bone contrasted with the straps of her undershirt and made him ache.

Although it could have been the hunger.

Or the pall.

Or the infernal drip, drip, drip.

26: Loonie, Loonie, My Loonie

"I'M COLD," SAID DEIRDRE, scrambling to her knees.

Rork could hear her rummage for clothes, the swishing of elbows as she got dressed, the zipper of the pack as she dug for whatever Hamish's pack might offer. He reached for his clothes, too. It was getting colder.

Deirdre held the torch while he attempted to light the camp-stove with their last match. The thing was more delicate that it should have been, given its purpose. Rork held his breath. Thankfully, the thing sparked alight. Rork caught a glimpse of Deirdre. Without the headband, her hair fell forward in loose strands, and her face was smooth.

They didn't have a lot of water left, but they scrounged up enough for half a cup of tea each. The tea was necessary as the temperature continued to plummet. Shufftie weather had proven itself to be rash and unpredictable, especially at the higher levels. Rork was hungry, as usual, but didn't want to mention it. He supposed he could manage with more hardtack, even though it had the texture of plasterboard and stuck in his throat.

His fingers were beginning to ache from the cold. He felt a knob of worry between his shoulder blades. They seemed to be between the proverbial rock and a hard place. He could hear the jangle of a sleeping bag zipper.

"Aren't you cold?" asked Deirdre, her teeth chattering.

"Aye," he said. "I'm perished. Let's both get inside the sleeping bag."

Deirdre acquiesced, but she wasn't exactly comfortable. She was stiff inside the sleeping bag, her forearms a fortress against his chest. He understood she wanted to be left alone — to meditate, let things settle, as she would say — and if they weren't at risk of hypothermia he would have taken himself off in order to give her the solitude she craved, even if he'd had to sit against a dripping wall. As it was, he was quiet and tried not to move. Between them, they created warmth, enough for him to hover in a semi-state between sleep and waking. He hoped they were preserving energy, although his backside was still exposed. Had they really battled through Shufftie and escaped the pall only to freeze to death on the Summits of No Return?

They lay face to face inside the sleeping bag. Deirdre's hair tickled his chin. Rork tried not to shiver. They breathed in synchrony. In. Out. In. Out. Rork wondered if the pall had anything to do with the falling temperatures, the atmospheric impact of powerful negative forces imploding. If all else failed: shutdown. Was the freeze-out retaliatory? Or perhaps he was being fanciful, imagining motivations where none existed. What was the pall anyway?

Images of Deirdre's skin flashed in his mind: their hands intertwined, the curve of her neck, the downy path of fine hair disappearing down her back. Forget me? Forget-me-not? Where was the banshee when they needed her? What kept her away for so long?

Rork had always thought there was something pure about a landscape covered in snow. Rork pictured how it might look outside the rock mass, across the summits. What was it about snow and ice that was so striking?

His gran had been energized by the turn of seasons, signaled by the longest night, All Hallow's Eve. She'd had a boarding house when he was young and cooked an evening meal for the boarders. The final harvest was always a bustle of activity as she put up pickle and chutney, her white head bobbing between kitchen and pantry. He would help, making sure to stay far away from the blasts of steam from the pots. His gran would store the thick-glassed jars in the shed in the back alley. He would be entrusted with a jar or two and remembered how important he'd felt, the bracing contrast of air between the kitchen and yard, the crunch of hardening ground, the layer of ice on the few remaining leaves of the plum tree, the dry stonework of the shed. Thanks to his Pinny-Full Project, he still had most of her cherished recipes.

Rork and Deirdre's breaths plumed in the frigid air. When Deirdre turned over, Rork closed the space between them, pulling the sleeping bag tighter around their spooning bodies, her long spine to his breastbone. Inside his eyelids he saw the imprint of her forget-me-nots. He imagined slow kisses down the length of her backbone, lingering on each bony protrusion. He flickered between his selves — self, shadow-self, self — losing energy. A creeping stupor stole into him. His hands settled on the sun of Deirdre's belly. He lifted a finger but couldn't summon the vitality to finish typing the word. What would he have typed? He couldn't remember. He wasn't uncomfortable, but his limbs felt bound by cold, maw of deepest sleep opening wider. It would be so easy to give up, slip away, let go of whatever it was that bound him to the present, to the banshee, to Deirdre. Damn the pall. Rork dreamed of snow and bandages.

Snow was a bandage, layer upon layer, shrouding. He drifted away from himself, sinking into a subconscious realm, brooding. He remembered having scarlet fever as a boy. He recalled he couldn't escape the furnace, the sound of his own blood in his ears. He'd been so hot he was cold, so hot his skin had blistered, peeling off his fingers. He remembered the floating face of his gran, nursing him. She had called to him in her singsong voice. He was covered in a rash. His skin was rough as sandpaper, sloughing off as if it did not belong to him. She had crooned, "Loonie, loonie, my loonie." The softest parts of him had been brittle, on the verge of shattering. It had ached to move, his throat barbed with pleas for relief. He'd been young, not fully understanding what was wrong with him.

"Loonie, loonie, my loonie." She dabbed a cool cloth on his forehead, dabbing the sides of his face, a poultice of aloe and other soothing herbs.

He smelled brine. He fought for consciousness. Sleep was a spider, spinning a web with its sticky strands. The doctors had taken blood. He hadn't cared what they did. He was infected with bacteria. Finally, they had figured out what was wrong. Strep-to-coc-cal. He hadn't learned to type yet. The bacteria produced a siege of toxins. This bad army was in charge, as destructive as the pall. His blood echoed the noise of their stomping boots.

Hamish had visited every day, sitting with him quietly, drawing.

"Loonie, loonie, my loonie."

He must have been delirious, muttering about the 'bad army' in his sleep. Hamish gave him a drawing: "Rork Fighting the Bad Army." Rork missed Hamish, the Hamish-before-he-lost-his-parents Hamish, that quiet companionship. "Rork Fighting the Bad Army" was Rork's screensaver. Before the tragedy, Hamish had had a unique ability. Deirdre possessed it, too. The capability to just be. B-e. His gran had been the master.

"Loonie, loonie, my loonie."

The maturation of year after year, filling the moments with her quiet presence. He had such a sense of her.

"Loonie, loonie, my loonie."

Half-dreaming, Rork thought he heard something in the distance, but he couldn't seem to move. He was numb with cold. An insistence like an ember of light in a tiny corner of his mind beckoned.

"Loonie, loonie, my loonie."

He tried to stir inside the sleeping bag. It sounded like his gran, but he was afraid to hope. Would the banshee really live up to her promise?

"Loonie, loonie, my loonie."

Once again, he fought for consciousness, peeling back layer upon layer of sleep. He thought he heard the chink of metal, a careful tread. His gran had had a pet rabbit she kept in the shed. It would hop out when it heard his gran's footsteps in the gravel. It recognized her walk. His gran had made a pet of the rabbit, its elongated back feet moving like a comma in the back alley.

"Loonie, loonie, my loonie."

Rork grew impatient with himself, his inability to make the simplest thing happen. Like move. Like emerge from the sleeping bag. He dreaded the terrible cold.

Deirdre elbowed him in the ribs.

Rork saw a light wavering on the jagged walls of rock mass. The light illuminated beyond the tight crevice where they huddled, where the shifting of rock created a slightly larger opening, jagged ceiling rising at a steep slant. Not expansive, but navigable by a slighter person. His tongue felt thick. He thought he saw the shadow of his gran, her bobbing pin-curled head. He couldn't feel his fingers or his toes.

"Loonie, loonie, my loonie."

She was so near he swore he could smell her baby powder. It was her one vanity. With a girlish puff, she powdered the varicose veins of her nose. There was something about the seascape village where they lived that caused veins to erupt on the skin of residents, dark red tributaries visible on cheeks and noses.

Light gathered. Was he delirious? He teetered, boyish and glad. How he always felt around his gran. Joyous. In her presence he felt lit from within. He listened for more footfalls on the crushed stones.

If there ever was an antidote to the pall…

In the flickering, Deirdre looked trapped by cold and the sleeping bag. Rork saw her eyes flit about, searching for the source of the steps moving towards them. Freezing, immobile, entombed in a rock edifice of negative energy and bone-sapping cold, Rork gave her what he hoped was a reassuring smile.

"Loonie, loonie, my loonie."

His gran swung her light, breaching the seam of rock. His gran! All four feet eleven inches of her. Strong like before she got sick. Rork tried to get up but couldn't. He groaned, speechless. The walls dripped, glinting in a cascade of lantern light. Rork could hear the lantern handle's squeak as his gran set it down on the ground. In its light she crawled through the crevice to kneel near him. She put her hand to the top of his head. Deirdre's, too. His eyes swung to her face. He could smell her powdered freshness. Or maybe his memory of it. When she turned, the lantern light reflected on her round wire-rim glasses. Her smile was a benediction of wrinkles, scrunched nose, blue sugar of her eyes.

"Loonie, loonie, my loonie."

"Gran," croaked Rork. "You found us." His throat was parched, his body shuddery from cold. His gran was wearing every outer garment he remembered, including fur-topped boots and red wool coat. Her pinny peeked out from beneath the coat, rooster-patterned.

"Aye, Rork. The banshee saved the best citation for last." She chuckled deep in her throat.

"Is there a way out? What about the pall?" asked Rork, feeling a prisoner in his own body.

Her arms pinned beneath her, Deirdre's gray eyes watched Rork's gran feel about the crevice.

"Och," said his gran, "that dark soul?" Her voice cut in and out as she explored. "Aye, he's still skulking about."

Suddenly she was in his ear again, his gran, whispering. "Loonie, can you crawl? Help the quinie?" He thought he was dreaming. The cold had hooks in him. He struggled to move.

His limbs felt leaden. With what felt like superhuman effort, he got himself to a sitting position. Only for his gran. Then to his knees, slipping out of the sleeping bag. He began to crawl. Once in motion the momentum of movement seemed to help. He willed it to happen, and his body began to respond. His fingers twitched. Mind to body, he thought, but didn't type. Then he helped Deirdre, encouraging her to her knees, folding up the sleeping bag and collecting their scant things in the pack.

His gran crawled ahead to the lantern, raising it to better assess the space they were in.

Rork and Deirdre moved on all fours to her, getting to their unsteady and numb feet. He and Deirdre could only stoop under the angled rock ceiling. He looked at his gran, her downy white hair, the look in her eyes. He felt weak with missing her, loving her. Tears sprung to his eyes.

His gran held her arms wide. "Give us a hug," she said. The lantern at her feet cast an arc of light around her small figure.

Rork dove into her opened arms. She squeezed him mercilessly.

"I can't breathe," he gasped, laughing.

"Aye," said his gran. "No apologies for loving. I will seize this moment." His gran turned to Deirdre. "You, too, quinie." Deirdre was squeezed around her middle until she motioned for release.

Once they recaptured their breaths, Rork's gran explained, "The pall is the absolute worst kind of ghost. Exiled and allowed to wander, extracting lesser ghosts, amassing dark energy." His gran clucked, her breath misting in the meager lantern light. "The worst kind of human becomes the worst kind of ghost."

"Are we stuck here?" asked Rork.

"No, it's not as hopeless as that." Her hand rustled in a pocket of her pinny. She pulled out two wrapped candies. "Sweetie?" she asked.

"Yes, please," said Rork, who bent down and kissed her wrinkled cheek.

"Thank you," said Deirdre, unwrapping the candy.

His gran also unwrapped a third candy, putting it carefully in her mouth. "Now come and look at this," she said.

She led them deeper into the rock mass, holding the lantern as high as she could, so they could pick their steps over the rock-strewn floor, clouds of their breaths billowing about their heads. The way was narrow and low, and they moved in a single line. Rork's gran brought them to an interior seam where the rock veered away from their feet. The rock had eroded over time — by pall or shuddering or both — creating smaller caves. There were caves within caves like catacombs. Intricate carvings covered the walls of these smaller caves.

"Oh," said Deirdre, squeezing Rork's arm, her head and shoulders hunched.

Rork took the lantern from his gran and reached it out, shedding more light on the drawings. He saw pictographs — animals, plants, other objects of early life, bowls, fire — inside large wheels, spiraling inside and around each other in an extraordinary and mystic design. Although Rork had seen remnants of similar drawings on the standing stones dotted around their village, he had never seen so many drawings in one place.

Rork trailed his fingers over the raised stone, reading the drawings like Braille. He couldn't explain the designs, how they made sense in some archetypal way. They were deeply familiar. A chorus of voices sprung to life in his head, chanting. The moving cadence of words, the porous texture of the rock, and the sure lines of the pictographs joined Rork to an ancient life force, filled with joy, triumphs, sadness, and pain.

Rork found a shelf for the lantern. His gran touched him on the inside of his forearm. He held Deirdre by the elbow. By necessity, Rork was learning the ways and means of survival — how to refocus his every waking moment to staying alive in Shufftie. But this was *else*. He felt the wall. It connected him to something bigger than himself. Was it love? L-o-v-e? Or G-o-d? Or B-l-i-s-s? He felt compelled to type, but he hesitated, the out of himself-ness giving him pause.

"Is it a message?" asked Deirdre. She bent over the coiled notebook and sketched the plant symbols, repeating their botanical names. *Asplenium bulbiferum* (mother fern). *Semper virens* (evergreen). She squinted in the partial light. Rork knew she felt keenly how narrowly they'd escaped the pall's tomb of rock mass.

"There are many Shuffties," said his gran. "Wee shifts. One degree left or right: Shufftie, Shufftie, Shufftie." She held Rork's hand briefly with her own. "We leave behind our stories, what we want remembered."

Rork, Deirdre, and his gran made a half circle. His gran tugged on his shirttail for emphasis. "We are reverberations of our other lives," she said. "We apprehend based on what we already know."

His gran crinkled another candy wrapper. "If we can only get out of the way of ourselves, we can get a clearer view of the writing on the wall."

Rork thought about the obstacle of himself, how by escaping himself he'd discovered Boo, and Deirdre, and a journey he didn't ask for, but needed, that reunited him with his gran and her wisdom.

Gran pulled away and crouched inside one of the smaller caves. The ground was wet with melting frost, and the brighter light in the distance made it shimmer. She rubbed her hands together. "This is where I arrived in your Shufftie, and although I'm not much of a spelunker," she said, in her understated way, "this looks like the way."

Incised in the rock of the smaller cave was the word "EPIPHANY," surrounded by more symbols, etched into the stone.

"I think I have a memory of you catching moonlight in a jar," said Deirdre, focused on Rork's gran, crouched in the cave.

Gran's round eyes got rounder, her forehead wrinkling in marvel. Rork explained in shorthand, "River of Forgetting. Shared and recovered memories. I typed the memories."

His gran stood up, looking from Rork to Deirdre. "You *typed* the memories?" she asked.

"Aye," said Rork, his fingers twitching reflexively. "Voices came to me, recalling images, experiences, memories, and I typed, impressing them onto her body."

"My mother, we think," offered Deirdre, "my grandparents. Others who knew me."

"Och, me," said his gran, opening and closing her hands in the pockets of her pinny. She spoke to the catacombs wonderingly. "See," she said. "We can't help ourselves. We must share our stories, our internal knowledge."

She trained her eyes on Deirdre. "Yes, quinie, I did that. The kind of life you have is what you choose to believe, I think. Memories are our stepping stones." The creases in her face orchestrated a smile from Rork's childhood, and then his gran moved forward on all fours in her thick tights and crawled into the Epiphany.

27: Beyond the Edge of Self

"NO DAWDLING, LOON," said his gran. "Keep moving."

Rork's breath huffed out in front of his face, adding to the discomfort he was feeling. He wasn't so sure he trusted epiphanies. The rock was a strange amalgam hewn of time and pressure and something indefinable. Water? A hidden river? He swore he could hear water, the rush of it. He worried about Deirdre. Would the sound of water in the rock bring back her experience with the River of Forgetting? But she seemed unperturbed, her curiosity piqued by his gran. A hidden river would explain the inexplicable drip down the wall.

His hands were freezing. He wished he had gloves. Also, the rock was so damp they'd probably be useless in a matter of minutes. Deirdre was exhaling into her hands, trying to warm them up. He looked back at her apologetically. Cryptic-smile. They continued on their knees: Rork, his gran, Deirdre. A reverential threesome.

Rork knew they were leaving the rock mass. He followed light in front of them. It seemed different than the monochromatic Shufftie gray they'd learned to tolerate. There was color! Only the blue-green section of the spectrum, but still a solace to his eyes.

Then Rork saw shades of color he'd never seen before — ancient, primeval — like blue rust thrust up from the center of the rock. Even in his own head that sounded farfetched. Maybe he wasn't thinking so clearly. His stomach growled. He couldn't remember when he'd last had a meal. He remembered the sheen of Deirdre's skin and smiled. He didn't know how much more his knees could take. He wondered at his gran, leading the way. He could forget the images of her sick and weak. The hues of blue-green made him think of a peacock's tail, eyes on an iridescent background. A rare few of the birds roamed the gardens at the castle in his village. When they opened their tails, the tourists would clap.

It was getting colder, if that was possible. A ream of ice seemed to have infiltrated the cracks in the rock. Rork pulled the sleeves of his flannel shirt down over his hands. His nose dripped. He rubbed it against the sleeve of his shirt, a maneuver he wasn't particularly proud of but served its purpose. They continued to crawl on their hands and knees, wincing from the cold and sharp stone. There wasn't much conversation.

They entered a cathedral of rock where light pooled, and there was space enough to stand. Rork's knees balked as he tried to stand up straight. He walked his hands up the nearest wall for support. Gradually, his knees became less stiff, and he flexed his legs.

The walls were ornamented with sculptured layers of molten-looking rock. It gave the appearance of monolithic sconces. The cavern was tall and wide, suffused with the blue-green light streaked around them. The large cavern had a wide opening like a bowl. Rork heard trees swishing, rock skittering, and distant water.

Rork helped his gran. She leaned on his forearm.

"Thanks, loonie," she said, plucking at her tights and tsking at the state of them.

He went to Deirdre. She put her hands in his. His hands covered hers completely. He typed quickly on the soft skin of her inner wrist: D-e-i-r-d-r-e.

Together they looked out of the bowl. This was where the Epiphany had brought them. After his eyes adjusted to the brighter light, he saw dense gray summits blanketed in snow and low cloud cover drifting along a horizon pierced by jagged peaks. They were at the edge of something, although he couldn't make out exactly what it was.

"It's beautiful," said Deirdre, "and terrible."

"It feels… beyond the edge of self," said Rork.

Where had that come from? The words startled him.

"Aye," said his gran, peering over.

Rork scanned the horizon, looking for a waymarking.

"There's no signpost here," said his gran. "This one you have to feel, loonie." She patted his chest three times with the flat of her hand and then leaned her ear against his breastbone like she could hear his far seas like a seashell. He drew breath. She was carried on his chest like a wave. Rork felt expansive, wedged between his gran and Deirdre, past and future.

The cloud cover shifted along the horizon's rim, revealing, not revealing. The cloud cleared for an instant, and they could glimpse the next peak on the far side of a ridge. It looked closer than it probably was. There was another bowl cavern, from which cascaded an aquamarine waterfall. The rush of water was the source of the blue-green streaking light, but what was more extraordinary was the sight of the waterfall not fully reaching the valley of the summits. It ended mid-air, leaving a gap of emptiness in the sky as though it was chopped off. Beneath was whiteness. Sheer. Brilliant. Whiteness.

"What th—?" said Rork.

"What, loon?" asked his gran. "What the inexplicable? What the miracle?" She stepped out into a drift of snow, arms outstretched. "Look," she said.

In the foaming water, Rork read: LEAP OF FAITH.

He swallowed what felt like his tongue. "You want us to jump?" he croaked.

His gran rocked from foot to foot, her hands deep in the pockets of her pinny. "Aye," she said, her eyes crinkling.

Deirdre's eyes were huge, feltish.

"Isn't there another way?" asked Rork, his throat dry. They'd only just survived the pall, and the River of Forgetting. Apparently, they'd been only practice. Could they survive another extreme experience? A leap into empty space?

"Maybe. Maybe not," said his gran. "The banshees only care about passing from plane to plane. A waterfall does that. Bryonna is impatient."

"I noticed," muttered Rork, trying to comprehend, but in Shufftie they had faced one fantastic thing after another. And now jumping was a way out? Hadn't the old clerk advised them that "going out was really a going in"? Perhaps a Leap of Faith made sense. Yet he had no desire, having found Deirdre, of risking it all. Rork's thoughts were in chaos, in an endless loop:

His gran.

Deirdre.

His computer.

His dad's acceptance.

Stranded thoughts that confused him. He didn't know what to think, or feel, and his confusion got tangled up in the notion of leaving Shufftie and its monotone otherworldliness. The guiding knowledge of his gran. The promise of a new direction with Deirdre. A return to himself with the recovery of his computer, and the freedom of his father's acceptance. Would a leap into the unknown really remove them from Shufftie? And what would happen to his gran? He'd just found her. Rork was both grateful and annoyed with the banshee. If she was so impatient, why wasn't she here?

Silently, Deirdre came to stand behind him, resting her chin on his shoulder. Rork felt her, but neither said anything. His gran stood in a halo of light. Soon he knew he would have to say goodbye to her. Again. Even though she was only a citation, she felt real to him. He clenched his jaw, typing m-i-s-s y-o-u on the coarse fabric of his trousers.

"Loonie," she cocked her head, "I am with you," she said softly. "Every place we've been, every skill I've taught you, what you've taught me. Every smile. Every embrace. Every memory. There I am. There we are together."

Rork went to her and stood awkwardly. She smoothed the flannel of his shirt. Finally, they hugged again, Rork curved in half like an apostrophe.

"I'm running out of time," said his gran, tucked beneath his arm.

"Must you go?" asked Rork.

"Aye, I have more to learn about dying."

He made a noise, stiffened.

"Och, it's not so bad," she nudged. "I have a plum tree."

As a boy in short pants, the plum tree next to the shed in the garden behind his gran's boarding house had been his oasis. When upset or frustrated — usually because of some altercation with his father — he would dangle his legs from one of the tree's twisted branches until his gran would entice him back inside with sweet tea and a story.

Rork looked past the summits, at the ruins of trees, withered and deformed, creating haunting outlines against the whiteness. There were peaks, snow, desperate trees, and very little forgiveness in between, except for the plume of blue-green from the waterfall.

"You can see your way now, can't you, loonie?"

Rork sighed with his whole being. "Aye, gran. Aye."

"A wee shift makes all the difference. You can do it."

Rork had a sharp sense of déjà vu from his youthful schoolboy days, dutifully doing his homework at the kitchen table, knowing his gran had secret knowledge.

"Wait," said Deirdre, "don't go."

His gran turned to her. "What is it, quinie?"

Deirdre opened her hand to reveal a flower, resting in her palm, a delicate cluster of five rounded petals, hairy leaves, tessellated center.

Rork's gran touched it delicately with one finger.

"Forget-Me-Not," explained Deirdre. Tremulous smile.

"Aye, quinie," said his gran, touching her cheek. "Rare."

Rork's gran turned back to him, and they stood together at the precipice. She held him around the waist. He gave her upper arm a squeeze, overwhelmed by her presence and the the view. What he'd wished for. What he'd dreamed of. His gran had helped him leave the pall behind. He hoped their reconnection would sustain him. He felt for the flash drive in his pocket.

"I lost the sixpence," he confessed. Her opinion meant everything to him.

She blinked up at him. "Did you mean to lose it?"

"No," he said. "How can you ask me that?"

"We don't always know why we do things." She rubbed his back.

Rork thought about it. Far off he heard the gathering steam of what sounded like a teakettle. Could that be?

"That's my signal," said his gran, starting to fade around the edges. "I'm sure the sixpence will turn up." Her fading face crinkled in an irrepressible smile. "I did."

"A teakettle?" asked Rork.

"Aye," said his gran. "It seemed fitting."

Rork swallowed around the lump in his throat. He missed the haven of her kitchen. The teakettle began to shrill.

"Love you."

"I love you, too, loon. Think of me whenever you hear the whistle."

"I will, gran. I will." He thought of their battered teakettle. The countless cups of tea she'd made him.

Rork watched her disappear, leaving him alone on the ledge. His arms felt empty, and he felt moisture on his face from the waterfall, or maybe it was something else. He typed g-o-o-d-b-y-e, looking for Deirdre, resolving to get home, so he could maybe mend things with his father and hear that battered teakettle's whistle again.

28: Sacrifice

AS RORK AND DEIRDRE skittered down the cavern bluff towards the ridge to the Leap of Faith, Rork was distracted, replaying his gran's fading away. She believed he could finish the assignment and get through Shufftie. He was feeling bereft, wondering if he truly had the potential in him, which was how he came to miss the banshee sitting on a ledge.

Deirdre stopped, and he bumped into her.

"What?" he asked. "What's wrong?"

Deirdre gestured towards Boo, and Rork turned his head, scowling. He found it easier to be angry than sad.

"And here I thought you'd be glad to see me," said Boo. She waggled one of her slippers, glowing against the rocky prominence.

"It's about time you showed up," said Rork. The sound of water grew louder. He drank what was left of the canteen. "You left us with the pall!" He wiped his mouth, narrowing his eyes.

"I couldn't help it!" replied the banshee, a little huffy, her lower lip protruding. "Wait a minute. Didn't your gran come?"

"Yes," said Rork, angrily.

Boo sighed, floating down reluctantly to the hillside. "You could show a little more gratitude."

Rork glared at her. Then his eyes rested on Deirdre. How had she gotten involved in all this? He was shocked that he hadn't considered that before. She was so beautiful and independent and *gifted*. He felt as close to her now as his gran. His gran. Even in death she watched over him, coming to rescue them from the pall in the rock mass.

"You're right," said Rork, still scowling, grateful to be alive but feeling so many other emotions, too. He didn't understand the banshee, her comings and goings. All her energies seemed to be put into channeling others. Was that what she was practicing in Shufftie?

Rork and Deirdre picked their way down the descent to the ledge. Rork carried Hamish's pack, quickly becoming depleted, knees straining against the decline. He glared at the banshee. She hovered over his left shoulder, glancing briefly at the plummet of water. Into nothingness.

"Technically," said Boo, ignoring Rork's challenging mood, "the pall is not really a ghost." She pulled her long, unearthly hair to one side, out of the way of the rush of water. Backsplash from the falls filled the air with droplets as they moved nearer the thunder of it.

"Not a ghost?" asked Deirdre, glancing at Rork.

"No," said Boo. "He was a banshee, one of us, but he failed to earn his hood. After repeated attempts, he threatened his advisor. So, he was sent away, banished. He's the ghost of a banshee. He no longer belongs anywhere. He's vengeful and occupies his eternity extracting souls. Over the millennia, he has morphed into absolute soullessness. A supernova of emptiness."

"Banished to Shufftie?" mouthed Deirdre.

"Shufftie is just one of our simulations. He could turn up anywhere."

"Exiled," whistled Rork. He tried to get his mind around what that might mean. "No wonder he's so pissed off. But he's dangerous! Deirdre and I could have died back there."

"Yes, his banishment could have been handled differently. My mother wasn't CEO then."

Rork harrumphed, feeling far removed from banshee affairs, although he was intrigued about Boo's mother. He stepped carefully, bending his knees to absorb the descent, a flash of reflection in his periphery.

"Unfortunately, he has insider banshee knowledge and knows our weaknesses," Boo continued. "He created a black vortex. I couldn't find you in the rock mass. I couldn't even see you on the heatmap. I tried and tried and tried. He kept obscuring the readings. Some call him the Un-messenger." She crossed her arms defensively. "Do you know how many mountains there are in Shufftie?"

"No," said Rork. "How many?"

"Too many," she retorted. "And the pall has created more in his banishment. Just to mess with us."

"How did my gran find us?" asked Rork.

"She had something you gave her. It helped guide her to you."

"Something I gave her? She didn't mention that. Do you know what it was?" asked Rork.

"Some locket or other," said the banshee.

"Locket?" Rork ran his fingers through his hair. "I gave her a necklace when I was a wee bairn. It wasn't much, had a chain like dog tags. Do you mean she kept it all these years?"

"She must have," said Deirdre.

Rork rubbed his eyes gruffly. He was stiff with anger and sadness and the exertion of climbing down the bluff. He remembered what his gran said. She was with him in every memory. He saw her ahead in her pinny, erect, alert, turning towards him with an encouraging smile.

The banshee was mesmerized by the falls. She couldn't seem to look away. Moisture collected in her hair and glittered. "All that power," she said, to no one in particular.

Deirdre tugged at the pack on Rork's back. He let it slip to the ground. She rearranged the contents, making the spare items more compact. She handed him the last crumbling square of hardtack. He chewed thoughtfully.

Rork could see the ridge now. It had a railing on one side and a low dyke on the other. The bluff disappeared on either side. Rork smacked at his jeans. Traversing the ridge would not be easy. They were tired, hungry, dusty, and slightly damp. He tried to ignore his nerves. The voices in his head soothed.

"There are certain plants that thrive in the vicinity of waterfalls," offered Deirdre.

Rork peered at the waterfall apprehensively. It was a relentless surge out of a rock bowl. They picked their way forward, close enough now to get a truer measure of how powerful it really was. The bluff they'd been shouldering disappeared, leaving them exposed to the cold from the mist off the falls and the dizzying emptiness of its huge height. The only way forward was the ridge and a precarious collar of rock that would take them over to the Leap of Faith. He could see switchbacks on the other side, rising to the precipice at the top of the falls. Did water normally flow at such high altitudes? If he'd had his computer, he'd research their geologic situation. But he didn't have his computer. His fingers typed on air, searchingly.

Perhaps it was worth chancing the leap. His gran had seemed to encourage that, and she had never steered him wrong in his life. Perhaps if he and Deirdre were insane enough to leap toward where the falls disappeared into nothingness life would go back to normal. *What was normal?* Perhaps he'd be reunited with his computer, and he'd be able to organize his feelings.

His eyes found Dierdre, and her colors cheered him, even dulled by dust and ordeal, their last few days in Shufftie, the rock mass, their limited options in apparel after they'd lost their backpacks. They'd only taken the basics from Hamish and Charboy's backpacks. Deirdre wore the sweatshirt and scarf like some kind of Bohemian fairy.

Would he continue to see her if they found normality again? Could there be normality without her? Where did she come from? Would his life be split? Before Shufftie? After Shufftie? He knew her family originated from the islands, and she called herself "the storyteller's daughter," but where had the banshee found her? He didn't know so many things. Was she at university? On break? Stuck in Shufftie instead of some botanic other life? What would his father think of her?

Rork's thoughts would have continued to unreel in this manner if they hadn't been pulled up short at the sight looming in front of them. Beck, Charboy, and Hamish blocked their access to the ridge. Somehow, they had climbed up from below the ridge. How was that even possible? It seemed superhuman. Rork looked at Beck, his face hard and stony. It was doubtful he played fair. Hamish's sweatshirt hood covered his face. He looked down, clutching a gnarled stick. Charboy smoldered in his fingerless leather gloves. Beck had a strange kind of cape draped around his thick neck, made of heavy material, peppered with holes.

Damn, thought Rork. Damn, damn, damn. Why did they have to show up now?

The banshee floated down to the ground. She gritted her teeth. The air started to crackle. "Get out of our way," she seethed.

"Ha!" said Beck. "We will take it from here." He sneered at Boo. "You didn't really think you'd beat me to the leap, did you?"

"How did you find us?" spat Boo through clenched teeth.

"Oh," said Beck, "I had access to your lesson plan from the first time you tried to earn your hood." His smugness was palpable enough to be a third person. "You should have changed it up. You are so predictable. Even Hamish here could have figured it out, and he has turned out to be a less than useful member of the team. Doesn't have the stomach for it."

Hamish retreated further into his hood.

Rork questioned Boo with a look.

"You didn't know this was her second attempt?" Beck asked Rork. He turned to Boo, "Something you neglected to tell them? And you say *I'm* underhanded?"

"I would have told them," snapped Boo. "Eventually." She bristled, inhaling deeply, preparing to fight Beck at a sonar level.

"Now, now," said Beck, snapping the cape loose from around his neck and draping it around his shoulders. The garment had a high collar. In it, Beck looked like a bat-banshee. "Like my acoustic invisibility cloak?" he asked. "Your infernal caterwauling will not get to me this time. Prepare to fail a second time!"

Beck motioned to Charboy. Charboy flicked an ember of fire towards Deirdre. It caught her on the hem of her shirt and flared into flame. She dropped to her knees and scooped loose dirt from the path onto the flames, tamping the fire with the flat of a large stone. The fire was out in seconds but left an acrid odor in the air.

Deirdre stood, looking furious, gripping the rock in her fingers. Her headband had slipped off and hung around her neck. She moved suddenly, her hair swinging forward, and with a shot-putter's aim, she flung the rock. It struck Charboy on the side of his head, near his temple. With a stare of astonishment, he teetered and fell to the ground like a charred chunk of wood.

The banshee laughed gleefully. "She beaned him. She really beaned him!"

"Get them!" said Beck to Hamish.

"You said no one would get hurt," said Hamish defiantly.

"You useless piece of shit," said Beck. Framed by the high collar of the acoustic cape, Beck's face contorted, his mouth making an ugly shape. Rork felt pressure between his ears, but he didn't hear anything. Boo, however, screamed, clutching at her ears.

"Stop, stop," she said, backing away until prevented from going farther by the bluff. Boo cowered, her feet continuing to peddle backwards.

Hamish hung back. It was clear he didn't want to fight. Charboy was out of commission, at least temporarily, which meant the real fight was with Beck. Rork looked at Boo, incapacitated by whatever Beck was doing to her. She looked helpless, and Beck gloated over her. Rork knew it was him or them. There was no truce with Beck. He would win, and he would win at someone else's expense, if he had the choice. They had to get past him, but how could they bring him down?

Alone, Rork was no match for Beck. Beck was bigger and much, much stronger. And a banshee. Deirdre aimed another stone at him, but he easily deflected it with one of his large forearms. "You'll have to do better than that, lassie," he ground out snidely.

Deirdre pressed her lips together, scouting the area. Plant life was scarce but not non-existent. Beck was focused on tormenting Boo and keeping a hold on his cape. It was stiff and unwieldy, forcing Beck to adjust his grip repeatedly.

Rork was on the higher ground, so with a running start he launched himself at Beck, wrapping his arms around Beck and the cape from behind. Somehow Beck managed to throw him off. Rork landed with a thud. He skittered dangerously toward the drop off that plunged below them. He scrambled to his feet while Beck struggled some more with the cape. It was crazy he was so worried about a dumb cape in the middle of a life and death struggle.

Deirdre crouched near Rork, fingering the waxy leaves of some kind of weed. "Do it again," she motioned to Rork.

Boo had collapsed against the bluff face, insensible, her delicate features seamed with pain.

Determined, Rork took a couple of steps backwards and threw himself again on Beck's back, this time holding Beck around the neck in a one-armed headlock. He tried to drive Beck toward the bluff face rather than toward the drop off into nothingness. He couldn't believe he had the courage — or madness — to do what he was doing. Beck spun back and forth, trying to loosen Rork's hold, but Rork hung on, using his other arm as a lever. Deirdre tossed a handful of dirt into Beck's face. Beck clawed at his eyes with his free arm.

Hamish cursed, pushed back the hood of his sweatshirt, and threw himself into the fray. But to Rork's surprise, Hamish sided with him and Deirdre, grappling with Beck.

Beck groaned at the weight of both Rork and Hamish, swaying like a huge humpbacked beast. "You, you –" he bellowed at Hamish. "You'll pay!"

Deirdre dragged a trail in the dirt, and the waxy gypsyweed snaked across the dry soil towards the thrashing Beck, winding its woody stalk around and around his ankles. Beck staggered and tumbled headfirst with a heavy "oomph." Beck, Rork, and Hamish rolled down the slope in a three-headed jumble towards the ridge and the huge drop off into nothingness.

Rork was caught between Hamish and Beck, both pulling at him as they bowled towards the ridge's disappearing point. Beck at last cast aside the useless cape and clutched Rork's arm with a vice-like grip. He held Hamish's hood with the other as they bounced forcibly in a downward heap. Dust and small stones skittered around them. The disappearing point got nearer and nearer, but Rork tried to hang onto sense. As they careened towards nothingness, he heard his gran whisper in his ear, "Don't lose your head, loon." He also felt Deirdre willing him not to panic as she ran after them.

Momentum caused them to fall faster and faster, somersaulting end over end. Rork's shirt rode up, exposing his skin to the sharp lacerations of rock. He knew he had to break Beck's hold and get back the use of his arms. On the next rotation, he kicked out with all his might and landed his instep in Beck's solar plexus. After years of forced participation, he wasn't much of a soccer player, much to his father's disappointment, but he did have something of a leg.

Beck yowled and let go of Rork's arm. Untangled from the others, Rork continued to roll, but with the use of his arms he was able to stretch out his full length — long arms and long legs — levering himself against the pull of gravity, braking with all ten fingers against the ground.

Beck and Hamish continued to barrel towards the ridge. Hamish, slighter than Beck, was tossed around like a chew toy. At full tilt, Beck banged into the pylon anchoring a small railing at the ridge's edge. A resounding crash echoed.

Rork found himself snagged on carpet grass. He dug in his heels to stop himself from sliding any farther. Deirdre caught up to him and held onto his legs.

Beck's body was twisted and mangled around the pylon, against which he'd slammed hideously, but he'd still managed to hang onto Hamish. The base of the railing buckled under Beck's weight. Poor, tragic Hamish, tethered to Beck by the hood of his sweatshirt, sailed away from him past the disappearing point in a slow arc and then hung in the empty air beneath the ridge. Below him was pure, white blankness.

"No!" yelled Rork, lurching towards the edge. Hamish hung limply, his sweatshirt hiked up around his ears. "Pull him up!" he yelled to Beck.

Beck just sneered, head cocked at an awkward angle. The railing continued to collapse around him. Caught on the pylon, he sloped towards his outstretched arm, on the end of which hung wretched Hamish. "Fat chance," he said.

"You'll *both* go over," said Rork.

Beck looked at him fatally. "Somebody has to die."

"No, nobody has to die." Rork crawled over the lip of the disappearing point. From his knees, he tried to reach Hamish but couldn't. Hamish dangled too low.

"Hamish," urged Rork. "crawl up his arm!"

Hamish looked at him, a lock of hair over one eye. "Can't." The chain on his trousers jangled.

"Why not?" asked Rork.

"Spent."

"No, no," said Rork. "Fight."

Hamish was silent, sunk in his sweatshirt.

"Hamish! Hamish!" yelled Rork.

"I'm sorry I wasn't a better friend," Hamish said from the folds of sweatshirt. "I just missed them, you know?"

"I know," said Rork.

Behind them on the ridge, they could hear Charboy starting to moan, returning to consciousness.

"Pull him up!" Rork yelled at Beck.

Beck began to swing Hamish, turning him back and forth. Towards the ridge, away from the ridge and towards emptiness. Rork turned helplessly to Deirdre who had come up behind him. She clutched Boo under one arm, who drooped, panting for breath.

As Hamish swung out and back, his face was a mask of horror and hope, horror and hope. Horror as he swung away from the ridge and pylon, and hope as he swung near. The sweatshirt started to strain, pulling away from Hamish's shoulders and arms. Hamish clawed desperately with his one free hand, finally fighting to survive. But it wasn't enough.

The look on his face when Hamish realized the inevitable — he was out of strength. He was out of options. In horrible slow motion, they all watched as Hamish slipped out of the hoodie and disappeared into the white nothingness below. That deathly expression on his face. His eyes closed. He did not make a sound.

"N-o-o-o-o!" yelled Rork. He dropped to his knees, his head brushing the ground. Poor Hamish. They could have been friends again. They could have. Rork could have given him new memories to ease his grief. Rork pounded the ground with a fist. "No, no, no!" He turned to look at Beck, eyes blazing.

Beck tried to rise but couldn't. He slumped against the piling. "Somebody had to die," he repeated.

"No, no," said Rork, looking at Boo. "The banshee said nobody had to die."

Boo looked stricken and pressed her lips together. She avoided looking at Rork directly. "I'm sorry, Rork," she said, hoarsely. Rork could hear the regret in her voice. "I never said *nobody* would die. Somebody did have to die."

"But you promised." But then Rork thought back to the tea shop and an awful truth descended on him.

The banshee shook her head as if reading his mind. "I said *you and Deirdre* wouldn't die. I didn't say anything about others. I was careful not to, and you never asked. I might not have told you the whole truth, but I am not a liar. It was the reason I failed the first time. I couldn't do it." Her knees started to tremor, and Deirdre clutched her more firmly around the waist. The banshee trembled. "I guess I have you to thank," she grimaced at Beck. "Enjoy it, because I am going to report you for using open channel against me. You know it's not allowed."

Rork saw a hint of her characteristic flash.

"And you thought failing Shufftie was bad." Boo's voice rasped, giving out.

Beck couldn't help himself. He flinched.

Rork sat back on his heels. His palms were bleeding, his head reeling. He looked at the banshee collapsed in Deirdre's arms. He looked at Beck quailing beside the pylon. He looked at the empty space where Hamish used to be. How had Hamish become the scapegoat? A part of him blamed Boo. She should have said something. She should have warned him. But what would he have done with the information? Could he have chosen between seeing his gran again and Hamish? Knowledge was only good if he was prepared to act on it. His father had taught him that much. He considered all the things he didn't know or understand. The inner workings of Shufftie. The inner workings of banshees. The despair of Hamish, hoping to see his parents again, agreeing to go with Beck.

Despair at least Rork understood. That's what drove him to leave with the banshee. Despair and rejection. He shifted his cramped feet. What was it with fathers? Why did Rork care what his father thought? Why was his father navigational to him? Like a compass point?

Rork looked at Deirdre, struggling to keep Boo semi-upright. Her paleness was extreme. Had the banshee done what was necessary? Had she spared Rork an impossible decision? "A wee shift made all the difference," said his gran. Perhaps he was in no position to judge. Perhaps she had her reasons. Perhaps he would find out.

29: Leap of Faith

"IT WASN'T YOUR FAULT," said Deirdre.

Rork groaned, the sound muffled. The sight of Hamish slipping away to nothingness replayed over and over in his mind. Was it worth the sacrifice, he wondered again? He felt like the string on a guitar, a cello, a harp. Plucked. Until everything about him was vibrating. Humming. Buzzing

Rork second-guessed himself for the umpteenth time. Could he have done anything differently? It had all happened so fast. He and Deirdre could only react. Why Hamish? Hadn't he suffered enough? Rork despaired. He'd lost his gran. And then Hamish. He had to make it all worthwhile by continuing the assignments.

"What did you say?" Deirdre stooped to slide the banshee to a raised rock on the ground. Rork held his head, walking back toward them. Inside, the voices were hushed, subdued by everything that had happened.

"I didn't say anything," croaked Rork. "What is there to say?"

"It wasn't your fault," Boo said, leaning over her knees. "It's mine." She was hoarse, washed-out, almost indistinguishable in the grotto. The experience on the ridge had taken its toll on her, too. "I'm sorry," she said. "I knew it had to happen, but I couldn't tell you."

"Why not?" asked Deirdre, her voice barely audible.

The banshee didn't answer.

Rork couldn't afford to dwell on it anymore. If he did, he'd be mired in grief and regret, unable to move, take action. They had to move forward. It was the only way to honor Hamish's sacrifice.

The waterfall's rush of water echoed in the grotto. Rork and Deirdre stood on the wet floor in the bowl just above the water's descent into blankness. Rork knew that their only chance to leave Shufftie was jumping. His gran had said as much, leading them to the Leap of Faith. The alternative was what? The next level? What next level kind of ghost would they encounter? Rork's mind balked at the idea of staying in Shufftie. He knew leaping was their only option. But knowing what to do and doing it were two very different things.

Boo recovered herself slightly by holding the wall behind them, unable to hover. The grotto was carved in sculptured rock formations. Rork could hear Boo pick at a seam in the rock. Crumbs of stone skittered to the ground.

"What will happen when we jump?" asked Rork.

"I don't know," said Boo.

"How are you still here?" Rork asked over his shoulder. Rork would've liked to be alone with Deirdre, and the banshee's presence was unnerving. Her agenda clear.

"I get Beck's —" Her voice died away.

The three of them were quiet for a drawn-out, sobering minute. Rork couldn't get Beck's last words out of his head.

"Leave me," he'd said, broken. Hamish was gone. Charboy had scarpered. Beck was without allies, without strength. He sagged against the piling, defeated. It had become apparent to Rork that the impact had been serious. Beck was injured. His ribs? Back?

Boo hobbled nearer. "You don't have to be left behind," she'd said. "You'll survive the tribunal. Your brother did."

"Did he?" lashed Beck with what little energy he still possessed.

"But what about the pall?" asked Boo. "He'll extract you."

"So be it," Beck had said.

Now the dead chimed in, unable to keep quiet anymore. They really were hard to ignore sometimes. Their clamoring voices in Rork's head joined the crushing sound of water. "Jump, jump," they chanted.

Rork wasn't sure the dead were his best guide at the moment. They had nothing to lose. He wondered whose interests they supported. His? The banshee's? Or a mishmash of their own?

Rork's legs felt twitchy. His fingers tapped on one thigh. "L-e-a-p of f-a-i-t-h." Then just "f-a-i-t-h." He looked at Deirdre, who stood next to him on the edge. He was rewarded with her enigmatic smile. This was it. This was where his gran said their journey led. How they'd complete their time in Shufftie.

"What was it all for?" asked Rork.

"Banshees learn through the simulations," sighed Boo, almost by rote. "Continually refining the experience of death."

But this wasn't just about banshees, Rork thought in protest. Hamish, Deirdre, and he were involved, too. "It seems a strange place to end up," he commented wryly. "Perched on a cliff, overlooking a waterfall to nowhere in particular."

"Oh, are you afraid of heights?" asked the banshee.

"No," said Rork.

"Well, then."

"The view is —" began Deirdre, unable to find the words. "Is that what possibility looks like, do you think?"

What a question, thought Rork. He could feel she was as reluctant about the leap as he was, and she was distracting him with larger questions, pretending the unthinkable was not all that daunting.

The view *was* spectacular. He could see almost all of Shufftie, its various terrains: The River of Forgetting meandering through, the incursion of Memory Trees, the rocky peaks of the summits. The light was silver, as if etched on the horizon.

"I guess," responded Rork. He felt the sheet of drawing paper thick and stiff in his back pocket and drew it out. It was one of Hamish's, sketched in pencil. Rork had found it on the ground. After. It was a drawing of Rork. Hamish must have drawn it years ago when Rork had been sick. His face was gaunt, his chin sharper than usual, a faraway look in his eyes. "The Fergus," it read, "The Chosen One."

"Jump already," said the banshee, weak and irritable. "Unless you plan to hike back?" She arched a pale brow.

"Jump, jump," repeated the voices in Rork's head.

Deirdre shrugged. "Maybe we should listen to your gran? After all, we came all this way." She looked intensely at Rork, communicating what couldn't be communicated. She had to be the bravest woman or man Rork had ever met.

In his shirt pocket, Rork found a sweetie stashed by his gran. He unwrapped it and put it on his tongue. He stood up and reached for Deirdre. Deirdre put her hand in his.

"So, after everything, all we went through, you're telling me Shufftie is basically a beta test for a better death experience?"

The banshee looked him straight in the eyes, tapping a slipper. "You humans do like your odysseys."

Rork kissed Deirdre quickly, squeezing her hand. "For Hamish?" he asked.

"For Hamish," she replied.

When he jumped, Deirdre did not let go.

COURIER PROJECT

A Voice.

DEATH IS. That's all I can say. It's death when your mind wanders. Where does your mind go? You have no idea. It leaves the room. Maybe it remembers. Maybe it regrets. You remember others, and there they are, foggy with memory. Proximity is something. A comfort, perhaps. There is something in the terrain of a face. The topography speaks to you at some level. You even dream about it. Yes, death and dreaming are hard to distinguish. Death-dreams give the pretense of days, passage of time. I suspect we are beyond time. It's a mirage we try to articulate, but words are experimental at best. You can never say what you mean. We try. I guess that's what eternity is for. If you believe in that. (chuckles)

30: When It's Time to Take Action, Take Action

THE FIRST TIME RORK remembered disappointing his father was on a fishing trip when he was maybe seven or eight. He didn't know why his father liked to fish. It was an activity wildly opposed to his basic nature. Casting a lure? Waiting? His father never had a thought he didn't act upon. It was at an early age, then, that he began to understand paradox.

His father was difficult, demanding. Even as a loon he'd recognized that. Where they lived, on one of the most prestigious fishing rivers in the world, it was difficult to obtain a fishing permit. His father had called in a favor from a mate, a local ghillie. It was high spring. The riverbank was burgeoning, overrunning its banks. The shore was wet, sloppy. It sucked at their boots as they maneuvered for the most promising spot.

His father carried the tackle box and two fishing poles. Rork nervously carried the container of worms as if it was precious cargo. His anxiety over dropping the container made his stomach clench.

It was a rare day in the Highlands. The sun was out, touching everything with its fiery spotlight. Tall grasses of the marshlands waved above his head. Birds flittered high in the trees. Rork liked the sound of the mud as he walked, a rhythmic base note to the higher pitched birdsong, swish of tassels. He was dawdling in the day.

"What's taking you?" shouted his father from up ahead.

Rork could see his broad back steamrolling through the grasses. The mud did not slow him down. The shine of his well-combed hair was incongruous in the setting, but Rork accepted the spit-and-polish veneer as part of who his father was. "I'm coming," he shouted back. He was tall for his age, but the combination of mud, grass, and soft-sided container of worms did not contribute to the speediest progress. He tried to run to catch up, but almost tripped and began to pant after a few steps. Mud clung to his boots.

When he finally did catch up, his father was already setting up his lines. He'd discovered an outcropping in the river, a solid point of land that overlooked a wide bend. Water collected here in a deep pool. Tree roots were exposed by erosion of the bank, so branches cast shadows at a slant. His father called the spot a "wee oasis." Rork liked the sound of 'oasis,' but his father sure got annoyed when his line got tangled in the riverbed's roots and rocks.

His father strung Rork's line for him and handed him a pole, nodding at the container of worms. Rork bit his lower lip. He did not even like to watch when his father put a worm on a hook, winding soft flesh around and through the barbed end to ensure it didn't fall off, worm ooze gushing out. Ugh. But he refused to ask his father for help. He was more like his father than he realized. Stubborn. By virtue of not breathing and squinting his eyes through the narrowest of peepholes, he got a worm on his hook.

"Good," said his father, exhaling smoke from his hand-rolled cigarette, the first of many during the long afternoon.

His father stood at the edge of the river, casting his line with one hand, smoking with the other. He watched ripples in the water with his fire-and-ice eyes, deeply engraved crow's feet. With his strung and baited pole, Rork moved upriver. He did not want to get their lines tangled. Also, he could use some practice casting. He'd been shown how to cast with an open bale many times, but his hands still fumbled with the lever and sequence of small actions. He hoped his father hadn't seen his first cast. The tip of his pole arched towards the water, but the line did not release. Stupidly, he'd forgot to lift his finger. The next cast was a little better. By the fifth he was feeling more comfortable and could perch on the stump of a felled tree, flicking his line. He liked to cast into the current and watch the bobber trail away.

Rork could hear the steel flint of his father's lighter open and close. Vaguely, he smelled the burn of amber leaf tobacco his father favored, but mostly his mind wandered. He wished he was in the kitchen with his gran. She was making scones today. His mouth watered at the thought. Her scones were the perfect balance of crust and moistness, filled with plump currants.

The sun moved across the sky. Rork let his bobber trail farther and farther down the river. When the wind would still momentarily, he could hear the rush of water around the next bend. It made him curious. The handle of his pole hung loosely in his hand. He felt a few nibbles, but nothing that required any kind of response from him. He knew his father had a couple of wax paper-wrapped sandwiches in his tackle box. He started to wonder about lunch when he felt an unmistakable tug on the line. He stood up, holding the line in both hands.

"Sir," he cried, "I think I've got one."

His father came crashing through the marshland. He'd broken a cigarette, which he flung into the river. He stood behind Rork a few paces, his eyes going from Rork to the line and back.

"Take it easy," he said. "You need to set the hook."

"How do I do that?" asked Rork.

"Let the fish take the line a bit. Then hold it steady. When you feel a distinct tug on the line, pull back sharply and reel it in." His father played with the lighter in his pocket.

Rork tried to do as his father directed, but he was anxious. And what would happen if he landed the fish? Would he have to pull the hook out of its mouth? Clean it? He could see the fish visibly thrash at the end of his line. He thought he'd hooked it, but after a few turns of the reel he felt nothing. It was a disconsolate feeling. His mouth was suddenly dry. "I think I lost it," he said.

His father didn't say anything. He waited until Rork reeled in an empty line. Even the worm was gone. The lighter clanged open and closed. A stream of smoke swirled about their heads. "Son," he said, finally, "when it's time to take action, take action. Stay in the moment. Don't be getting ahead of yourself with your two minds."

It was good advice Rork was not yet ready to hear. He felt the sting of tears behind his eyes, and he boyishly wished he'd followed the sound of whitewater in an adventure upriver, away from his father.

31: White Woman

RORK FELT THE LID OF HIS EYE being peeled back.

"Are you awake?" asked the banshee.

Rork tried to speak, but it seemed his whole body was asleep. His limbs felt unearthly heavy. Like they didn't belong to him. He heard plinking and whirring. Where was he? The side of his face was pushed into a porous surface that smelled strangely of wet rock. The image of a riverbed floated in his mind. Did he dream it? The voices in his head murmured concern.

"Are you awake?" Boo asked again, louder, peeling back his other eyelid.

Again, he tried to speak. It came out, "#M$a*k."

"Are. You. Awake?" the banshee asked again, even louder.

"Iii'mmm aaawwwaaakkkeee," mumbled Rork, managing to move an arm.

"About time," said Boo, crouching beside him.

"Where ammm I?" asked Rork, flopping to one side. He was reacquainting himself with the rest of his body. He couldn't seem to focus, and the banshee's face swam in front of his eyes.

"Transmission room," said Boo.

Rork listened to the plinking, whirring, tapping, and whooshing. Once he got control of a hand, he checked to make sure he still had the flash drive and was reassured by its sharp edges. He'd already lost the sixpence. The thought of losing the flash drive was unbearable.

"And wwwhere exactly is the transmission room?" he panted, getting to his hands and knees. A Leap of Faith took a lot out of a person, he realized.

"In the banshee complex." Boo crouched nearer.

Rork tried to shake the fog from his brain. He had zero idea what a banshee complex might be. He imagined long hallways, white walls, sky.

"Where's Deirdre?" he asked.

"She woke up a long time ago," said Boo.

"Where is ssshe?"

"You'll see."

Rork started to stand and, raising a knee, teetered. "Isss Hamish still gone?"

"Yes."

Rork hung his head.

Boo stopped outside a sliding glass-paned door. "My mother," she deadpanned. A frisson of something crossed her face. Rork looked at the door, then back to Boo. Two sliding doors met on a corner. "Is Deirdre in there?"

"Yes," said Boo without expression.

"Corner office?"

"Yes," she said, knocking. "A corner is a place of converging."

Rork looked up and read on a placard above the sliding doors, PLACE OF CONVERGING.

"Come in," said a rather melodious voice.

A woman sat at a desk that floated in the center of an ethereal office. The floor was squares of glass tile, covered by a bamboo rug.

"Hello," said the woman, a mature banshee. Rork could see a hint of her features in Boo. Same gap teeth, same gray eyes, same flyaway hair. Hers was cut short in a bob that tucked behind her ears. Her gown was like Boo's, but what was most noticeable about her was her hood, which was thick, plush, and a deep iris-purple. Rork blinked rapidly, surprised he could see in color. In his head, the voices held their collective breath, sensing importance.

Rork immediately found Deirdre already seated in front of the desk. His breath caught in his throat. She wore a clean T-shirt, her colorful scarf laundered of trail dust, and another of her preferred tiered skirt. She loosely clasped her hands in her lap. He could glimpse one of the forget-me-not tattoos inked on her inner wrist.

"Welcome, welcome," said Boo's mother, suspended in the air beside her desk. Behind her on a cream wall was a painting of a mandala. Kaleidoscopic colors and shapes — squares, circles, triangles — covered a large section of the wall, giving the room a psychedelic aura.

"I've heard so much about you, I've been anxious to meet you." She looked to Boo, waving the pair of them to the other chairs in the semi-circle in front of her desk. She motioned Rork to sit. Rork took the chair nearest Deirdre. He imagined taking off her headband, unwinding her scarf. Instead, he gripped the arms of his chair. The sweetness in the air grew complex, liquorish, like vanilla.

"Hi," he said to Deirdre, under his breath.

"Hi, she said back, equally hushed, lowering her green lashes.

Boo's mother bustled about. "How are your eyes adjusting?" she asked. "We try to bring back color in stages, so our Shufftie wayfarers are not too overwhelmed."

"Thank you, I'm good," said Rork. "I missed color, actually."

"Yes, color does add a certain dimension." Boo's mother glided to the floor, settling herself in the fourth chair, tugging her robe into position. Her slippers matched her robe. She looked at Rork, cocking her head to one side, a gesture not unlike her daughter's. "You look familiar," she said.

"Do I?" said Rork, stretching his legs. "Tall, curly-haired? I guess we all look alike."

The banshee laughed.

Rork liked the shape of her mouth.

"As you know," she breezed on, "I'm my daughter's advisor. A little irregular, I know, but we make it work." She smiled at Boo, who was unusually quiet in the presence of her mother, despite the curious looks she kept shooting at Rork.

"Yes, ma'am," said Rork. He felt his gran poking him in the ribs, reminding him, "Politeness doesn't cost a body anything, loon."

"Oh, you may call me the White Woman. Most do," she said. "Would anybody like tea and biscuits?"

"Yes, please," said Rork. "Ma'am," he added.

"You may dispense with the 'ma'am.'" She punched into a handheld device, reminding Rork how much he missed his computer. He drummed his fingers on his knees.

"I told you," piped up Boo.

"Yes, yes," said the White Woman. "Persistent hunger is not unusual in intermediaries. It seems to accompany the yearning." She assessed Rork from head to toe, not unkindly, lingering on his fidgeting hands. "Do you have any ideas for your project?" she asked her daughter.

"Well," said Boo, sitting forward in her chair, "I think there's something in the memory-typing Rork discovered in Shufftie."

"What?" asked Rork, caught off guard.

"What, indeed," said the White Woman.

Boo's words came out in a rush, as if she'd been thinking about them for a while. "I don't have it all worked out yet, but Rork, the way you described how Deirdre's ancestors came forward with memories as you typed on her skin. It just sounded so…so…so elegant. I was thinking we could build a project around it."

"A portal for the dead," said Deirdre, eyes shining with her own brand of yearning.

Rork's mind was spinning. What was happening? The memory-typing had been an intimate exchange between Rork and Deirdre, a breakthrough for Rork as an intermediary, as go-between. Did he want to share it? *Should* it be shared? If he did agree to work with the banshee and share it, would it give him more opportunity to work with Deirdre? Would his father sense the accomplishment in him? Rork really didn't know what he wanted. Only a moment ago, he'd been content to survive the Leap of Faith with Deirdre.

"Like that face note thing you humans are so obsessed with?" asked the White Woman.

"Facebook?" asked Rork.

"Face note…face book." The White Woman waved her hand nonchalantly.

There was a light rap at the sliding door. The White Woman collected the tea tray and brought it back to her desk. "Milk and sugar?"

"Yes, please," said Rork and Deirdre in unison.

The White Woman handed out two teas and resumed her seat, crossing her legs at the ankles. "The idea has promise," she said. "What would you call this portal?"

"Spirit Talk?" suggested Boo.

Deirdre wrinkled her nose.

The White Woman considered. "It doesn't really say 'Courier Project,' does it?"

Boo crossed her arms, deep in thought.

There was a long pause. Deirdre was clearly okay with sharing her memory-typing experience, and it *was* a breakthrough. Rork could understand why Boo was excited by it. It was the very definition of an act of interlife moment.

"How about SoulSpeak?" suggested Rork, getting into the spirit of the discussion. He was the best version of himself when he was solving a problem, and with Deirdre beside him how could they not pull it off?

"What do you think?" Boo asked her mother.

Before the White Woman had a chance to reply, Deirdre spoke. "Soul*Seek*. It should be SoulSeek." She smiled broadly at Rork and reached for his hand.

Rork looked at his hand clasped in Deirdre's. Mother and daughter banshees exchanged a knowing look, but Rork didn't care. Deirdre and Boo approved his memory-typing and thought the concept worthy of a Courier Project. They were in this adventure together!

Rork tried out the name, typing it on his knee. S-o-u-l-S-e-e-k. He heard approbation from the voices of the dead. In fact, they besieged his head with cheering and clapping, which he did not appreciate. He really didn't. Deirdre tugged on his hand, and he tried to ignore the clamor. Perhaps his father would share memories? Rork knew he'd lost a lot of friends in the military. He felt a pang for the missing sixpence.

The White Woman smiled at Deirdre. "As always, in every world, we defer to the stronger opinion."

"SoulSeek," repeated Boo. "It's bold. I like it." She flashed her gap teeth at Deirdre.

"You would," said Rork, although he was thrilled with the challenge and Deirdre's continued involvement.

"I think you're onto something," said the White Woman. "Of course, it needs more thought and development, perhaps a visual interpretation of some kind." She reached for the teapot. "More?" she asked.

Rork held out his cup.

"I think I know an artist who might be able to help you bring the project to life." Slyly, she smiled.

Rork thought it an eerie turn of phrase, considering, and wondered if it was intentional. He tended to think yes. He didn't believe the White Woman did anything by accident.

"You can come in now," called the White Woman.

Rork turned, looking for another door.

A section of the mandala wall opened. The newcomer chinked as he entered the room, flicking his lank hair in a familiar gesture.

Hamish!

Alive and slouching!

Alive and smirking!

"Hamish!" shouted Rork, bounding up from his chair. He felt a rush of —. His emotions were so knotted up he couldn't exactly describe what he was feeling. Adrenalin? He interrogated Boo with a look. What the —?

The banshee turned up her hands. "You had to believe he'd truly died. Grief is how we learn."

"I can't believe you made us think he died!" said Rork.

"As long as you help me."

"Each of our teams' experiences and emotions — positive and negative — enhance the simulation of Shufftie, helping our banshees-in-training better understand their roles as messengers," explained the White Woman. "We pick our teams very carefully."

Rork heard with only one ear. He hesitated, his eyes on Hamish, then, not able to contain himself anymore, he took two steps forward and hugged Hamish, lifting him off the floor.

Hamish groaned. "I missed you, too, mate," he managed to get out. He sounded bemused by the whole situation. As if falling to his death had been just a bad dream he barely remembered.

Rork set him down but continued patting him on the shoulders, needing to reassure himself that he was really, really present, standing in front of him. Hamish. Skinny as a fencepost. Hair pulled back in a ponytail. Hands fluttering with their crosshatching of scars. Jangle of chain at his belt.

To Rork, Hamish looked more like the old Hamish, the before-the-accident Hamish, his eyes brown, frothy as porter. He looked like he was, finally, happy to be alive.

"I saw them, Rork," Hamish whispered. "I saw my parents."

32: Courier Wing

"WHERE ARE WE GOING?" asked Rork.

"Courier Wing," said Boo, hovering in front of them, leading the way. Rork, Hamish, and Deirdre followed quickly behind. Rork's imagination was rewarded with glimpses of the complex, which included long hallways, white walls, lots of glass, and sky.

"Is that a joke?" asked Hamish.

"Why would it be a joke?" asked Boo, turning to regard him.

"Courier? Wing?" Hamish elbowed Rork.

"It's a wing of the complex where teams work on courier projects. Simple as that."

After two sharp turns, they arrived at a pair of double doors. The banshee flung them open. "Here we are!"

The doors swung open on a cozy bungalow.

"Oh," said Deirdre, squeezing past Rork and Hamish.

The bungalow reminded Rork of a holiday cottage he'd stayed in once with Hamish and his family. There was a great room with stucco walls and ceiling beams, a galley kitchen. He saw doors to bedrooms, leading from the great room.

"You found my computer!" he shouted, spying his laptop on an end table in the great room.

"Of course," said Boo, hovering out of reach. She was no fan of Rork's huggish enthusiasm.

Rork ran his hands over the surface, thumbing the catch. He turned the computer on and waited for the telltale chiming. His fingers played over the keys.

"Yes, we recovered it from Shufftie," Boo said.

"You didn't find anything else, did you?" asked Rork.

"Like what?" asked the banshee.

"Never mind," mumbled Rork.

"I'll take this room," said Hamish, calling unseen from one of the bedrooms.

The banshee hovered near Rork, turning the lights of a wrought iron lamp on and off.

Deirdre unwound her scarf and draped it over the back of the great room's large settee, adding a splash of color. She wandered into the kitchen.

"Now we can get to work," said Rork. He sat on one end of the sectional with his computer in his lap. Although he was focused on the Courier Project, a part of him was brainstorming a web show for Deirdre. He didn't trust words, and he wanted to show her how he felt.

"Yes," said Boo. "Let's get to work."

Deirdre opened the door of the fridge.

Rork heard the unmistakable swish of air. "Is there anything to eat?" he asked over his shoulder.

"What was it your gran called you?" asked Boo, exasperated.

"A gannet."

Deirdre tossed him an apple, which he snatched out of the air.

The banshee shook her head.

"Close your eyes," said Deirdre.

"You know I can see even if my eyes are closed," said Boo.

"Pretend," said Rork. He struggled to cross his legs on the wood floor. The hamstrings were tight, so his legs refused to bend. How had he let Deirdre talk him into this?

"Breathe," said Deirdre, taking in a deliberate breath and expanding her ribcage.

Rork, Deirdre, Hamish, and the banshee sat cross-legged in a circle, hands open like scoops on their knees. A subtle sweetness hung in the air, stirred by a ceiling fan. There was no shortage of project ideas, but they were having trouble coming together. Hamish was fidgety, suggesting composition after composition. He'd gone through half a sketchbook. Deirdre wanted to delve into each idea, exploring its meaning, its narrative. The banshee agreed to everything, thinking it would hurry them along. Worse, the voices in Rork's head yammered, full of zeal, intent on contributing to SoulSeek.

"Sink into yourself," said Deirdre. "Breathe deeper."

Rork's mind skipped around. His legs were falling asleep.

In other words, they were stuck. Deirdre wanted to try mindfulness. She swore by it. Well, it couldn't hurt, Rork supposed.

"Stay in the moment," said Dierdre.

Rork tried to rein in his skittering thoughts. How should SoulSeek behave? What should it answer? There were so many ways it could go. He thought of his Pinny-Full project. What had made it successful?

"Soul meets body…"

The whir of the fan added a certain languor to the experiment.

"Soul meets mind…"

Pinny-Full had been grounded in an image. This had been largely intuitive on Rork's part. For him, his gran had been connected to her pinny. She'd worn one every day of his life. She had even worn one in death. Rork couldn't explain it in scientific terms, but he believed there was something in the psyche that needed physical objects as handholds for thoughts and memories.

"Soul meets soul…"

"What if," said Rork, clearing his throat. "What if we let their treasures talk for them?"

Three pairs of eyes swiveled to him.

Deirdre rocked side to side, considering. "You mean, like the language of keepsakes?"

"Yes," said Rork. "I think that's what I mean." His problem-solver mind was humming. He snatched at words to explain.

"We let each artifact tell its own story?" asked Hamish. He opened and closed his lighter. He'd promised Deirdre he wouldn't smoke, but he still fidgeted with the paraphernalia.

"Yes!" yelped Boo. "*Love letters in things.* I can't wait to tell my mother."

33: Open Citation Day

"I CAN'T SEE THE END of the line," said Deirdre in a rush, moving around the kitchen creating trays of appetizers. She had shed her long-sleeved blouse and wore only a tank top.

"Mmm…" said Rork. He looked over the top of his laptop at Hamish. "I like that look," he said, "although we may need to rearrange some things. Let's see what happens as we capture more."

Their computers faced each other at the kitchen table in the great room. Rork sat on the edge of a kitchen chair, intent. Hamish jiggled his leg while he worked, chewing on a pencil. The settee and other furniture had been moved out of the way to create space.

Deirdre stopped at Rork's computer with a full tray. "What about —?" She pointed to his screen, making a flourish.

"Good idea!" He filched an appetizer from the tray.

The White Woman had agreed to declare it Open Citation Day. Any ghost in good standing from any level who was interested in participating in SoulSeek was welcome. The transmission room worked overtime as all walks of ghosts materialized from the simulations, other worlds, or wherever in the ether, lugging their ghost mementos of other lives. It was a temporary measure, of course. The long-term goal of SoulSeek was a self-serve (ghost-serve?) portal.

This was what Rork loved. Engaged in problem-solving. Creating out of nothing. Coding meaning within meaning. Organizing the chaos. Occasionally he'd observe Deirdre move about, a virtuoso in the kitchen. Or he'd watch Hamish work. How his face twitched as he moused concepts. Rork hadn't realized how much he'd missed his friend, another point of orientation in the vast, unfriendly universe.

Deirdre adjusted her headband, flashing him a conspiratorial smile. She stirred some concoction in a bowl. She was obviously at home in the company of ghosts. Rork could see the forget-me-not tattoos as she assembled trays, placing small circles of mushroom bruschetta in rows with a sprig of some herb on top.

Boo helped her serve, smiling at the ghosts in line as they helped themselves to the appetizers, licking their fingers appreciatively. Open Citation Day gave them temporary privileges. Eating was a big hit.

The kettle whistled.

Hamish looked up, rapped his pencil on the table. "Ready?" he asked.

Rork nodded, arrested by the sound of the kettle.

"Next!" called Hamish.

One-handed, Deirdre ushered another ghost into the guest area. "We're so pleased you are offering your keepsakes. We can't thank you enough," she said. "Bruschetta?"

The next ghost juggled a bundle of papers under her arm as she nibbled at the bruschetta. "That tastes earthy," she said. "Rosemary?"

Deirdre gave the ghost citation a quick nod. "They'll see you now."

The next ghost citation was a tall, sturdy woman with light hair, round spectacles, and plump cheeks. She held her bundle with freckled hands, plucking at the twine that bound it. She had a tall person's stiff-legged gait.

"Want me to sit here?" she asked, pointing at the lone chair in the great room.

"Yes," said Rork, "to start. Tell us your name and what you've brought."

"My name is Colette," she said.

Rork thought she had a sprite's smile despite her years and ghostliness. Her voice had a lovely singsong tone.

"I've brought my parents' love letters." Colette loosened the twine.

Hamish was sketching madly on a digital board. One of Rork's suggestions, he thought it would help them be more efficient. There were *a lot* of ghosts.

Colette unfolded a letter. It had yellowed with the years, growing fragile. "My father was an officer in the American army. My mother was a WAC. They were forbidden to fraternize, but that didn't stop my father."

"Can I see?" asked Rork.

The greeting was effusive — "My dearest dear." The handwriting was spidery but had a certain swagger. The tails of the "g's" and "y's" were very distinctive.

"He had a way with words," said Rork.

"Yes," said Colette. "He worked as a journalist when he came out of the service. He was working on a book when he died."

Rork handed the letter to Hamish, who studied it, holding it myopically to his face. He then placed the letter carefully in the 3D scanner. The other letters followed suit.

"Colette," said Rork, "I need you to do one more thing."

"Yes."

"I need you to place your hands on my shoulders and try to recall your best memories of your father and mother."

Colette looked to Hamish. Hamish smiled his hackneyed smile but nodded reassuringly. She re-bundled the letters and settled them on the seat of the chair. Then she stood behind Rork diffidently, holding her hands above his shoulders.

"It's okay," Rork said. "I'm an intermediary."

"A what?"

"An intermediary." There was something validating about his saying it out loud. "If you lay your hands on my shoulders, your memories will transfer to me, and I'll be able to memory-type them into the project."

"Oh," said Colette, not fully understanding but reassured, and she placed her hands on his shoulders. "My father," she rambled, "had spent long hours in his study, writing articles, transcribing their letters. To a young girl after the war, it had seemed like he was writing himself back into the world, into equanimity."

Her hands were airy. Ghosts did not have the heat of humanity. Rork could hear Colette's shallow breaths. Her breath became a tunnel, which he followed trance-like until it was all about the voice, a new voice coming forward, more prominent in the endless sea of voices in his head.

My dearest dear. (Mannerisms of a man, a father. Deep baritone. The scratching of a pen by desk light.) *I cannot tell you where we are. We are boots deep in the middle of a maneuver. We pray it makes a difference. I think of your smile. The way your hair wisps around your face. The freckles you hate so much. I think of your capable hands, the work you will do one day. Thankless perhaps but necessary. We will win or lose based on the incidental things. Will supplies reach their destination on time? Will troops? We are at the last resort. Would it be better to die than live in a world of tyranny? That is the question we ask ourselves daily. Most days we are sure of the answer. Others, we're not sure there is an answer. I am battle weary, jittery to the core, wishing for the noise to stop. I love listening to your heartbeat. I would fight for that.* (A child's leap into the studied lap of a father, smell of binding, ink, black tea.)

Rork hunched over the keyboard, typing harder than he needed to on the keyboard, transcribing Colette's father's *voice* in his head. It was the voice of the letter collaged with a child's memory of a father. The task made Rork remember his own father, the happy moments before the anger, recriminations and rejection. Sitting next to his "Da" in his gran's kitchen as he laced up his boots for work. The feel of his knuckles in his hair. The wink as he nabbed a corner of toast from Rork's plate as he ducked out the door.

He wished he had more happy memories of his father and was more than willing to co-opt Colette's. When had his relationship with his father become such a source of conflict? Rork tried to piece it together. His gran had always been the knowing one in their family, and he tried to channel her intuition. His thumb moved over the shape of the flash drive in his pocket. When his mother died? Rork had been so young. He hardly remembered her, although he did recall his mother begging his father, "Talk to me! Why are you so stubborn?" It had made him think of a locked door. An industrial one with a lever and bolt.

After the accident his father was inconsolable — dragged himself to work, sat in the gloom of the back parlor until well past Rork's bedtime. Rork was dazed, in shock. His gran stepped in to give him hugs, comfort, and encouragement. His mother's death had made him feel vulnerable, lost.

"Should I go to him?" he'd ask his gran, feeling responsible, in his preschooler way, for his father's sadness.

"No, loon," she'd tsk, shaking her head, the kitchen thick with the yeasty smell of bread. "He's thinking all the things he wished he'd said."

Rork knew his father had loved his mother, but perhaps he couldn't express it. Not in words. Like Bazzie the ghost, Rork thought. And what was it Susan had said? After all her books? Live each day like it was the last? And the labyrinth? How walls can spring up between people over the stupidest things? Like pie? Rork had learned from Bazzie that love can be articulated in ways other than words. Like a sixpence.

Rork suddenly wondered what other lessons Shufftie had been trying to teach him.

After Colette, there was Rachel with her mother's ruby ring, Gustav with his father's tools, and Sanjay with his grandparents' lamp. Rork pounded on his keyboard frenetically. Faster and faster. The more citations they could talk to, the more chances someone would come forward with the sixpence. He *needed* the sixpence.

"Rork, Rork," said Hamish, disrupting the frenzy of his thoughts.

"What?" said Rork, not wanting to look up, impatient.

"Take it easy, mate," said Hamish, considering him. "You'd think the pall was after you."

Rork looked at Hamish blankly.

The pall?

Had Shufftie shown him what *would* happen if he and his father didn't reconcile?

A vast, soul-sucking emptiness?

34: The Nature of Dreams

RORK'S WRISTS ACHED, but he couldn't sleep. For almost eighteen hours straight, they had collected "love letters in things," as Boo called it, and although they had aggregated a good base he was beyond exhausted. The project would grow and grow. All they had to do was demonstrate the idea and its preliminary implementation to the White Woman to fulfill Boo's in-training assignment. No one had come forward with the sixpence, and they were missing something else. Some uniting force, some metaphor for the whole endeavor. Rork knew it but couldn't resolve it. He was *so* tired and anxious for the missing sixpence. Probably the culmination of Shufftie and the extreme swings in emotion. He wished Deirdre were with him. The answer was just beyond the edge of his current thinking. The voices weren't helping either — their cacophony, their jumble of thoughts.

Rork paced the bedroom he'd chosen in the Courier Wing. Bed. Night table. Lamp. Dresser. There were sensors in the ceiling connected to the light switch. The ceiling reflected a night sky, including a sliver of moon and spray of stars, as if the dark fabric of night had worn through. The bright North

Star pulsed. Or perhaps it was a star just like the North Star but located elsewhere in the universe. Rork was no longer convinced he could comprehend the parameters of the known universe. Or universes. He was only beginning to understand the complexity of the world.

There was a soft rap at the door, and Deirdre softly entered. She'd slept fully clothed in her tiered skirt, scarf, and headband.

"I heard you," she said, closing the door. She came to him and kissed the lids of his two eyes.

"What?" he asked, inhaling her green fragrance. She must be a mirage. He couldn't believe she was in his room. That he had wished for her, and she had come.

"I wanted to be near you," she said.

Rork and Deirdre slow danced under the cloak of stars, room spinning in the gravitational pull between them, the attraction of their shadow selves. They whirled — light and color — their closeness chinking in the shadows.

"You know," Rork whispered, "if we keep working on the portal, your mother must come forward. I hear her. I know she's close by."

Deirdre's gray eyes shone in the twilight of his room. She rested her forehead against his.

"Perhaps my mother, too," he said, not realizing he wished it until he heard the words.

Rork wrapped his arms around her. Deirdre moved closer. Something seemed to have been decided between them. Something important, like connection.

Glow of her stitched headband. Dark aureoles. Sinuous line of her neck, long arms.

She clutched his hair. His mouth drank her in. Where did the hunger come from? Shadow eyes saw the filigree of forget-me-not, forget-me-not in the darkness.

In between the in-between worlds, Rork and Deirdre created skin memory, sound memory, smell memory, and soul memory in a kaleidoscope of feeling, sensation, and breath.

Was he dreaming? Was he not?

Deirdre brought him access to his feeling self. Perhaps relationships and kinships were worth the risk? She also brought him a solution to what was missing from SoulSeek, a way to beautifully "see."

"I knew you looked familiar," said the White Woman, gliding into the bungalow in her effortless way, her majestic hood flowing behind her.

"Huh?" asked Rork, looking up from his computer, momentarily alone.

The White Woman perched on a chair, her hands disappearing up the sleeves of her hood. She looked about the room as if seeing it for the first time. "I've been a messenger for a long, long time, shuttling people between life and death."

Rork stopped keyboarding.

"Certain shuttles you remember." Her gray-violet eyes focused on Rork. "I don't know why. Some combination of occasion, emotion, circumstance, I suppose."

The White Woman sighed, heart heavy. "Times of war were the worst. In so many ways."

Rork stopped breathing, sensing the White Woman was on the verge of some revelation.

"You look like your father," she said.

"Do I?" asked Rork.

"I met him in Morocco," she said. "During the allied invasion. According to your history a successful operation, but at great, great cost. Your father was in the parachute regiment, correct?"

Rork nodded, his mouth dry.

"Many men died that day. We were very busy." Her mouth twisted in an unknowable expression. "I found your father half-dead, surrounded by other soldiers who were very dead. They'd been cut down by the French."

The White Woman sat cast away in thought, remembering. Rork held his tongue.

"The separation between worlds is not perfect. We are only meant to appear to those already dead. But your father saw me. I'm not sure how, but I could tell by his agitation. His injuries were nearly fatal. He grew frenzied. I feared for his recovery and put my hand to his forehead. Touching, as you might imagine, is not advisable. For good reason. He passed out."

The White Woman concentrated on Rork. "I don't know why I'm telling you this. It seemed I should. A story I could tell you about your father."

Rork swallowed with effort.

"I regret that I still haunt him," said the White Woman.

Rork thought of his father, striving to be in control. Always. Did the White Woman appear to him like a dream? Or a nightmare? Having endured the ghost experiences of Shufftie, Rork felt for his father.

"I have something for you," said the White Woman, standing. "I thought it might serve the 'love letters in things.'" She smiled.

"What is it?" asked Rork.

The White Woman held out her arm, and Rork opened his hand. As if in slow motion a round metal object dropped into his palm. Rork looked at it incredulously. The sixpence! She'd found the sixpence!

"These pass down from soldier to soldier, you know. I'm sure it has a story or two. Perhaps you can ask your father?"

Rork stared at the sixpence overjoyed. When he looked up from his reverie to thank her, the White Woman was already drifting out the door.

35: Banshee Graduation

"WE NEEDED A FRAMEWORK," said Rork to the White Woman, a private look passing between them. Other banshee board members, ranged around a large table, followed their exchange in shades of quizzical. "We took inspiration from a toy," continued Rork. "It took us in a new direction."

Rork, Hamish, Deirdre, and Boo stood at the end of the table in another skylit room, reflecting a strawberry, golden light. The subdued pink put Rork on edge, but on edge in a positive way. Rork was alert, nervy, as if affected by Hamish's perennial jitteriness.

Deirdre leaned near him to double check the audio-visual connections, just to be sure. He was calmed by her presence.

The White Woman leaned forward as if she were going to add a remark but then thought better of it. Her face relaxed. "It's your project," she said to Rork, but looked at her daughter.

Rork stood in a row with the team. Deirdre held herself at full height. Hamish jangled his chain, and Boo tapped one of her tiny slippers, counting down to her cue.

"We wanted to add to the interlife experience," she said. "Our idea was to give you love letters in things." She was nervous, paler than usual.

Rork took a deep breath and launched the web show. He'd asked the White Woman for a Smart Board® and very deliberately rapped its frame. They had timed the web show to be a succession of images with a lyrical undervoice and narration by each team member in turn.

The first image was the zoomed-in center whorl of a red rose. Hamish had added a layer to each image, recoloring them to make it appear as if the sun burned in the background. Each large image dissolved into a cascade of smaller images filling up the screen.

"Beauty," said Rork. He rapped through a quick series of other images: a sunset over water, a baby's foot in the palm of a parent, a raindrop suspended on a leaf.

Music began to play. They had deliberated long and hard about what song to play during the presentation. Their tastes were so diverse, and they didn't want the song to overshadow the content. In the end, they collaborated on narration, recorded against a background of plinky acoustic guitar. When she wasn't shrilling, Boo's voice could be incredibly melodious.

Beauty is a bell we trill from within.

A tingsha bell resonated with the guitar.

"And form," said Boo. Rork rapped through more images. Gothic architecture, stone arch silhouette, frame of a face, shards of colored glass.

Ghost-shapes of memory drawing us in.

"And watchful minds," said Hamish. Rork drummed through images of eyes. Old eyes. Young eyes. Asian eyes. Tearful eyes.

We share images as a mosaic of meaning —

"Beauty, and form, and watchful minds," repeated Deirdre. More images.

...our dream of being, a collective believing,

Rork rapped faster. The images displayed in quicker succession, flickering.

...our souls keeping, our souls speaking.

The guitar got softer.
The flickering panned back to a white screen, a hyperlink.
Rork rapped the hyperlink.
The Smart Board® opened to a website.
"Introducing Soul…Seek," said Rork. The homepage was a kaleidoscope of images in the shapes of tiny pieces of glass.
"This is our beta site," said Boo. She avoided looking at her mother.
"Each shard opens to a ghost object." Hamish reached past Rork to tap a pocket-watch shard. The shard became a larger image of a pocket watch against a blaze-of-sun background with a carousel of other pocket watch images below. Swiping down, Hamish opened another window, which revealed the tale of the pocket-watch. The room could hear the ticking of the watch.

I am the pocket watch of William Grant, father, son, husband. I was a gift from William's mother, Isabella. William received the watch when he left home for the first time to join the boy service. He'd been adopted when Isabella was overcome with grief after her first husband died suddenly. The adoption had been prescribed by her physician. Time had stopped, but when the young fire-haired mother handed her young Willie to Isabella, somehow the hands of time began to tick again. (Lacy pattern of a young lad's lashes superimposed over the scroll of the watch.) *Read more…*

…our souls keeping, our souls speaking.

"We named the site SoulSeek," said Deirdre. "We mean seek in the sense of finding." She and Rork held each other's eyes.

"Seek in the sense of looking," said Rork. One hand typed on his thigh. No one could read what it spelled.

"Seek in the sense of range," said Boo. "Range of perceptions, thoughts, or actions. The combined experience of the dead."

"Beautiful forms," said Hamish. He tapped on more shards. More interior pages opened — page upon page. He tapped and tapped, conveying the range of content.

"SoulSeek," said Rork, "embeds keywords. People — 'Father,' 'son,' 'husband' — and things — 'pocket watch,' 'wedding dress,' 'love letters.'"

"SoulSeek is available for counseling of the living," said Boo.

"You might not find *your* mother, but you will find *a* mother," said Hamish.

"Many mothers," said Deirdre. "Because you can be served with other people's memories. There's a community of memories."

"If you like the stories, you will absorb them. They will become part of your own memories. Memories are the core connection between beings."

"We humbly submit SoulSeek as our Courier Project, our project of interlife moment," said Boo. The guitar continued to plink while a botanical drawing of a forget-me-not scrolled and unscrolled across the ending screen. Deirdre had painstakingly drawn forget-me-nots in various aspects, which Hamish had animated together. All four shifted nervously at the edge of the conference table. Boo squeezed Rork's forearm and mouthed, "Thank you."

The SoulSeek images propelled on screen, mixing-and-matching in a kaleidoscopic effect. Finally, the Smart Board® went blank.

Rork, Deirdre, and Hamish were carried along in a crowd of banshees, humans, and visiting ghosts into an echoing auditorium.

Rork saw Morag in the crowd, the Crazy One who lived at the turn in the lane, his gran's great friend. Worse, she saw him. She wagged a finger at him and cackled. He could hear her across the room. Why was she here?

Deirdre pointed to chairs in the middle of the auditorium, and Rork ushered them quickly to their seats.

They sat.

Others milled around them chaotically.

Rork found Deirdre's hand. She interlaced her fingers with his. This was a big day.

The White Woman walked to a podium on the stage.

Hamish sketched rapidly on one knee with a small drawing pad.

The room erupted in applause. Rork and Deirdre clapped louder than the rest.

Behind the White Woman sat a row of banshees-in-training, including Bryonna, or Boo, looking rather resplendent in a long gown with silver slippers, her hair secured in a low, side ponytail. The combined glow of the banshees was blindingly bright.

Rork was astonished and elated to see that his gran was the keynote speaker. She stood on a box behind the podium, a special guest of the White Woman. He smiled from ear to ear, feeling like he'd won the jackpot on a game show, getting to see his gran again.

His gran winked at him from the podium. Boo watched him from the stage, as if gauging his reaction. Her proud-as-punch smile told Rork she must have had something to do with his gran's reappearance.

"I died," said his gran to those assembled. "Leukemia." She tsked. "The White Woman shuttled me across the worlds." She smiled at the White Woman, standing in the wings of the stage. She looked out into the audience, found Rork, her grandson, and held his gaze.

Deirdre craned her neck, looking around the auditorium.

His gran's voice carried. "It helped to have a messenger, a messenger to guide me without judgment, a messenger without opinion. About my life. Or my death. It is not a calling for everyone. Beings, I am honored today to present the latest graduating class of banshees, banshees determined to evolve the transition of death."

The crowd clapped.

Rork's gran sat down.

The White Woman looked to Rork's gran on the stage. "What our guest speaker forgot to mention is she helped me get my hood when I was only a banshee-in-training, so I understand the importance of this day. She opened her arms wide, the gesture encompassing Rork's gran, the banshees on stage, all the beings in the audience. She then called each banshee forward, and her attendant slipped a hooded cape over the shoulders of each banshee.

In her hood, Boo smiled at the audience, hugged her mother, and waved at Rork, Deirdre, and Hamish. She smiled her gap teeth. "We did it," she yelled, thankfully at an audible level comfortable for humans.

We did it, repeated Rork to himself, looking proudly at Boo. We not only survived Shufftie, that wee shift, but took away experiences — life and death lessons — and successfully applied them to SoulSeek, a project of interlife moment. Rork looked around the room at the impossible mix of banshees, intermediaries, minders, and humans. Weren't they all just souls seeking other souls?

Rork looked down the length of the banquet table. Deirdre sat next to him. His gran on his other side. Morag sat next to his gran. Hamish also sat at the table, fiddling with his lighter. Boo sat at the end, sniffing a three-tiered cake, an ornate confection with white frosting.

"Banshees like cake?" asked Rork.

"Banshees *love* cake," said Boo.

"*That's* what you smell like!" Rork shouted, smelling the scent of buttercream frosting.

The banshee smiled her gap teeth, lifting a shoulder unapologetically.

Rork held Deirdre's hand under the table. She wore a simple sleeveless dress. His index finger followed the outlines of forget-me-nots.

Rork leaned into his gran, "Why is she here?" he asked, nodding towards Morag.

"Now, loon, I taught you better than that. You two have a lot in common. She was my intermediary." His gran pulled on the locket that hung around her neck.

Morag smiled wildly at him. That did explain some of her crazy.

"What's that?" asked Rork, touching his gran's locket.

"You don't remember?" She rubbed the locket like a wishing stone.

Rork shook his head. "Is there something in it?"

His gran opened the locket to reveal a fragile sprig of Forget-Me-Not. "You gave me this locket when you were a boy. You saved up your pocket money for months."

"Boo said that's how you found us hiding from the pall in Shufftie," said Rork, remembering.

"Yes. Memories are like waypoints for our unconscious." His gran turned toward him and brushed her fingertips across his forehead. "Forget-Me-Nots symbolize memory meaning," she said. "Isn't that what your memory-typing preserves?"

"Aye," said Rork.

"Here," said his gran, unclasping the necklace and locket and pressing it into his free hand. "You can have it," she said. "For SoulSeek."

Rork clasped it tight. "Thank you." He sat at peace, observing the antics of the table, sitting between Deirdre and his gran, the voices mildly gossiping between his ears. He was still mystified by the memory-typing but would continue to explore its capabilities as they continued work on SoulSeek. He squeezed Deirdre's hand. "Ouch," she mouthed, while across the table Hamish gave him a conspiratorial look. Yes, thought Rork. They were all integral to the banshee's accomplishments this day. Yes.

The banshee modeled her new hood, draping it across her shoulders, pulling it up around her face.

"It suits you," said Hamish. "You don't look like such a ghost."

"She's *not* a ghost," corrected Rork.

"She's a fantastical being," added Deirdre, "heralding death and moving between the realms."

"You got that right," said Boo happily.

36: Home

BACK IN THE VILLAGE, Rork scraped his feet on the stoop and entered the house. The door closed with a whoosh, as the wind whipped down their street. He heard sighs of relief in his head. "Home. Home. Home." He had the flash drive in one pocket and the sixpence in the other.

Rork touched his gran's pinny, still hanging on a hook in the dim hallway, a pattern of purple star clusters on a yellow background. Peering closer, Rork saw that the design was bunches of forget-me-nots with golden centers. How had he missed that? He reached into one of the pockets and found a sweetie, which he unwrapped and placed on his tongue. He considered how lucky he was. He got to see his gran again!

Rork looked forward to memory-typing about his gran's locket, which was stowed away in one of the pockets of his backpack. The continuing work on SoulSeek gave him more opportunity to be in touch with Hamish and Deirdre. His gran was right about her. She *was* rare.

His father stuck his head out from the kitchen through the low lintel doorway. "You're home, then?" he asked.

Rork heard another chorus from the voices of "Home. Home. Home."

"Aye, Da," he said, pulling off his outer shirt. He set the bag of his things on the floor. Before Shufftie, his father had always seemed to him a craggy edifice, rugged and rocky and unbreachable. Now, feeling more confident, knowing a small thing about him, maybe even a secret that rattled him that he'd told no one, he saw his father a in a softer, more accessible light. Flawed. Hard-working. Weather-beaten. Tongue-tied. His hair all of a sudden more gray than ginger. His father raised an eyebrow at him, wiping a cup with a tea towel, his fire-and-ice eyes quizzical. Rork usually called his father "sir." "Da" was an endearment.

"Tea?" asked his father.

"Yes, please."

Rork ducked into the kitchen after his father. His father fussed with the tea things, his large hands and meaty fingers spooning sugar daintily into teacups. Rork considered the kitchen table, his usual chair facing the wall, and shifted a degree or two. He sat at the end of the table, where he could see the sun high in the sky above the stovepipe flues of their neighbors, the rosebushes in the back garden, the tiny flowers of rock cress that looked like forget-me-nots but weren't, and he could see Angus spinning in a circle on the paving stones. The tea kettle whistled in approval. Rork smiled to himself, stretching his legs underneath the table. Aye, gran. A wee shift makes all the difference.

Rork's large feet jogged the leg of the table, and his father's mobile phone flashed alight. Rork saw Pinny-Full opened on the screen. He remembered his gran had insisted his father download it.

His father handed Rork a steaming cup with the handle out. He saw Rork see his phone. He cleared his throat. "I miss her, too, you know," he said.

Rork nodded, taking a sip of hot tea. "I have something of yours."

"What?" asked his father, sitting with his back to the window.

Rork slid the sixpence along the surface of the table with two fingers.

Rork's father followed the coin with his eyes. "Where'd you find that?" he asked.

"Gran said you wanted me to have it," said Rork.

His father squeezed the sixpence in one hand, then released it into his other hand. "It feels different," he said.

"Does it?" asked Rork, seven ghost levels and a leap of faith later.

"Aye," said his father. "Lighter." He flipped the coin, and they watched it spin. His father grabbed the sixpence out of the air and gave it back to Rork. "Keep it," he said.

"You're giving it to me?" asked Rork.

"Aye," said his father. "You're my son. Your turn to 'keep the faith.'"

Rork inspected the coin, the intertwined foliage of rose, leek, shamrock, and thistle, and returned it to his pocket. The word 'son' thrummed through his body like circuitry, turning on a power source, many points of connection.

"I met a girl," Rork said.

"Did you, now?" asked his father.

"Aye."

His father lit a cigarette, blew smoke in a stream to the ceiling. "I take it," he said, squinting, "you have no interest in becoming a mason tender."

Rork took a long drink of tea. "No, Da." He held the gaze of his father's fire-and-ice eyes without shying away.

His father nodded to himself.

Rork heard a collective sigh between his ears and for once was in perfect sympathy with the crowd.

His father looked around the spare kitchen and then at Rork. "Are you hungry?"

ACKNOWLEDGMENTS

THIS BOOK WOULD NOT BE POSSIBLE without the following very important people in my life. My husband Douglas Welhouse for the space and support he grants me every single day. My daughter and son Arabella Welhouse and Fergus Grant and stepson Devin Welhouse for their inspiration and encouragement. My father Michael Koller for believing in me. My brother Mick Koller for daring me and being my creative collaborator. My sister Trudy Strand for helping me remember the important things. My early advisor Christine DeSmet from the Writers' Institute for the tough love and novel-writing tools. My early readers Katie Vogt and Shoshannah Smyser for their honesty and candor. My writer friends Annette Langlois Grunseth for her cheerleading and Thomas Davis for the generosity of his time and insight. My editor and publisher Laurisa Reyes from Skyrocket Press for helping me understand what a novel can be and for urging me to imagine better.

ABOUT THE AUTHOR

TORI GRANT WELHOUSE is the winner of the Skyrocket Press 2019 Novel Writing Contest. She earned an MFA from Antioch University-International. She published a chapbook *Canned* with Finishing Line Press (2012), and her poems and reviews have appeared in many regional and online literary magazines. She is an active volunteer with Wisconsin Fellowship of Poets and lives in Green Bay. *The Fergus* is her first novel. Early chapters earned honorable mention at the University of Wisconsin-Madison's Writers' Institute (2012).

Visit her website at: https://www.torigrantwelhouse.com/

Thank you for reading

THE FERGUS

We invite you to post a review on Goodreads
& your favorite online book retailer.

For a free e-book, join our mailing list at:
www.SkyrocketPress.com